Sarah Fisher is the author of *A Private Collection*, available from Black Lace in print and digital editions. She also writes women's fiction under a variety of pseudonyms.

# SARAH FISHER

# A Private Collection

BLACK LACE

3 5 7 9 10 8 6 4 2

First published in 1995 by Black Lace, an imprint of Virgin Books
This edition published in 2013 by Black Lace, an imprint of Ebury Publishing
A Random House Group Company

Copyright © Sarah Fisher, 1995

Sarah Fisher has asserted her right to be identified as the author of this Work
in accordance with the Copyright, Designs and Patents Act 1988

The Random House Group Limited Reg. No. 954009

Addresses for companies within the Random House Group can be found at:
www.randomhouse.co.uk

A CIP catalogue record for this book is available from the British Library

The Random House Group Limited supports The Forest Stewardship
Council® (FSC®), the leading international forest-certification organisation.
Our books carrying the FSC label are printed on FSC®-certified paper.
FSC is the only forest-certification scheme supported by the leading
environmental organisations, including Greenpeace. Our
paper procurement policy can be found at
www.randomhouse.co.uk/environment

MIX
Paper from
responsible sources
FSC® C016897

Printed and bound in Great Britain by Clays Ltd, St Ives PLC

ISBN 9780352346766 *5407 5782* 05/14

To buy books by your favourite authors and register for offers visit:
www.blacklace.co.uk

# Chapter One

'Come on, there's no one here,' Chris whispered, struggling to lift the heavy iron gate; rusty hinges shrieked in complaint as he forced it open. Behind them on the far side of the sea wall, an afternoon tide sighed gently over the deserted beach below.

Walking a few steps behind, Francesca had to duck under the arched gateway, pushing aside a great veil of dusty ivy. 'If there's no one here, why are we whispering?' She laughed.

He turned and beckoned. 'We don't want to disturb the ghosts. Come on.'

The view in front of them was hidden by bedraggled shrubs. Chris hurried along an overgrown path, leaving Francesca to pick her way between dried tussocks of grass and piles of fallen masonry. When she drew level with him he grabbed her hand, pulling her through the bushes.

'This is it,' he announced, arms spread wide.

She looked up and gasped. 'Oh, Chris! It's beautiful.'

In front of them lay a huge, unkempt garden; it rose up from the sea wall, climbing unevenly over crumbling terraces towards a grand Victorian villa.

Francesca ran her fingers through her hair and turned to him, grinning with delight.

Around them the overgrown garden was bleached with summer sunlight; trees shaded pools of cool green grass, while ivy tumbled over fallen urns and twisted across crumbling walls. The air was heavy with the musky smell of sun-bleached foliage. It was a magical place.

Chris turned to face her, so close she could smell him; a subtle mixture of heat and wind-blown cotton. He reached towards her and, with one suntanned finger, traced a line down her long neck. Her skin tingled under his delicate touch.

'I found it during the winter,' he murmured. 'Paradise lost.'

She smiled and leant into his caress. 'And what do you think we ought to do now we've found it?' she whispered huskily.

He moved a little closer. 'You have no idea how long I've waited for this moment, Francesca,' he whispered. 'I know just what we're going to do.' He left the implication hanging between them. His intense brown eyes caught her gaze and a ripple of anticipation trembled up her spine, whilst above him the sun spun his grey-streaked hair into a halo.

Slowly his hand moved towards the buttons on her thin, cotton shirt. She shuddered; any doubts she had were pushed aside by her body's aching, hungry need to be touched. Under the lightest brush of his enquiring fingers she felt her nipples rise and harden. He smiled appreciatively and began to undo her blouse, his dark eyes never leaving hers.

'I want to be with you for ever,' he murmured as he pushed the thin material down over her narrow, suntanned shoulders.

The heat had added subtle jewelled highlights of salty perspiration across her collar-bones and between her flushed rounded breasts. His fingers traced the dark outline of her tightened nipples and she let out a thin moan of desire, shivering despite the heat of the sun.

'I want you naked in paradise. I've always wanted you,' he whispered, as he pulled her towards him.

She turned and moved even closer, her pulse racing, opening her mouth in anticipation of his kiss. His eager mouth pressed home to meet hers, his inquisitive tongue slipping between her moist lips. Desperate and needy, his hands moved to the band of her skirt and pushed the flimsy cheesecloth down over her hips, taking her knickers down with it. She let them slide to the ground and whimpered as his hands moved to caress her buttocks, cool fingers kneading her firm flesh.

She smiled under his kisses and pushed her body towards him teasingly, brushing the hair of her sex against the front of his jeans, her eyes dark with desire. He sighed and his lips, hot and wet, slid down into the pit of her throat, licking at her throbbing pulse.

She held her breath as his tongue moved on, tracing

the salty hypnotic path down between her breasts. The hot kisses cooled on her skin despite the heavy summer heat; a tantalising sensation that left her trembling. His eager mouth nibbled and sucked, tongue moving back and forth over her erect nipples.

Cool inquisitive fingers feathered down across her thighs, whilst his teeth nipped her breasts lightly. She pushed against him, shuddering at the sharp, acidic contrast of sensation.

The tip of his tongue slid down over the swell of her ribcage. The feelings electrified every nerve ending as he lapped hungrily at her hot salty body, murmuring endearments and whispering little animal noises of pleasure and desire.

Between her legs she could already feel the soft silky wetness of her excitement trickling down on to her thighs; felt herself opening for him, aching for him. Sensing her need, Chris's fingers moved towards her sex, softly, gently, brushing against the hair and the sensitive tender flesh of her inner thighs, parting the folds; his caress a languid exploration of her hungry body. As he slid a finger into her she let out a sigh of pleasure whilst on her belly his tongue, as if drawn by a magnetic compulsion, moved to join his fingers as they glided into her, anointed by the silky fragrant moisture. Sinking slowly to his knees on the grass in front of her, his tongue lingered for an instant in her navel before travelling lower still in an ancient act of worship.

He pressed his lips into the dark curls above her sex, his kisses tentative, fleeting, as if he were breathing in the essence of her body. She opened willingly under the potency of his desire, his tongue gliding lower, seeking out the hard, engorged ridge of her clitoris. His lips mouthed softly against her silken folds and as his fingers slid deeper into her she felt her muscles tighten around him. Clutching frantically at the soft hair at the nape of his neck she arched towards him, relishing the compelling caresses.

Around them in the garden the raw heat of summer echoed the intense heat that grew between them. Somewhere close by a grasshopper stroked out a compulsive vibrato rhythm. Francesca shivered and threw back her head, pulling Chris's tongue into her, her hips thrusting forward against him. She whispered his name, letting the intense sensations wash over her. Beneath her fingers she could feel the compelling tremble of his desire as their excitement rose.

At one of the windows in the old house there was a fleeting glint of reflected light. Unaware of it, Francesca slipped her fingers into the familiar moist contours of her sex and held herself open for Chris's enquiring tongue. He moaned with excitement and she felt him probe her deeper, relishing her wetness – drinking her – lapping at her. She wriggled closer, and in response his tongue moved to the delicate contours of her inner lips, guiding its sensitive tip into her again and again before slowly lifting to lap at the throbbing bud of her clitoris.

Gasping now, Francesca could feel the bitter-sweet ripples of tension building in the pit of her belly. She pushed her body hard against him, desperately chasing the moment of no return. Her pulse throbbed, rising insistent and hypnotic in her ears. Her whole body cried out for fulfilment. She felt the first tentative white-hot waves of her climax and shuddered, opening herself wider, compelling him to take her to the very edge.

To her horror he pulled his lips away; she gasped in disappointment.

'Please . . .' she whispered huskily. 'Don't stop. Please.'

He looked up at her, eyes dark and glinting, his lips wet with her juices. The air between them was electric with the magic of their desire as his fingers trailed her fragrant wetness over her thighs and up over her nipples. In the sunlight it glistened like spun silk. She moaned with bitter frustration as his touch sent a tremor of expectation through her.

She stood still, every nerve ending beneath her skin alight and trembling as he slid back to look at her. She shuddered as his eyes moved appreciatively across her nakedness, drinking in the darkness of her taut nipples still wet from his kisses and her own fragrant juices. Her skin flushed with desire, pupils dilated. His gaze lingered on the dark hair of her mound; a startling contrast to the swollen inner folds of her sex.

Slowly he pulled himself to his feet; she moved towards him furiously, frustrated now, desperate for a conclusion. One hand tore at the buttons of his shirt whilst the other moved quickly to his belt. Below, the straining bulk of his cock pressed aggressively against his jeans; she fought to free it, her hands trembling.

He grinned at her and she crushed his mouth to hers relishing the taste of her own excitement on his lips, her flushed breasts pressed hard against his chest whilst her sex strained against him. Almost angrily, she ripped his shirt down over his broad shoulders. The tight curls of the hair on his chest brushed against her nipples, sending a *frisson* of delight down into her belly. Maddeningly close, her arousal lingered unsatisfied and vulnerable as she fought with his zip. He eased himself away from her and slipped off his jeans and canvas shoes.

His cock was heavy and thick, deliciously engorged, a single droplet of moisture clinging to the end of it. Francesca moved towards him; desperate to maintain her excitement, her fingers sought out her throbbing, aching clitoris. She began to stroke rhythmically, her eyes never leaving his as she brought herself closer to her climax. His smile hardened into something colder as he grabbed her wrists, and he pulled her hand away.

'No,' he whispered tightly. 'Don't ever do that, let me.'

As she moved closer he grabbed her arms and spun her around. She felt the brush of his cock against her and the heat of his body as he pushed her down on to her hands and knees amongst the fragrant sun-whitened grass. His roughness took her by surprise. Grabbing the back of her neck, his other hand reached between her legs to brush her clitoris. She cried out and instinctively dropped her belly to let him enter her.

Maddeningly, he pulled away from her and she let out a hiss of desire as, exposed and vulnerable, she waited for him to take her. The seconds heightened her sense of anticipation. Slowly she heard him creep closer and felt the merest fleeting brush of his belly against her back. She swallowed hard, dosing her eyes as the heat of his body overwhelmed her. The light sensation as the tip of his cock brushed her inner thigh sent a shiver down her spine. She whimpered and begged him to take her.

He parted the lips of her sex and she felt the hard urge of his cock between the delicate folds, felt its quivering silken entry as he pressed slowly into her. She drew in a sharp breath as her body engulfed him, her inner muscles tightening gratefully around his thick shaft. His hand lingered, stroking the wet junction of their flesh as be began to move slowly in and out. He stroked the scented juices of her body down over her inner thighs.

'You're mine,' he whispered in the space between their breaths. 'All mine. I've waited so long for you.'

Shuddering, she arched her back against him and he pulled her closer, grabbing at her hips, locking her bare, cool buttocks against his thighs as he pumped into her – deeper and deeper. Every thrust renewed the exquisite sensation of her muscles tightening around him and brought her closer to the moment of climax.

His hand lifted from where he entered into her, teasing, brushing, tickling, seeking out her clitoris. And then it was there – glowing, straining – swollen under the insistent caress of his fingertips. She let out a soft moan of pleasure and desperately arched again, her body baying for satisfaction as he forced himself still deeper into her.

The silvery waves of her climax gathered like a summer storm in the pit of her belly. She felt her muscles contract rhythmically around him, drawing his passion and desire to its height. From over her shoulders she could hear his breath roaring in her ears, his belly brushing against her arched back. She pushed back against him, every nerve ending alight, every sensation engulfing. She heard herself roar with satisfaction as the brilliant white-hot waves of orgasm crashed through her. In the distance – lost amongst her own ecstasy and fulfilment – she felt Chris falter for an instant as he reached the point of no return, then buck against her as the shuddering tidal wave of his own orgasm engulfed them both.

Alicia Moffat put aside her binoculars and returned her attention to Ralph Cormac, her GP, who was loosening the blood-pressure cuff around the top of her slender arm. He pulled the stethoscope from his ears and sat beside her on the *chaise longue* near the window.

'It's up a little today, Alicia. What are you watching in the garden? Birds?'

Alicia lifted one perfectly plucked eyebrow and handed him the binoculars. 'Why don't you take a look for yourself, Ralph? Everyone should have a hobby.'

Indulgently the middle-aged doctor hoisted the glasses to his eyes and turned to peer into the tangled garden outside the sitting room. For a few moments he let the lenses play across the litter of shrubs and ruined flower-beds. He paused for a split second and hastily swung the glasses back to a spot he'd just passed.

Alicia smiled broadly and leant forwards to pour the tea.

'Good grief,' hissed Cormac on a long outward breath. 'Oh my goodness.' Red-faced, he looked quickly back at Alicia who was adding milk to one of the bone-china cups. 'Have you seen this?' he stammered, waving the binoculars at her.

Alicia calmly handed him a cup and saucer. 'Only this afternoon. I was really terribly cross when you arrived, Cormac. I'm sure I've missed all the best bits.'

Cormac stood up and moved to the other side of the room, before folding himself self-consciously into an armchair.

'I'll put a stop to it for you, Alicia. Have a quiet word with them,' he blustered, stirring the tea enthusiastically.

Alicia looked fleetingly at the not-inconsiderable bulge in the front of his cavalry twills and waved her hand. If he caught her glance, he gave no signs of it. 'No, don't. They probably think the house is empty, and they're hardly vandals, are they?' She paused. 'What were you going to do, rush out there and throw a bucket of water over them?'

The doctor shook his head. 'No. Hardly do that, could I? Thought I'd wait until I see them in town and have a discreet word.'

Alicia clapped her hands and laughed with delight. 'I would be most interested to hear which discreet word you would use. But don't, Cormac. Not a word, please. They're not doing any harm. Can I safely assume you recognise them?'

Cormac glanced surreptitiously at the binoculars.

'By all means have another look if you're not quite sure,' she whispered playfully.

He looked away quickly, blushing furiously. 'He's called Chris Pearce, some sort of artist chap who's bought the old boat yard on Tolman's Creek and she . . .' He paused, his mind instantly filled with sunlit images of the woman's narrow arched back straining eagerly against her lover's thighs, her half-closed eyes, mouth open, the movement of her tiny pert breasts as he'd pushed deeper into her. Cormac swallowed hard; he could almost smell the delirious aroma of the woman's damp inviting sex.

'She's just moved here too. Renting the old fisherman's cottage down on the quay. Name'll come to me in a minute; some sort of writer,' he spluttered desperately, trying to regain his composure.

Alicia picked up the binoculars and turned to look out of the window.

'Are they still there?' asked Cormac too quickly, getting to his feet.

Alicia's immaculately painted face was totally devoid of expression when she looked away from the eyepieces. 'I was watching the gulls,' she snapped acidly.

Early the following morning, Alicia Moffat's vintage Daimler drew up on the quayside. The day was already cloudless and bright, promising a classic summer's day. From the driver's side of the car a large uniformed man stepped out on to the cobbles and crossed to the fisherman's cottage. Pausing for an instant to glance around the deserted quay, he knocked on the low door.

'I'm coming, I'm coming,' Francesca called crossly as she slipped out of bed. She pulled on a cotton wrap and tied the belt before pulling her thick dark hair back into an untidy knot. Slipping on her mules, she hurried across to the bedroom window and flicked aside the curtains. Outside, the quay seemed empty except for a black car parked by the railings at the edge of the harbour wall. Heading out of the bedroom she paused mid-stride to look in the minor; blue sleep-bright, morning eyes glanced back at her mischievously. She pushed her hair back a little and ran a finger around her lips.

Downstairs there was another knock at the front door. Francesca cursed. If it was Chris she'd kill him; she'd told him she was never up before ten. Despite the temptations of his tender lovemaking, she felt (when they were apart) that he was pushing her too far, too fast. Since she'd moved in he seemed to spend all his time at the cottage and she doubted she'd get her latest novel finished for the deadline if she couldn't persuade him to spend less time in her company.

Below her on the stairs lay a bundle of crumpled clothes and a pair of shoes. Crossly, she scooped up the debris and threw it in the hall cupboard before unlocking the door.

Flinging it open, she snapped, 'It's far too early for a social call, Chris,' and then froze as the words caught in her throat.

Framed in the doorway in silhouette against the

bright summer morning stood a tall uniformed man. Francesca screwed up her eyes against the light to try and make out his features.

'I'm so sorry,' she stammered, trying to compose herself. 'I thought you were a friend of mine. Can I help you?'

The liveried man nodded, almost a bow, and removed his peaked cap. 'Good morning, Mrs Leeman?' His voice was deep, each word enunciated with a crispness that suggested English wasn't his first language.

'Yes?' Francesca felt slightly confused as she didn't recognise the man nor his impressive olive-green uniform. As she glanced down she realised he was also wearing what she thought might be gaiters.

'I have a message for you,' he said, stepping into the little hallway.

Thank you,' murmured Francesca. As she took the envelope from him she sensed his eyes moving slowly over her body, drinking in the details of her undress. His gaze lingered for a second on the soft curve of her breasts and the lightly tanned V of flesh where the edges of her robe overlapped.

She felt a little flush of anxiety as she tore the envelope open and fought back the temptation to pull her wrap closer around her.

The typewritten note contained an invitation to discuss a possible commission for – Francesca let her eyes wander down to the name below the signature – Mrs Alicia Moffat, who would like to meet her for lunch at the Crown at 1.00 p.m. to discuss her proposal.

She glanced back at the man who was now gazing beyond her into the gloom of the hall. In profile his features were rugged and intimidating; his square jaw and finely sculpted bone structure gave him a cold, almost brutal look.

'Do you have any idea what Mrs Moffat has in mind? I'm afraid I don't know your name?' she said evenly, ignoring the tight flutter of panic in her stomach.

She saw the slightest flicker in the man's expression as he glanced back at her. Almost instantly his face settled back into an impassive unreadable mask.

'Catz, Mrs Leeman, Randolph Catz,' he purred. 'I am Mrs Moffat's chauffeur and I'm afraid I am only the messenger. Have you a reply?'

Francesca hesitated; she should have refused the invitation. Barely halfway through the rewrite of her book, she hadn't time to consider another commission, but the invitation and its bearer aroused her curiosity and stirred something deeper, something undefinable. Catz looked like something out of a black-and-white movie; even his name compounded the sense of mystery. She looked at him again.

He was over six feet tall, somewhere in his late thirties, with an intimidating brooding presence. The chauffeur's uniform was skilfully tailored to parade his powerful physique, gold buttons placed to emphasise the breadth of his shoulders in relation to his narrow waist and hips. Above his muscular neck the fine bones of his suntanned face made him unnervingly handsome, although his eyes remained cold and distant. He ran his fingers through his light close-cropped hair and turned back to face her. Under her unguarded scrutiny his blue eyes narrowed.

Francesca looked away, feeling her colour rise. Quickly regaining her poise she said slowly, 'Tell Mrs Moffat I will be delighted to meet her for lunch, although I think it would be only fair to tell her I'm working on something else at the moment.'

Catz nodded briskly. "Thank you, Mrs Leeman. I'll pass your message on to Mrs Moffat.'

He stepped back through the doorway but not before turning to let his eyes move slowly back over her body, lingering for a few seconds on the outline of her nipples where they pressed against the thin fabric of her wrap. Francesca shuddered and practically slammed the door shut behind her.

She leant back against the closed door, unnerved to hear the excited throbbing pulse in her ears. She glanced across at the hall clock and wondered if Chris would be in his studio yet; it was almost nine. Picking up the phone she dialled his number. He was bound to know something about Mrs Moffat and the intimidating Randolph Catz. The phone rang, but no one answered.

From outside came the soft hum of the Daimler's engine as it started up. She glanced towards the door, her mind rerunning the cold undisguised interest with which Catz had surveyed her body. It sent an alien chill up her spine. She shivered and lowered the receiver into its cradle, relocked the door and hurried upstairs to shower and dress.

On her bedside table lay a single wilted dog-rose; it had been Chris's parting gift to her from the faded paradise garden. She hesitated and then lifted the blossom to her lips; a hint of fragrance still lingered amongst the soft creamy petals.

Chris had been friends with her husband Paul for years before the accident. At one time they had worked together and, for Francesca, Chris had been a gentle supportive companion in the hollow empty months that followed Paul's death. At first he had been her comforter, her shoulder to cry on – and now? Now he told her he was her friend and, in the weeks since she'd moved to the cottage, her lover. But she wondered; there was something about the way he treated her. She couldn't define exactly what it was, but she knew that he would never be content with friendship alone.

She closed her eyes. It had been his suggestion that she moved to the village in the first place. He'd practically insisted on it: he'd found her the cottage on the quay, helped her to move in. Looking down at the faded rose she knew Chris was spinning an enticing trap for her to fall into. She lay the rose back amongst the books and went into the bathroom. In her mind Chris's face faded abruptly, to be replaced by the cold exciting features of Randolph Catz.

At lunch-time Francesca set out across the harbour, keeping to the cool shadows. The midday heat was oppressive. Around the quay a sprinkling of tourists wandered about, stopping to gaze out over the brilliant shimmer of the incoming tide. The air was white-hot, wringing every last breath out of the day.

In a narrow side-street she caught sight of her reflection in a shop window. She wore one of her favourite outfits: a soft and faded blue chambray cotton shirt that echoed the colour of her eyes, loosely tucked into a bold abstract cotton skirt which hung in soft pleats to mid-calf. The effect was feminine and comfortable. She smiled confidently at her reflection; the dark image smiled back, revealing the delicate tracery of lines around her eyes. A few tendrils of dark hair had escaped from her loose bun, framing and softening her small features. Casually she brushed the soft strands back into place and set off towards the Crown.

Chris hadn't answered her calls, despite her dialling several times. His absence vaguely disturbed her and she would have been interested to hear what he had to say about Alicia Moffat and her mysterious chauffeur before her lunch date. But another part of her was relieved he'd been out; she found his need to know where she was and what she was doing oppressive. Since Paul's accident she was slowly learning to live alone again, to make her own choices and decisions, and despite their new, more intimate relationship, she knew she wasn't ready yet to fall into Chris's silken web – however tempting the bait.

The Crown was at the far end of a quiet backstreet; a relic from a bygone age when the small fishing village had been a prosperous and bustling sea port. Popular with the locals and famous for its wonderful food, parts of the building dated back to the reign of Charles II. Under its magnificent thatched roof, mullioned windows and narrow arched doorways gave it a secretive and romantic air.

Francesca walked around the back of the building under an archway that led into a shady flagstone courtyard. The terrace was set out with tables and colourful sunshades. Glancing across into the car park she spotted the sleek distinctive lines of Alicia Moffat's black Daimler parked in the shade.

She stepped into the cool dark foyer and was momentarily blinded after the brilliance of the sunlight outside. She hesitated, waiting for her eyes to adjust to the gloom.

When her sight cleared she spotted the unmistakable figure of Catz standing by the bar with a tray. His brutal good looks made her shiver but, despite the little flutter of anxiety, her eyes lingered on his muscular frame. He looked up as if sensing she was there, and nodded in greeting.

'Good afternoon, Mrs Leeman. Would you like a drink?' He nodded towards the waiting barman.

She moved closer, aware of the subtle smell of his cologne. "Thank you, I'd like a white wine, please.'

The barman smiled and Francesca glanced around the low cool interior of the bar, trying to find the unknown face of Alicia Moffat. Catz shook his head as the barman added Francesca's drink to the tray. 'Mrs Moffat is in the dining room, if you would like to follow me,' he said, indicating the direction with his eyes.

Falling into step behind him Francesca followed Catz through the pub to a long panelled room overlooking the paved terrace. They stopped at a table set in a shadowy alcove. Francesca looked across at her host and froze.

Alicia Moffat was tiny, no more than five feet tall. She was dressed in an elegant and softly tailored cream suit; a matching bandeau pulled an abundance of sleek white-blonde hair back from her tiny heart-shaped face, whilst discreet pearl earrings set with diamonds twinkled in the soft light. Alicia extended her gloved hand towards Francesca and smiled.

'Good afternoon, Mrs Leeman. How good of you to come.'

Francesca took her hand and was rewarded with the slightest pressure against her fingers.

Alicia Moffat was certainly not young, though it was almost impossible to guess her age. She was, however, astonishingly beautiful. High cheekbones gave her an angular, almost sculptural beauty whilst her intense violet eyes set in the palest of ivory skin enhanced the image of fragile perfection. In spite of herself Francesca gasped. Alicia Moffat was truly beautiful. No, more than that; she was stunning.

Francesca smiled politely as Catz continued the introductions and removed their drinks from the tray. Alicia dismissed him with a wave of her hand and indicated that Francesca should sit.

'I am delighted to meet you, Mrs Leeman; I hope

you don't mind my contacting you. I am told you are a writer.' Alicia's voice was as smooth and soft as velvet.

Francesca slipped into the seat opposite her and as she did she caught a hypnotic breath of Alicia's subtle perfume.

'Of course I don't mind you contacting me, but I'm not really sure I can help you, Mis Moffat. I –'

The woman silenced her with a wave. 'Catz has told me you're already working on a book, and please, call me Alicia.' She paused and looked across at Francesca. 'How long have you been in the village?'

'Almost six weeks; I've rented a cottage for the summer. I'm working on a novel at the moment.'

Alicia nodded, her eyes never leaving Francesca's face. 'And is it a good novel?'

Francesca smiled and shrugged. 'I think so, my agent thinks so.'

The older woman picked up her glass and held it to her exquisitely painted lips. 'And do you live by your talents?'

Francesca shook her head. 'No, not yet, but I hope to.'

'I need a writer,' Alicia continued, 'to do some work for me. My late husband travelled extensively and left me a collection that I think would make the basis of a wonderful book.' Francesca felt herself shiver unexpectedly under Alicia's undisguised scrutiny. 'A collection of what, exactly?' asked Francesca lightly, trying to recover her composure.

Alicia waved a hand dismissively. 'All kinds of things, books, photographs, artefacts, prints. You'll have to take a look at the collection before you can fully appreciate the scope of the material.'

As she spoke, a waiter arrived with the menus. Alicia glanced fleetingly in his direction. 'I'd like a green salad with a little chicken,' she said crisply, in a tone that clearly indicated his dismissal.

Francesca smiled at the bemused man. 'That will be fine for me too,' she said, turning back towards Alicia. 'You must understand, I have other commitments; even if I look at your husband's collection I can't promise I'll take another book on at the moment. I might be able to recommend someone who could do it, particularly if you need the work doing soon. I write mainly fiction.'

'I understand. May I call you Francesca? All I ask is that you take a look.'

Francesca nodded. 'Thank you. Tell me, how did you come to contact me?'

Alicia smiled. 'My doctor, Ralph Cormac.' She hesitated. 'Though he did mention he hasn't met your husband as yet.' Alicia tipped her head in gentle enquiry.

Francesca smiled politely. 'I'm not married, or at least not now; I'm a widow. My husband Paul died in a car accident several years ago.'

Alicia's face gathered itself into an expression of polite sympathy; Francesca murmured her thanks.

'And what he left you allows you to write?'

Francesca nodded. 'Yes. I manage.'

The older woman grimaced. 'What an awful expression that is. Tell me, Francesca, have you never longed to be free?' Her voice rose a little.

Uncomfortably, Francesca glanced around the almost empty dining room. 'I'm not sure what you mean. I think I am free,' she began. Through an open door she caught sight of Catz. As if sensing her, he looked up, his eyes bright and hungry. Francesca looked away quickly.

Alicia, catching the exchange, laughed lightly. 'Don't mind Catz, he's been with me for years, he's totally harmless.'

Francesca shuddered. "There's something about him,' she murmured, without thinking.

Alicia smiled. 'Oh indeed there is. Let me tell you a story.' She paused, sensing Francesca's discomfort. 'Or perhaps now is not the time, or is it that I'm boring you?'

Francesca sipped her drink self-consciously. 'I'm so sorry, I didn't mean to be rude. Please carry on.'

Alicia took a little wine from her glass. 'I am not a young woman. Before you make ridiculous inane remarks about how wonderful I look or how beautiful I am . . . Trust me, I have spent a great deal of time and effort to ensure that I maintain every vestige of youth. I work hard to look like this.' She raised a hand to indicate her body and lifted an eyebrow as if to invite Francesca to comment. Francesca said nothing.

Alicia smiled again, her voice dropping to no more than a conspiratorial purr. 'I was married at sixteen to Edgar; he was forty. I was an exceptional prize: pure virgin stock, a shy and rather fey little creature spirited away from my family before I'd had a chance to experience anything of real life. Edgar sought perfection. He was a collector, a connoisseur. He wanted a creature he could train; mould to his own particular requirements – please note that I didn't say a *person*.'

Alicia took another sip from her glass. 'He was a very old man when he died and he left me an extremely wealthy woman, a perfect wife, a trained monkey. In return for his largesse I had given him my youth. Where does one go to find a companion at my age?' She let her eyes move slowly across the room towards the doorway and Catz.

Francesca swallowed hard.

Alicia laughed at her uneasiness. 'Catz is an expensive toy. He does everything for me that I ask him.' Alicia paused and raised the wine to her lips; for an instant the moist tip of her tongue appeared and she trailed its wetness around the rim of her wineglass.

Unable to look away, Francesca felt an unexpected flutter in her belly. She could feel herself flush.

Alicia smiled easily. 'Oh come come, don't be embarrassed, Francesca. You're a writer; aren't you fascinated by other people's lives? Wasn't there an instant there, a fraction of a second, when you let your mind consider what it is that Catz might do for me? Look at his beautiful cruel face.'

Unable to prevent herself, Francesca felt her eyes drawn to the darkened doorway. Bright feral eyes stared back. Francesca knew her colour was rising and she swung round to Alicia. 'I'm sorry,' she stammered. 'I don't think I can help you. I'm not even sure what it is you want from me.'

Alicia laughed. 'No, I'm not sure either but I instinct-ively feel we are being drawn together. I want you to understand the true nature of freedom.'

Francesca began to gather her things together. 'I think this is a mistake,' she began.

Alicia leant across the table and laid one gloved hand on top of Francesca's. That isn't true, Francesca. You feel something stirring inside you when you look at Catz, don't you? There are things that you only dream about. Tell me you want to be free.'

Francesca blushed violently and looked away. 'You're wrong,' she stammered, 'I. . .'

Alicia removed her hand and the intensity left her voice. 'Why don't we forget lunch? We can eat at my house. Come and take a look at my husband's collection. Then,' she said with a shrug, her tone light and inviting, 'if you still feel you're unable to help, you can leave and we'll forget the whole idea.'

Francesca hesitated, every instinct telling her to leave. But there was something darker and more compelling that pressed her to accept Alicia's invitation.

Alicia stood up slowly as Catz crossed the dining room towards them.

Francesca struggled to her feet, feeling the pulse hammering in her ears. She fought to control the intense feelings that bubbled up inside her. After all, her rational mind argued, she was a grown woman, and this was simply a commission – one she could easily decline – but the other, darker side of her mind knew that the invitation held more than a chance to view a collection of dry books or photographs; the unspoken possibilities excited her.

Catz looked at her speculatively as he took Alicia's arm.

She heard herself saying slowly, 'I would be interested to see the collection.' There was the slightest tremor in her voice.

Alicia nodded. 'Wonderful. Catz will settle things here.'

In the Daimler, Francesca felt a sudden ripple of panic. Seated beside Alicia, she watched as Catz silently closed the doors. He climbed into the driver's seat which was divided from the passenger compartment by a sheet of glass. Her eyes were drawn again to the outline of his broad shoulders under the smooth fabric of his uniform. In the taut muscular lines of his neck she could see the steady throb of his pulse; the tiny movement sent a dark flurry of anticipation through her and she swallowed hard and looked away.

The engine purred into life, its sound barely more than a low hum in the rear of the car. The interior was deliciously cool, upholstered in pale-tan leather. The heady combination of Alicia's perfume and the subtle undertones of the old leather made Francesca feel dizzy. Alicia, relaxed and perfectly at ease, glanced across at her.

'I think you will enjoy my late husband's trophies,' she said, as the car pulled out from the car park into the narrow street beyond.

Francesca tried to keep her mind on the scenery as

it passed; they turned at the next junction out on to the old coast road. The car seemed to glide along under Catz's direction as they drove out beyond the village into the shade of a small copse beyond and slowly up a steep hill overlooking the bay.

Francesca stared; there was something unnervingly familiar about the view. Then she recognised it. It was the view she had seen from the cliffs when she'd been out with Chris. In the same moment she realised where she was, the car turned off the road through an ornate pair of heavily weathered gates. Beyond the gates the driveway was lined with unkempt conifers, giving it a dark dusty look even in the full sunshine. The wheels of the Daimler purred out a salty dry rhythm on the gravel while ahead of them, almost obscured by trees, stood the Victorian villa. Francesca gasped. The house,' she murmured. 'We . . .'

'You were here yesterday, I believe,' said Alicia, not looking at her.

Francesca swung round. 'I didn't know there was anyone living here. Chris said it was deserted,' she spluttered.

Alicia shook her head calmly. 'Please don't apologise.'

The car purred to a standstill in front of the ornate porch.

'Here we are,' Alicia said softly.

In the driver's compartment Catz had slipped on his peaked cap and got out to open the passenger door. Francesca could feel the glittering tendril of panic rising again in her belly. Alicia touched her on the arm.

'There is no compulsion to stay, my dear, none whatsoever. You may leave now if you wish; Catz will drive you home. Remember, Francesca, you are free.' The older woman's voice was barely above a whisper. As she spoke Catz swung the passenger door open and, taking Alicia's hand, helped her on to the uneven gravel drive.

In the doorway Francesca could see the tiled floor of the porch; weeds grew up in clumps between the black-and-white marble squares. The ornate doors and window frames were peeling and around them thick dusty creepers snaked up towards the roof. The atmosphere of the villa was cloaked in fading genteel splendour.

Francesca hesitated for an instant and Catz leant into the passenger compartment, offering his outstretched hand. Francesca glanced at him and then slowly placed her hand in his. He smiled triumphantly as he helped her out into the bright sunlight.

# Chapter Two

The large hallway of the villa was dark and cool after the brilliance of the day outside. Francesca remained still while her eyes adjusted to the light, trying to get her bearings and quell the strange bubbling excitement she felt inside. Though outside the house was ramshackle and neglected, the interior was spotlessly clean. The entrance hall was square, panelled all the way round in dark wood, with a marble tiled floor echoing the chequer-board effect of the porch. In front of them an ornate wooden staircase swept up from the centre of the room. Either side of the hall were double doors set into the dark panelling and beyond those, shadowy corridors went off into the darkness beyond.

Alicia Moffat smiled and turned to her. 'Don't be deceived by the exterior, Francesca, it's an act of pure rebellion. My husband wouldn't have so much as a blade of grass out of place.'

As Alicia spoke, Francesca was aware of Catz standing behind her. She could almost feel his breath on her neck and his eyes lingering on her back. She shivered at the thought; a subtle mixture of fear, and on another deeper level, the glistening thrill of anticipation.

Alicia glanced past her. 'Catz, we'll have a tray of tea in the sitting room if you please.' She hesitated and turned back to Francesca. 'Or would you rather have something stronger?'

Francesca shook her head, 'No, tea will be fine.'

The older woman nodded a dismissal to Catz and beckoned to Francesca. She followed silently. They walked into the intriguing darkness of the corridors beyond the staircase, their steps ringing out on the chequered marble floor. Alicia opened the set of double doors set into the panelling and Francesca stepped forward to look inside.

Beyond the doors was a large square sitting room which overlooked the garden; Francesca knew instinctively it was the room overlooking the cliff wall. Alicia smiled and stepped inside before turning and beckoning for Francesca to follow. Francesca followed apprehensively.

The sitting room was decorated in the palest cream, its furniture discreetly upholstered in soft pinks and greens, but the room's character was totally dominated by a huge picture window set in the far wall. The room was designed to turn the eye outwards to what had once been the magnificent gardens, with their view of the sea beyond.

Alicia indicated a chair beside the marble fireplace. For a few seconds they sat in total silence facing each other, the only noise a tight meticulous tick from a carriage clock on the mantelpiece.

Francesca glanced around the room, her eyes drawn again and again to the window overlooking the garden. 'You watched us,' she said softly, feeling the insistent flutter of panic pressing up again.

Alicia's expression was unreadable; only her violet eyes flickered. 'You were worth watching,' the older woman said softly.

Francesca felt dizzy; it was all she could do to stop herself from getting to her feet to look outside, as if she might catch herself and Chris still engaged in their passionate all-consuming embrace.

There was a discreet knock at the door, followed by the appearance of Catz bearing a tray of tea. Attentively he began to pour it – the perfect manservant. The silence hung electric between the three of them as Francesca and Alicia received their tea.

As she picked up the cup and saucer, Francesca realised her hands were trembling. She swallowed hard and struggled to control the sense of expectancy that rose up like a silver flame in her belly. Her growing sense of unease didn't seem to affect Alicia, who made polite conversation.

Across the room, framed in the doorway, Catz stood unmoving, his eyes never leaving her. Only the almost imperceptible rise and fall of his broad chest gave lie to his being alive.

Finally Alicia smiled and got to her feet. 'I think we'll begin our tour,' she said, glancing at Catz. 'Leave the tea tray and come with us instead.' She turned back to Francesca. 'If you'd like to follow me, Edgar's collection is kept in the gallery. I'm sure you will find it fascinating.'

Francesca nodded and followed Alicia from the sitting room.

They walked silently through the vast house, their footfalls ringing out on the marble floors. Francesca fought desperately to suppress the fluttering anxiety in her stomach as Alicia led them through the maze of cool dark corridors away from the main hall. Finally they came to a small door set back amongst the panelling. Catz moved forward to unlock it and opened the door for Alicia, before stepping back to let her through.

Inside was a small dark lobby with a cast-iron spiral staircase rising up from the centre to a patch of sunlight above. Alicia stood with one hand on the banister and indicated that Francesca should climb. Francesca glanced towards her in the gloom.

'I can't climb the stairs,' Alicia said softly as if answering Francesca's unspoken question. 'Catz will show you what you need to see.' She paused and glanced across at the uniformed man. 'He is an excellent guide.' Alicia lifted Francesca's hand, inviting her to climb.

Francesca hesitated, part or her feeling she should resist. She glanced around the darkened room, knowing that her hestitation betrayed her fear.

'Or,' continued Alicia conversationally, 'Catz will take you home. The choice is yours.' Her strange violet eyes flickered with a dark unreadable brilliance.

Francesca took a deep breath and mounted the first step defiantly. She looked back over her shoulder in time to catch an electrifying glance passing between Alicia and Catz. She decided that she had come this far, and something inside that refused to be denied longed to discover more. Taking another deep breath, she hurried quickly up the other treads. Behind her, Catz followed silently like a predatory animal.

At the top, the stairwell opened up into a long gallery, and Francesca hesitated before stepping out into the room. The light was subdued; large windows set well back in the walls were hung with cream linen blinds which gave the interior a soft warm quality, the delicate glow reflected by the highly polished boards that covered the floor. Ornately panelled walls echoed those in the hall and were hung with a huge collection of framed oil paintings and prints. Beneath them, standing against the panelling, were a variety of glass-fronted cabinets and cases. At intervals along the centre of the room dark plinths displayed sculptures and statues.

With a sense of relief – almost anti-climax – Francesca moved over to the first sculpture. It was a dark wooden carving depicting a beautiful oriental woman stooping forward to pick up a heavily ornamented vase. The workmanship was breathtaking, every detail perfectly picked out in the softly diffused light. Entranced, Francesca circled it and froze, her senses stunned by the secret imagery of the statue.

From the front, the statue of the woman looked innocent, her full robe carved into a replica of perfect soft folds brushing against the vase. From behind, Francesca could see the intricately carved fabric was gathered up around her waist, exposing the ripe full curve of her buttocks. Between the woman's legs a grotesque pot-bellied man crouched, his great hands forcing the woman's naked buttocks apart while his unnaturally long tongue lapped greedily at her sex.

Francesca gasped and stepped forward, unable to control the compulsion to look closer. Every detail was perfect, every crease faultless. The broad lips of the woman's inviting slit seemed to almost drip with saliva and her juices. The pot-bellied man's eyes were wide open, fascinated and hypnotised by the vision of her exposed body above him. His heavy robe was dragged back to reveal the bulky engorged shaft of his erect cock. Around it was the tightly grasped hand of a smaller woman who lay wrapped around the feet of the other two figures, making up the base of the statue. The second woman's other hand was pulling up her own robe; one long dark finger inserted into her perfectly carved mound.

Francesca could feel a subtle change in her as the heat began to rise from low inside her belly. The statue was exquisite, breathtaking in its realism. She could almost hear the noises of their pleasure; the soft excited moans of the bending woman, the grunting pig sounds from the pot-bellied man, and beneath them the prone woman chasing her own satisfaction whilst her other hand worked against the rigid hardness of her master. Between her legs Francesca could feel the warmth and the wetness of her growing excitement. She shuddered, unable to take her eyes off the figures.

As she stared, absorbing the erotic intensity of the image, Catz moved closer. Francesca's eyes were drawn again and again to the intricacies of the carved figures. She tried to compose herself and circle the plinth, tried to tear her eyes away but the image was too vivid, too compelling. What she had taken at first glance to be heavy bracelets were complex carved handcuffs, securing the standing woman over the vase. The carved woman was tied for her master's pleasures. Franceses felt an intense ripple of pleasure surge through her. The bound woman's eyes were half-closed in ecstasy, her lips drawn back. Francesca was so close now she felt she could almost hear the woman's intense moan of satisfaction as her master brought her closer to the edge of paradise.

Francesca glanced around the gallery and knew then that she had stumbled across a breathtaking collection of erotica. The images on the walls and plinths and cabinets now screamed out at her, not as artefacts but as living, breathing records of the extremes of passion. She caught sight of Catz creeping towards her, his piercing blue eyes alight. She swallowed hard, feeling the heat coursing through her, and stepped away from the carving. She wanted to say something – anything – but no words came. Instead she was only aware of the intense heat in her belly and the rising sense of desire throbbing in her sex.

Catz stood still for a moment – unearthly still – and then one broad hand moved up towards the buttons on his tight uniform jacket. His voice, when it came, was low and hypnotic. 'I can give you anything you want,' he whispered, 'anything you have ever dreamed of.'

Unnerved Francesca glanced again around the room.

'I don't know what I want,' she stammered, gauging the distance between herself and the stairwell. Catz followed her gaze.

He smiled thinly. 'There is everything here, lady. Perhaps you would like to look at something else?' He held out his arm in invitation.

Francesca shook her head, the blood pulsing in her ears. 'No, no I don't want to look,' she whispered, but there was no conviction in her voice.

Catz smiled again; the effect on his brutally handsome face was unnerving.

'Let me show you, then. Perhaps I can tempt you,' he whispered and beckoned to her. He half turned, his long boots cracking out the beginnings of a rhythm on the polished floor. Mesmerised, she followed him as he made his way along the gallery.

As they stepped into a pool of shadow Catz suddenly spun round and sprung towards her. She cried out and stepped back but too late to stop him grabbing her wrists. Her handbag slipped from her fingers and clattered to the floor. His eyes glittered dangerously in the half light.

Francesca instinctively pulled away, trying to fight him, push him off. He smiled down at her. 'You only have to tell me to stop,' he whispered triumphantly. 'But isn't this what you dream of, lady, when you are alone at night?'

He stepped closer, taking both of her narrow wrists in one of his hands. His fingers lifted to cup the softness of one of her breasts; she let out a thin desperate moan and pulled against him. His face set in a narrow grin as he stepped closer, still forcing her to step back. Desperately she tried to resist him; feeling the panic in her gut, she whimpered and struggled to free herself. His expression didn't change as he forced her roughly up against the panelled walls. The coolness of the wood through her thin blouse made her shudder as she strained against him, frustrated at being unable to match his strength. She struggled helplessly, her face contorted with panic. He glanced upwards, as if judging a distance and, unable to resist, she followed his eyes.

Above her, screwed into the panelling, was a pair of manacles secured into rings. She screamed and kicked out; to her horror he threw back his head and laughed, whilst his hands jerked her wrists upwards. She bucked and wriggled as he lifted her higher, dark desperate fears flooding her mind as she sobbed and curled her body away from him, trying to slip from his tight grasp. Even as she resisted him she was aware that some compelling part of her mind craved what he was offering, the paradox unnerving her as she twisted again.

He pushed her back firmly and forced her wrists back and up towards the metal cuffs; there was a distinctive snap as they closed automaticaly; around her. Francesca felt her shoulder joints stretched in complaint as the cold metal bit into her flesh. To her surprise Catz stepped back. His expression hadn't changed but now he seemed to be considering something else. He leant forward and adjusted the chain on the restraints so that the balls of her feet rested on the floor, taking the strain out of her shoulders.

If Francesca had doubted it before, she now knew she was in the control of her tormentor. This was a complex game; one in which she could call the shots if she wanted to. He glanced at her, his face cold and impassive. She let out a strangled breath and her momentary certainty vanished as he stepped back towards her, his hands raised. She let out a thin moan, her eyes never leaving his brutally handsome face. His fingers moved back to the buttons of his uniform jacket and slowly began to undo them. Francesca licked her lips, her fear mingling again with the dark sense of anticipation.

The cut of his jacket did not lie: his shoulders were indeed broad; sculptured slabs of lightly tanned muscle accentuated the triangular shape of his torso as it narrowed down to his waist. Between hard rounded pectorals a light covering of curls added a subtle highlight to his rugged shape.

Francesca shuddered; he was as stunningly beautiful as his mistress. He moved closer under her unguarded scrutiny, and she could feel her eagerness growing, struggling with the sharp glittering shards of fear. She swallowed hard, aware that she was salivating in anticipation of his assault on her. The paradox of her fear and deep aching desire confused and exhilarated her, bringing tears to her eyes.

He cupped her face in his large hands, pulling her towards him, and she tried to pull back but his mouth refused to be denied. His tongue forced her lips apart, his teeth nipping at their soft contours, compelling them to open under the hot invasive arrow of his tongue.

Intense and unstoppable he ran the tip of his tongue along the delicate arch of her palate. She shuddered, trying to close her mouth against him.

His mouth moved relentlessly against hers, his vicious kiss leaving her dizzy with sensation. Abruptly, his hands dropped to the collar of her shirt and with a single outward movement he ripped the front of her blouse open. Somewhere close by she heard a button clatter on to the wooden floor. His strong hands hovered over her nipples, swollen and hardened in expectation of his touch. He pulled away from the kiss, leaving her mouth bruised and tingling. His cold ice-blue eyes glanced down at her straining breasts before he leant closer and closed his teeth around one nipple. She held her breath as his teeth closed a fraction more, tightening, teasing, threatening. A thin whimper of fear escaped from her reddened lips. Slowly he released his bite, whilst his tongue lapped fleetingly across the darkened bud, caressing her before he stepped back.

The effect was galvanising. Suddenly her vulnerability and terror bubbled to the surface; she kicked out at him, ignoring the protest in the muscles of her arms. His eyes moved over her slowly, watching her face as she gasped with desire and fear. To her surprise her attack made him smile. She kicked out again, wildly, swinging on the chains. She could feel the cold sting of the manacles as they bit into her wrists. Desperately she lunged at him again. With almost casual ease he grabbed one ankle: she swore and tried to wriggle away. Calmly he bent down and grabbed her other foot, his hands tugging at the heel of her sandals, easing them off.

Moving forward slowly he lifted her narrow foot to his lips. She cried out, writhing under his touch as he ran his tongue between her toes: the sensation made her whimper. His fingers slipped into the sensitive crevices, teasing, tantalising. She twisted against his hold, her face contorted in confusion.

He looked up at her and she thought she could see a triumphant ice-cold flash of pleasure in his eyes. Then she moaned in expectation as he ran his tongue along the sole of her foot. She yelped and tried to pull away from him.

A calm measured voice halted their struggle.

'Perhaps you would like these, Catz?' Alicia Moffat said quietly as she appeared from a concealed door in the panelling.

Francesca felt her colour rising; heat coursed through her. She looked around wildly, straining against the bonds. Her thin blouse was ripped at the front, revealing the curve of her breasts, their nipples dark and tight with anticipation, her hair wild and dishevelled. But more revealing than this, she knew Alicia could sense her excitement.

Alicia was carrying a pair of leg irons; she walked slowly across the gallery towards them, barely glancing at Francesca, and dropped them to the floor. The noise as they crashed on to the wooden surface was startling. Despite herself, Francesca looked up and caught the look in Alicia's violet eyes – they were excited too – eager, shiny with another, darker desire.

'What are you doing to my poor Catz?' she murmured as she moved closer still. Her hand lifted to stroke the huge man's arm; one perfectly manicured finger traced across the taut outline of his shoulder muscles.

Francesca looked away, speechless, humiliated by her nakedness and undisguised excitement.

'I thought you liked to be watched,' Alicia said slowly, her eyes lingering on Francesca's hot dishevelled body.

She glanced up at Catz.

'Perhaps I'll watch another time,' she said and walked back slowly across the gallery; at the door she hesitated, and turned back towards them for a second as if to fix the scene in her mind. Then she was gone.

Francesca heard the faint hum of a lift. Reddened and embarrassed, Francesca renewed her struggle with Catz.

Catz, his face set in a grimace, held her ankles tight and jerked her legs further apart. Francesca moaned again and tried to pull away from him. Catz grinned and, bending at the knees, picked up the items of bondage then snapped them closed around her ankles. The touch of cold metal against her flesh made Francesca flinch. Slowly he lowered her to the floor.

The irons held her ankles rigid, forcing her legs further apart; she was exposed, secured for his pleasure and helpless against his advances. Kneeling, Catz locked the irons into a short chain set in a ring on the floor. Francesca felt her sex contract with an electric flicker of desire. Her helplessness and vulnerability added to her excitement.

With a slow deliberation he stood up, his great hands running up over her feet, over her calves and knees, over her thighs. He pressed his face against the hard swell of her mound, rubbing, smelling, nosing against the soft folds of her sex. She moaned, writhing at the humiliation and was stunned to feel the dark glittering part of her mind take control. Her hips pushed forward instinctively at his touch; he looked at her, unable to disguise the look of triumph in his eyes as his hands moved away, on over the swell of her hips, over her belly, brushing up over her naked breasts.

Inside she could feel her desire lifting higher. Her need for his touch stopped the breath in her throat. She was wet for him and the dark gifts he offered; between her legs she could feel her knickers clinging to every fold and contour of her sex. He moved up her body until his face was barely a foot away from hers, his eyes hard glittering pinpricks. Leaning closer he ran his tongue wetly around the outline of her lips whilst his hands came up to the remains of her blouse and ripped them away. She cried out as the material bit into the soft creases of her body. He kissed her again before standing back to admire his handiwork.

Again Francesca felt the intoxicating mixture of fear and desire; her breasts ached for him to touch them, rub them, cradle them, suck them. She wanted him and the knowledge terrified her.

He moved back towards her, the mask set once more as he caught hold of her under the arms. She tried to press against him, longing to feel her naked breasts against the hard glistening heat of his chest – the restraints prevented her – instead he coldly turned her around to face the wall.

Francesca began to protest, struggling feverishly, but stopped instantly as he leant against her and murmured softly in her ear. 'All you have to do is ask me to stop, Francesca.' His voice was low and emotionless; the tone made her shiver.

His hands lingered for a fraction of a second over the curve of her naked breasts. She shuddered in delight and was rewarded by his wet tongue tracing slowly over the tortured muscles at the nape of her neck. His breath warmed her shoulders. 'Tell me you want this,' he whispered.

Francesca gasped.

'Tell me,' he said again, his hands moving to her hips.

She stiffened as he dragged up the material of her skirt, his hand lingering on her rounded buttocks for an instant before he grabbed hold of the band of her knickers. His fingers slid into the top, jerking the material tight up into the wetness between her legs.

His tone was firmer now. 'Tell me you want this.'

'I want this,' she whispered, her voice scratchy, barely above a breath.

'I can't hear you,' he said sharply, jerking her knickers harder. 'Tell me again.'

'I want this,' she said, barely any louder.

'Not good enough,' he said softly.

Letting go of her, she felt him reach up towards the manacles; his bare chest brushed her back while above her she could see his fingers searching for the catches.

'No,' she said desperately, trying to find a voice. 'No!'

'Tell me, then, tell me now,' he said softly.

'I want this. I want this,' she shouted huskily. As she strained to call out, his hands moved quickly back to her hips, dragging up her skirt and ripping away the thin silk of her sodden knickers.

'Then you shall have it, lady. You shall have it all,' he hissed malevolently and grabbed at the waistband of her skirt. She heard the material of her skirt rip like paper between his hands. Intense waves of desire rippled through her as his hands moved down across her buttocks. His fingers moved nearer to her moist aching opening. She was so certain with each movement that he was going to touch her, so desperate that she held her breath and then gasped as his fingers moved slowly away. She groaned between gritted teeth, feeling his breath warm and moist on her body, sensing his cold eyes taking in every inch of her vulnerable nakedness.

She strained, arching her body back towards him. She wanted him to fill her up, to take her, wanted to feel his cock buried deep inside her; instead he moved away. She let out a hiss of frustration. 'I want you,' she whispered. 'Please, Catz.'

'What did you say?' he said evenly. His voice seemed far behind her.

'I want you. Please, please -' she implored, her voice crackling with emotion. She heard him laugh softly.

'You'll have me, don't worry, you'll have me, Francesca,' he murmured.

There was a strange noise behind her. She turned, straining to see what Catz was doing, but too late to see the short arc of the switch as it cut through the still air in the gallery; the blow caught her low on the buttocks a split second later. The pain was a lightning-hot flash in her mind – she screamed as much from shock as pain. Her back arched, the second lash came before she had time to protest or recover from, the first.

'Please, please,' she hissed, not knowing whether she was begging him to stop or pleading with him to continue. Great hot tears ran down her face; her breath came in ragged sobs as she heard the switch cut the air behind her.

The third blow was higher and she bucked away from it. Screaming as it cut a hot, burning welt across her body, she felt her breasts pressed against the cold panelling. The fourth and fifth came in a blur of electric sensation. The feelings heightened the paradox; part of her mind screamed out in indignation and pain, but another part she had never heard or experienced before delighted in the white-hot sting and humiliation.

Then there was a split second of silence – a dark cool silence. Francesca held her breath not knowing whether there would be more blows. Her buttocks and back were on fire, the heat echoing and heightening the glow between her legs. She tried to be quiet so that she could hear Catz, but it was impossible now; the roar of her breath and the echoes of her strangled sobs cut out the sound. She knew he was directly behind her; as her sobs subsided she could feel his breath cooling the heat of her back. She heard the sound of liquid being poured and then his hands were on her, spreading something cold over her stinging flesh. She shuddered.

'How did you like it?' he murmured. 'Is it how you imagined it would be?' His voice was a low hypnotic purr.

Francesca could find no words to answer him; instead she leant into the soft circling of his touch. He moved his hands across her back with the subtle deft touch of a masseur, working the balm into the red-hot glow of the pain.

She found herself moving with him, soaking up his every touch; her tormentor and healer. A soft stilted moan trickled from her lips as his fingers eased the pain away. But as she felt her tense muscles begin to ease under his touch she knew it wasn't over. His cool hands moved higher, reaching up under the sensitive curve of her armpits, stroking, smoothing, turning. His expert fingers trailed along the stretched muscles of her inner arm, whilst his other hand began tracing the bones of her spine. He was playing her like a piano.

She could smell him, hear his breathing. Turning as far as her bonds allowed she glanced across at his broad muscular chest. The unguent he was spreading over her back was smeared across his body in a gleaming sunlit arc, its light perfume in stark contrast to the sharp pungent odour of his sweat. He caught her eyes, and his own narrowed. She looked away, but not before seeing the icy glint in his eyes and watching his hand as it dropped to the buttons of his trousers. From behind her she heard a soft throaty growl that made her shudder in expectation.

She knew instinctively he was naked beneath the finely cut trousers and in her mind's eye she could see him, imagine his every curve, every single hair. The broad stretch of his chest, narrowing to the tight flat plain of his belly and below – the images made her tingle. She felt the brush of his chest against her tortured back, cool and exciting, as his hands slid up from her waist to cup her throbbing breasts. She eased herself back towards him and was rewarded by the merest fleeting brush with his erect cock. The smile she had begun to form was ripped away as he savagely twisted her nipples, nails biting into them. The respite of tenderness was over.

His teeth sunk into the soft muscles of her shoulder and she cried out; her body instinctively bucked to escape from his teeth. His hands dropped to her hips, pulling her sharply back towards him, one hand snaking round to explore the contours of her sex. His fingers were brutal, probing, forcing her lips apart before they plunged into her, deeper and deeper. Over her shoulder she could hear the rawness of his ragged excited breaths and she knew then he desired her as much as she wanted him. The knowledge heightened every sensation.

His thumb lifted to press down on her clitoris, and she cried out, desperate for release.

She gasped with frustration as his fingers moved away. Once there was the sound of something being poured – and then his hands were back, cupping a puddle of something cool that trickled between his fingers on to her aching hot body. Changing position he slid one arm around her belly, pulling her out from the wall, whilst his other hand, cupping the liquid, slid lower dripping cold liquid over the curve of her buttocks.

'You want this,' he purred. 'Remember, you want this.'

His hand snaked down between her legs. Spreading her wide, he smeared the liquid around the folds of her slit; she wondered fleetingly why her juices, thick and fragrant, were running down on to her thighs. His fingers worked on feverishly whilst his other arm, taking her weight, jerked her back towards him opening her to him, exposing the soft pink swollen depths of her body. Oiled and warm, his fingers moved back still further, sliding towards the tight forbidden closure behind her sex. She gasped as his fingers brushed over it, tracing the line of tightness. Horrified, she tried to lunge forward but his progress was unrelenting.

The cool oily liquid trickled back into her sex and she could feel it mixing with her own liquid heat. She closed her eyes as his oiled finger slipped into her most secret place. She whimpered, not from pain but from her body's betrayal as it opened willingly under his sensitive and delicate touch. His finger began to move slowly in and out; with every gentle movement she gasped at the intensity of the sensations.

He lowered the arm that was holding her. Moving slowly round to her dark mound his fingers parted the lips of her sex, seeking out her engorged clitoris. The merest fleeting stroke was enough to send her jerking backwards, impaling herself on his finger and cursing herself for her desire.

With the pulse beating hypnotically in her ears, she heard his voice softly in her ear.

'Come to me,' he sighed, his dark voice no more than a whisper on an outward breath. She could not resist his entreaty, and began to move against him, her body drinking up every new sensation, aching for a conclusion. She was rewarded by a soft mewling sound of satisfaction deep within Catz's throat.

His fingers began to move slowly in total harmony, rubbing her throbbing clitoris, probing deep inside her darkest places, smearing more and more of her juices around the base of his fingers. Inside her head the insistent rhythm had begun the spiral that would lead to her climax. His fingers slowly slipped out from tight dark muscles behind her sex. She let out a sigh and was rewarded by being pulled back further. Now she knew what Catz had planned for her, she felt the great bulk of his rampant cock stroke her thighs and she glanced down. Between her legs she could see the raging bulbous head of his shaft, its ferocity undisguised by the smooth outlines of a silvery transparent sheath.

Continuing the soft pressure and touch on her clitoris, he slipped his cock in between the engorged lips of her sex. His first violent thrust made her lift against the sheer power of it; her muscles tightened spontaneously around him and she let out a desperate gasp. He filled her brutally, forcing himself deep inside her. Under other circumstances it would have been enough, but she felt the thread of his desire, the path of his lust, and she knew this was just a beginning. His fingers trailed scented juices over her helpless body. She could hear his breath, under control now, like an athlete finding his stride.

She began to ride him, the lights in her head glinting in the middle distance, within reach, fast approaching. His fingers worked more quickly, defining frenetic circles around her clitoris, encouraging her to impale herself on him, suck him deep inside her body, grasping at his bulk. She pushed again, but as she reached the lowest point of her thrust, he slid out of her sex and grabbed her hips. She hissed in panic, afraid to fight against him; sensing what was coming next, she felt him push slowly into the tight bud that beckoned behind her throbbing sex. She heard herself scream out; the sensation was dark – breath-stopping – a violent intense tightness that threatened to consume her.

His gentle controlled push inwards was accompanied by his renewed and speeded up attention to her clitoris. She couldn't hold back; she wanted him to bring her to the top of the arc, wanted to feel the waves of ecstasy crash over her; despite her fear, she thrust back against him, her aching empty sex longing for his cock to be there too. As if reading her mind, he pushed his fingers deep inside her as contrast to the thrusts in the deeper, darker places of her body.

She heard him lose control of his breathing; a thin animal moan of excitement escaped from his lips and echoed in her ears. With a sense of elation she moved against the taut sweating bulk of his body, revelling in her knowledge that his dominance and his control were almost lost.

The combination of sensations and the confirmation of his longing was almost unbearable. She could feel her excitement growing, could taste the sweat on her lips as it rolled down her face and feel his electric desire pushing him onwards. Against the contours of her aching arching back she felt the raw heat from his body as he impaled her again and again with fingers and cock and heard the roar of his breath as they moved together and then it was there – the rush, the triumph – as he electrified the glowing bud of her clitoris.

Gushing white-hot waves filled her head and crashed up through her belly. She felt her whole body tighten around him. Somewhere between the desperate waves of delight she heard herself cry out again and again and heard Catz scream in ecstasy as he joined with her, his hot body pressed close against hers.

Afterwards, there were the moments of shuddering awareness. Francesca glanced down at the heap of rags that lay around her feet, felt the burning sensation between her legs and noticed the trails of lotion and sweat on her belly. Below, amongst the matted tangle of hair around her sex, Catz's fingers were still buried deep inside her whilst inside she could feel the last spasms of her orgasm shuddering through them both.

With great care Catz slipped out of her. She assumed he would let her down now and she braced herself in anticipation; instead after a few seconds he stepped back and she suddenly felt desperately cold. There was another noise behind her of something being ripped open, and his hands lifted her gently up towards him again. She shuddered at the exposure as he began to wipe the swollen, pounded closure of her bottom with a sheet of moist disposable cloth. She felt herself colour as the cool material cleaned her, his touch fur-soft. A moment's pause and he smeared her aching secret places with ointment. Another soft ripping sound and he cleaned her sex with a second cloth; tenderly, like a nurse, touching the swollen tight folds with something akin to devotion.

Finally he knelt and released her ankles.

As he stood up to undo her arms he murmured gently, 'Don't try to move. You'll fall.' His voice was soft, tender, almost caring. She breathed in as he reached up; he smelt of bitter heat and the sweet perfume of the soothing balm. His body was glistening with sweat. Looking across she watched the taut knot of muscles in his arms as he stretched, and felt the last flutters of her orgasm tighten in her belly.

As the wrist-cuffs slipped off, he was there to hold her up. She allowed him to take her weight and turned towards him, heady and exhausted. His naked body was a masterpiece. She could not bring herself to look at his face. Instead, her eyes moved over his magnificent body and downwards to where, nestling amongst the coarse curly hair of his belly, his limp sex still glistened.

Without speaking he picked her up in his arms and carried her towards the panelled door of the lift. She closed her eyes, leaning against him, revelling in his heady scent, and allowed herself to be taken. She heard the soft hum of the lift and felt the cool air inside. Moments later the doors slid open and she wondered fleetingly where he was taking her. Opening her eyes a fraction she saw they were in a broad corridor. Catz walked without hesitation up to a door and pushed it open with his foot.

Francesca peered from between half-closed lashes; inside was a double bed set in the centre of a huge pale-pink room. On one wall, windows extended from floor to ceiling, giving the room a panoramic view out over the sea beyond. The sheets on the bed were turned back and ready. Francesca wondered if Catz had prepared the room earlier in anticipation of her visit. Had he done it in the morning when he'd come back from giving her Alicia's message? The thought made her shiver.

Catz placed her gently on the bed and pulled the heavy coverlet up around her shoulders. Francesca didn't move though she longed to turn to admire his exquisite naked body. He moved on silent catlike feet around the room and drew the full-length curtains closed, cutting out the sharp inquisitive sunlight. His outline against the windows made her draw in a breath of admiration; he glanced across at her, his face calm and impassive.

Quietly he turned and left the room, closing the door with a sharp click. She lay in the gloom for a few seconds, her feverish mind conjuring up the images from the gallery. Her body ached from the bitter-sweet assault. From outside she could hear the soft rush of the ocean, a hypnotic gentle breath against the eager and responsive sand. She let her body relax into the sweet-smelling sheets and didn't fight when sleep claimed her.

# Chapter Three

Catz watched impassively as Alicia Moffat posed in the dressing room that adjoined her bedroom. She was naked except for a pair of delicate high-heeled satin mules, her bandeau and her favourite diamond earrings. The large windows behind her were draped with heavy cream gauze which reduced the summer sunshine to a delicate, more flattering glow. Her slim body was almost translucent, the colour of finest porcelain. She turned so he could admire the lines of her skilfully preserved body in the gentle glow of the diffused sunlight. She caught his expression and smiled provocatively, lifting one hand to stroke her small uptilted breasts which owed their shape more to surgery than genetics. Her fingers lingered teasingly on the tiny, tight pink nipples.

Catz, seemingly unmoved, watched her reflection casually. She smiled back at him and moved gracefully into another pose. 'Do you love me, Catz?' she purred, her hand tracing down over the tight lines of her waist and belly.

He said nothing, turning instead to take an intricately shaped bottle of massage oil from the dressing table before slowly rolling up the sleeves of his collarless shirt. He knew exactly what she wanted from him and intended to delay the moment as long as he could.

She turned a little to let the warm light play across her torso before glancing at him. Her eyes were bright with expectation. His expression was determined, unreadable. She pouted at his reflection. 'You look so serious, Catz. Am I still beautiful?' she asked teasingly. Behind her, the reflection only served to confirm her perfection.

Catz poured a little of the oil into his palm and stepped closer to her, the delicate fragrance growing stronger in the warmth of his hands. He watched her move to and fro, admiring the elegant lines of her body whilst he let the oil warm through. Finally she stood in front of him and allowed him to smooth it gently over her narrow shoulders. He used delicate strokes as light as the caress of a summer breeze, and she turned appreciatively into the curving motion of his fingers. Beneath his fingers her skin felt like the most delicate silk, every muscle, every fine, delicate curve of her familiar bone structure revealed itself beneath his knowing touch.

'Ummmm,' she moaned softly, 'that feels so good.' She leant closer to him.

He caught her eye in the mirror and she laughed back at him; the light amused sound of genuine good humour.

'Come on Catz, why so silent; wasn't this afternoon blissful? Tell me you love me.'

Catz's expression didn't falter for an instant, his hands tracing intricate circles across her shoulders, the pressure never changing. She pouted at his reflection and lifted one elegantly slim arm to remove her bandeau. Her luxuriant highlighted hair fell loosely on to her oily shoulders. She shook her head and he hesitated for an instant before picking up a hairbrush. Her loveliness never ceased to captivate and fascinate him.

Still naked, she turned and sat down at the dressing table. Catz followed her. For a split second they were both caught in the mirror; his own face still and impassive, hers softly lined and animated. He rested his hand on her shoulder, applying no pressure. She stretched lovingly against his palm and stroked his strong fingers; he revelled in the coolness of her body: she was so tiny, so perfect. The tenderness and love he felt for her glowed inside him like a clear-blue flame, though she would have teased him unmercifully for his sentimentality were she able to read his mind. He looked up into her eyes, knowing that his face would not betray his inner feelings.

'Are you warm enough?' he asked, glancing at the delicate silk negligée she had discarded on the dressing-room floor.

She snorted and pulled a little face of displeasure. 'Don't spoil it, Catz. I'm admiring myself.' She paused. 'I have to admire myself, you know, because no one else will tell me how beautiful I look.'

Catz, in spite of himself, grinned back at her reflection. Her beauty was self-evident, it didn't require confirmation; the mirror said it all. 'You're ugly,' he said. 'Always were.'

Alicia threw back her head and laughed. Catz leant closer to brush his lips along the fine iridescent skin where her shoulders narrowed into the long arc of her neck. Her skin was warm and fragrant from the oil, soft and inviting like a sleek animal pelt. Beneath his lips he felt Alicia quiver. He lifted one hand to cup her small breasts; the fragrant oil gave them a delicate golden highlight. She snorted playfully and wriggled away from his fingers.

'Catz, instead of teasing me why don't you tell me about Francesca,' she said. Her voice had dropped to a low hypnotic purr.

He looked away. This was what she wanted from him, the dark electric secrets of the afternoon in the gallery; every moment, every intense engulfing second. She needed to share in his passion, explore every sensation by proxy. Her eyes were bright with expectation; under his fingers he felt her pulse quicken.

'Tell me,' she said more forcefully, her eyes diamond bright, though there was still an element of teasing in her tone. 'Tell me. How did she feel, did you taste her? Tell me about her heat; was she good, Catz, did you enjoy her?' Her questions came slowly, softly, in a voice barely above a whisper.

He stepped back and took the brush from her, laying it down on a shelf. Keeping the details from her would be impossible, but the game was to resist her as long as possible. He turned back. 'Why didn't you come back to see for yourself?' he said lightly, retrieving her wrap from the floor and hanging it back on its hanger.

She shook her head. 'I didn't want to inhibit you. Did she call out, did she fight you? Tell me what she said.'

It was impossible for her to hide the eagerness of excitement from him. Catz pulled up another chair so they sat almost side by side, both caught in the silvery rectangle of the mirror.

'What do you want from her?' he said quietly.

In the mirror Alicia shrugged. 'I thought she might be able to write a book about Edgar's adventures around the world. My GP says she is a very talented writer.'

Now it was Catz's turn to laugh. 'I'm not talking about her writing ability, Alicia. I was thinking more of Edgar's activities.'

Alicia tutted. 'His charity work, Catz; his acts of philanthropy, his travels.'

Catz still looked amused, unable to keep the smile from his face.

Alicia smiled too. 'She will, of course, have to be very selective about what she includes.'

Catz lifted an eyebrow. He had seen and enjoyed all of Edgar's collection over the years they'd been together.

'All right, all right. Extremely selective,' she said, with a snort. 'And then,' she said more slowly, 'I thought we might be able to get her to help us dispose of Edgar's collection.'

Catz leant closer to her, so close he could see the delicate rise and fall of her breasts. 'Are you sure you want to be rid of all your toys?'

Alicia nodded and waved him away. 'Yes, it's time we got rid of everything.' She hesitated. 'I want it disposed of before I die. It would be far too easy for some nosy journalist to get wind of the collection, and then God knows what the press would publish about me and Edgar.'

'And you think Francesca is the one to help you?' As he spoke her name, his mind conjured an image of her. He remembered the subtle mixture of desire and fear on her face and the way her slim naked body turned and bucked under his touch. His mind replayed the intense animal heat of her desire as she had raced towards her climax. She had screamed out as she had impaled herself on him, fighting her own excitement, fighting her own reluctance to accept her body's dark and desperate longing.

He looked away from Alicia's reflection for a split second, knowing he wouldn't be able to disguise the excitement of the memory. He felt a tightening in his gut, a soft stirring in his groin.

Alicia glanced across at him. 'I think she will be ideal. I'll ring Gerald Foxley at the auction house and suggest Francesca goes to see him. Perhaps they could meet at the London house.'

Catz sighed, suppressing the intense images that threatened to undermine his steely control.

"Why her?' he asked quietly, though in his heart he knew. Francesca echoed some distant memory in Alicia's past. Francesca was the kind of woman Alicia might have been if she had never met Edgar.

Alicia leant forward to examine herself in the harsher light of the mirror. 'It just seemed a perfect opportunity.' She looked up, in order to hold Catz's gaze. 'She just seems *right*.'

Catz nodded. He knew the kind of woman Alicia preferred, and Francesca fitted Alicia's criteria exactly. Intelligent, attractive, slim and, most of all, restrained.

It was almost as if Francesca had walked through life up till now in a deep sleep. They would awaken her; he had recognised the dark mysterious longing in the younger woman's eyes. Between them they would set it free.

'Now tell me about her, Catz,' Alicia murmured as if reading his mind. 'I've waited quite long enough; I want to know about her. Please.'

Catz spread his great hands in resignation, and got up. 'First put on your negligée and let me get you some tea.'

Alicia wrinkled up her nose in displeasure. 'Stop treating me like an old lady.'

He slipped the negligée off its hanger and held it out like a matador's cape. She compliantly allowed him to slip it over her narrow shoulders, and stood still whilst he tied it around her. Even through the thin material, Catz could sense her excitement. 'Now go into your room. I'll bring a tray up,' he said firmly.

Alicia pulled her lips into a small pout of displeasure. Catz gave her a sharp look and she held up her hands.

'All right, all right, I'm going,' she said lightly and stepped through the door into the main bedroom beyond.

*

Alicia's bedroom was curtained in the same way as the dressing room; the centre was dominated by a great four-poster bed decked with swathes of cream lace. Glancing over her shoulder to see that Catz had gone, Alicia crept across the room and slipped under the delicate lacy covers.

Eagerly she encouraged the feverish images of Francesca to flood through her mind. She had been compelled to find Francesca after seeing her in the garden. Catz's description of Francesca's interest in him had encouraged Alicia further. He had been right about her; Francesca was perfect.

In her mind Alicia replayed the scene in the library; Francesca's secured sweating body, her thin blouse in tatters, the tight curve of her small breasts pouting eagerly towards Catz. There had been a brilliant spark of desire in her eyes, echoed by the darkness of her nipples. The desire had stretched along the long curve of her waist and her muscles had tensed as she struggled against her captor. Alicia shuddered with delight at the memory.

When Alicia had opened the lift doors Catz had been holding Francesca's ankles, forcing her legs apart; her skirt had been rucked back to reveal the soft curves of her thighs and beyond. Barely covered was the dark damp bulge of her sex pressing against the thin fabric of her knickers.

She closed her eyes, imagining Catz's hard animal-bright eyes as she had stepped into the room. There had been a smell of warm bodies in the air. Feasting on the images she let her imagination linger on the thick knotted bulge of Catz's penis straining against the thick material of his trousers.

In his expression she had seen the almost imperceptible signs of animal arousal. Francesca might have thought him unmoved but Alicia knew him better; she had recognised the tightening of his jaw, the sustained effort to keep his breathing to a steady, rhythmic, seemingly unaffected level as his eyes moved back and forth across Francesca's vulnerable body.

Alicia had seen his eyes move towards the light leather whip lying on one of the display cases and had known exactly what Catz was planning for Francesca. The thought brought a flush of colour to her alabaster complexion. She wished he had let her stay. She ran the moist tip of her tongue around her lips as the images unfolded behind her closed eyes.

Edgar had taught her to appeciate the pleasures of being an observer. He had developed in her the ability to perceive what every player in the erotic game felt, what they thought, how their bodies ached, every sensation, every aching heat kissed, each passion-filled moment. She was grateful for his tuition; it sustained her now when other pleasures were denied her.

She wished Catz could have seen Francesca with her lover in the garden. The wish took on a life of its own, twisting other images into Alicia's memory of Catz and Francesca. She imagined the other man, Francesca's lover, Chris, standing beside Catz as Francesca hung naked, spread-eagled against the wall. As Catz stood back clutching the light whip, his face tight in concentration, Chris now, in her imagination, stepped forward from the shadows, his hands circling Catz's narrow waist, eyes alight with desire. Alicia shuddered in anticipation of the scenario that her mind was about to unfold.

In the dark sensuous mind that existed behind her violet eyes the fantasy Chris turned Catz towards him, eyes intense, mouth open, a gloss of sweat over his suntanned face and naked torso whilst his eager hand dropped to cup the bulk of Catz's sex. Catz shuddered, his composure lost as he leant forward to kiss Chris, his tongue pushing deep into the other man's eager, waiting mouth. Behind them on the wall the agonised figure of Francesca strained against her chains, whimpering softly.

The sound of the door opening broke into Alicia's dark fantasy. Angrily, she opened one eye. Catz looked at her.

'Started without me?' he said softly as he padded across the room carrying a tray. She pulled herself up on to one elbow.

'You were so long,' she snapped petulantly. He placed the tray on the bedside table and sat down beside her. Slowly he slipped off his shirt, revealing his broad, muscular chest; his almost sculptural torso was high-lighted with a sprinkling of soft tight curls. Alicia purred appreciatively.

'Why don't I tell you about Paris instead?' he asked, leaning towards her. 'Or Kenya?'

Alicia pulled a face.

'Or that night in New York? Would you rather hear about Berlin; do you remember Berlin?'

She pulled the bedclothes up to her face like a naughty child. From behind the cover she whispered, 'I remember everything, every moment. It's one of the blessings, or perhaps the curse, of being my age; every face, every body – every look. I remember everything.'

She paused for a second. 'If you won't tell me about Francesca, tell me about Rio; tell me about the blond man.' She caught the slight flicker of emotion cross Catz's face and pressed home her advantage. 'Tell me about his body and the things he made you do. I want to know it all; every sensation, every last pulse that passed between you.'

Catz turned towards her, eyes alight. He grabbed hold of the bedclothes and jerked them out of Alicia's hands. She let out a little squeak of surprise and then smiled. Her negligée had fallen open. He glanced up at her face before spreading the soft material around her so she was totally exposed. She giggled.

Beside his brutal, animal strength her body seemed pale and delicate, though she knew it still retained the lithe, athletic shape she had had as a young woman. Her rounded hip-bones lifted her pearly-white skin in delicious curving contrast to the flat bowl of her white belly. She watched him as he surveyed her body and let out a soft hiss of contentment. The slightest vibration of her excitement rippled through her with a sharp, diamond brilliance.

*

His voice was soft as he started to tell her his story.

'I was nineteen, good-looking – hungry – straight up out of the sticks,' he began. 'I wanted a job, any job. I was prepared to consider anything to set me free from the grinding poverty of life in my village. I remember coming up to the city on the bus. It was hot and crowded, people were pushing and jostling as it jolted along the unmade-up roads. All I could smell was the stink of chickens and unwashed peasants.'

As he spoke, she closed her eyes, letting his voice take her. She had taught him how to bring this delicate game to its conclusion. She had taught him well.

'I went first to the house of my uncle Leo in the poor quarter. He had promised my mother that he would find me a good job if I ever wanted one, serving in his bar. It was dark when I got to the outskirts of the city. The city is alive at night, like a dangerous wild animal. At every turn there were sounds and sights and smells that dazzled me. I was afraid to linger, and hurried to find my uncle's place. I used the last of my money to get a taxi. The cab dropped me at the end of a shabby little side street. When I got to Leo's house it was in darkness, the shutters closed, door locked.

'Night was closing in around me, I was alone in a city I did not know. Bright lights shone from the streets beyond my uncle Leo's establishment, city lights, crowds, bars, the smell of food cooking. My guts rumbled, but I was penniless and afraid. I put my bags on the steps and knocked again. There was no sound from inside.

'I decided to see if there was another way into the house, so, leaving my things tucked away in the shadows, I went down the street looking for a side alley that would take me to the back of my uncle's house. From a bar came the sounds of music and laughter.

'Outside, standing in the light from the bar, there was a group of girls. They were leaning against the open windows: beautiful girls with blonde hair; dark girls in short skirts so high that you could see the lips of their sex; girls with heavy breasts that strained against the thin material of their T-shirts, nipples jutting; slim girls with tiny breasts cradled in bikini tops, their painted nipples peeping out over the spangled cups.

'I could feel the stirring in my crotch. I had only ever touched one girl in my home village. I remember the smell lingering on my fingers, the way she had moaned under my touch.'

As Catz spoke, Alicia reached out and drank in the images Catz was painting for her; she could smell the heady perfume of the village girl, drink in the cheap perfume of the painted street girls. Her mouth began to water. His voice filled her head, and she moaned softly as he continued.

'I walked towards them nervously. They looked like cats, wild dangerous cats. I asked the first girl I came to if she knew where my uncle was; her expression was mocking. She shrugged but moved closer to me; lifting one of her long smooth legs, she stroked it across my thighs. She was wearing a thin white T-shirt and a short, red leather skirt. Under the T-shirt you could make out the hard outline of her nipples through the thin cotton. I knew she was naked beneath her skirt. Her hair was black as a crow's wing; long, falling on to her shoulders. Her skin was the colour of pale coffee and she smelt of heaven. Her hand lifted to my chest and through the cheap fabric of my shirt I could feel the heat of her hand pressing against me.

'I made as if to push her away, shaking my head and telling her I had no money, trying to explain about my uncle and the job he had promised me. She didn't move away. Instead her hand slipped inside my shirt, her long painted fingernails seeking out my nipples. She nipped, and I could feel the throb of my cock against her leg. Suddenly I wanted her more than anything. Her fingers moved around my chest, fluttering, her touch electric.

'I remember she leant back, her dark eyes alight with mischief as she held on to me, then she guided my nervous hand down under her skirt; I didn't resist. I felt the chill of the leather and then my fingers brushed the dark coarse curls of thick hair between her legs. I felt the dampness trickling from her open sex; the sensation of her against my fingers made me whimper. She grinned, her predatory brown eyes holding mine.

'"You want?" she whispered, holding my hand against her naked body. Her tongue lifted to trace around the soft folds of my ear. I could barely speak, my pulse was beating like a drum inside my head.

'I grunted, "Yes" and she stepped back, letting her fingers trail back across my chest.

'She was beautiful in the hothouse fleeting way of street girls in Rio. Her lips were smeared with carmine red, her dark eyes painted around in black kohl, making them into sharp catlike points of light. I was drawn towards her and she beckoned me to follow. I followed, hypnotised. On my fingers I could detect the slightest smell of her; salty, inviting. Around us the other girls were watching. Some were laughing and catcalling, some teasing, but I was lost. All I could see was the hard dark outline of her nipples pressing against her T-shirt, the curve of her heavy breasts as they moved beneath the thin fabric, and from beneath the skirt the promise of her hot wet sex. I can remember every detail of her, the smell of her, the heat and my driving, unstoppable desire . . .' Catz's voice faltered.

Eyes tightly closed Alicia whispered, 'Don't stop, tell me about the blond man, Catz.'

His voice was darker now, the tone compelling and intense. 'The whore took me into a dark alley; I followed like a child. At the next turning she paused to make sure I was still with her before opening a low door set back into the wall.

'Inside was a small room dimly lit by an oil lamp hanging from the ceiling. The interior was simple; there was a bed and a table. Sitting beside it was a tall, blond foreign man reading a newspaper. He was wearing a white vest that showed off his slim, lightly tanned frame. He looked up as we came in; he didn't seem surprised. Instead he smiled at the whore and then glanced across at me. She told him in English that

I was looking for work and, glancing back at me, said that I wanted her.

'I felt a ripple of fear, the man looked me up and down and said something to the whore in a dialect I didn't understand. She turned to face me and slowly lifted her skirt. Between her legs the dark triangle of her hair seemed to highlight the soft honey colour of her thighs and belly. Her fingers teased around the thick hair of her bush. I glanced at the blond man and swallowed hard. He got up and walked towards me. He was tall, muscular; his eyes were staring and intense now.

'"You want her?" he asked, ignoring her busy fingers and soft excited moans. I didn't know how to answer him; he looked down at the aching bulge in the front of my jeans for his answer and grinned.

'My eyes kept being drawn from his face to the girl. She was standing to one side of the room. With one long painted fingernail she was teasing her nipples through the material of her top whilst with the other hand had pulled up the leather skirt a little more. She was slipping one finger in and out of the livid gash that had opened up amongst the thick curly hair of her sex. I was rooted to the spot; she moved a little closer, then took the finger from inside herself and stepped forward to trail it across my open lips. My tongue sought out the flavour of her. I shuddered and nodded.

'"Yes, yes. I want her, I want her," I stammered, trying to find words to describe my desire, my need of her body.

'The man held up his hands and shrugged. "Then you

have to have money." He turned away as if dismissing me.

'I felt my colour rise. "But I haven't got any –" I began. "I've come to the city to find work."

'His face didn't change. "I have a proposition for you, boy. I will give you a little job and then you can have her." He glanced across at the whore. "Any way you want."

'I nodded. "Yes," I said without thinking. "Yes. I will do the job for you."'

Alicia knew that, despite the evenness of his voice, Catz was watching her reaction. Knowing he could sense her excitement added to the thrill.

'What happened then?' she murmured quickly. 'Tell me, what happened next?' She knew he was trying to control the rise of her excitement; he knew she liked to have the moment prolonged. The longer his story took, the better it would be. His tone didn't falter as he continued his story.

'The whore stepped towards me, and began to undo the hook of my belt. I glanced at the man; he nodded, watching whilst she undressed me. She moved slowly, like a sleek cat. With every movement she brushed against me, her breasts grazing me, the cool leather of her skirt stroking my thighs. As she pushed down my underpants my cock sprang out like a snake. She smiled and knelt forward to let the ends of her hair trail across the very tip. It took my breath away. I stepped out of my trousers, almost forgetting in my excitement that the blond man was watching us, I wanted to possess her, pull her to me and drown in the sensations of her hot liquid body.

'As she peeled away the last of my clothes I caught a flicker of movement behind her and saw the blond man was undressing too. His eyes were drinking in my body with the same intensity of desire I had for the whore. Between his legs his thick meaty penis stood forward, engorged and defiant.

'Suddenly I was cold and afraid. But instead of the fear killing my ardour, something about the sensation intensified my desire. He moved closer until he was standing immediately behind the whore. I imagined his thick sex pressing up against the red leather of the whore's skirt. His pale hands snaked round to her breasts and then he grabbed the neck of her T-shirt and ripped it open. The effect was galvanising: her heavy breasts fell forward, their great brown nipples puckered up into tight folds, and I heard myself gasp. He cupped them in his palms, his fingers pinching at the dark nipples.

'I reached out instinctively and his hands caught hold of mine, encouraging me to take the weight of her breasts, to stroke her nipples. I could feel her breath on my face. As I held her, his hands left mine and slid down to her skirt. I heard the sound of him fighting with the zip. With a little grunt as it gave under his fingers, he pushed the skirt down and she was naked except for the rags of her T-shirt. I glanced down between her legs.

'Between her honey-coloured thighs I could see the

very tip of his pink cock as it lay cradled between the dark curls of her sex. The whore lifted her hands to my head and pushed me downwards and I knew then what job it was that the blond man expected me to do.

'I lapped hungrily at the salty dark folds of her sex, pushing my tongue deep into her, shuddering with the pleasure at the smell and taste of it. All the time I was aware of the aggressive jut of his cock pressing between her legs. She pushed me down harder and almost without hesitating I slipped my lips around the glistening throbbing end of his phallus. Her sex was splayed open against my face, my cheeks wet from her excitement. From behind the girl I heard the blond man moan.

'Unexpectedly he bent his knees a little. Without hesitation I followed, my mouth sucking in his hardness. As he moved, the whore lifted her leg; she stepped over me where I was crouching amongst my discarded clothes on the floor. With no one between us I found myself kneeling in front of the tall blond man, his cock throbbing in my mouth. Instinctively my hands went up to cradle his heavy balls. The whore stood to one side, deliberately in my field of vision. Inches from my face she started to play with herself, leaning back so her heavy lips hung open, her fingers rubbing back and forth across the dark bud of her clitoris. She paused for an instant before sliding one long finger inside then smearing the thick glistening juices out over her lips.

'In my excitement I grabbed the man's shaft tighter

and began to pull his reddened skin back and forth; above me I heard him gasp with pleasure.

'The whore moved closer, trailing a scented damp finger under my nose and around my lips where they met the hard flesh of the blond man's cock. She leant closer, her heavy breasts brushing my arms, her nipples tantalising. I closed my eyes as she crouched beside me, wriggling ever closer. Her hand grasped the base of my swollen shaft. I sucked in air around the man's penis and she wriggled closer still, dragging her breasts across the tip of my cock, mouthing eager little noises of animal pleasure and encouragement. Her head went down and her eager wet mouth closed over me. I shuddered, and felt her laughter as she sucked my cock into her bright-red gaping mouth.

'The sensation of her lips against my desperate flesh made me gasp; for a split second everything was still. The man looked down at me. I could feel his sharp shiny eyes on me, and then his hand came around and gently pushed the back of my head, encouraging me to take more of him into my mouth. I took him as far as I could and below the whore instantly started to move her lips around my cock.

'It was like a game. Every suck, every kiss against his engorged shaft seemed to be echoed by her. I licked around the sensitive tip of his cock, then pulled back his foreskin gently, dropping my mouth lower down so I could run my tongue around the thick reddened ridge of its swollen head; a second later her tongue seemed to follow the same course. Her nimble fingers were grasping at the root of my penis, working expertly at the soft gathers of skin whilst her other hand cradled and nipped at my balls.

'Her hot wet mouth drew on me, pulled me in, nipped and nibbled. I could feel the excitement building inside me; a core of intense light building in the base of my gut while, under my tongue and hands, above me I could feel the same tension building in the blond man. His hands moved gently through my hair, thick fingers stroking the nape of my neck, pulling at the lobes of my ears. All the time he was encouraging me with his hands to take him further, take him higher . . .

'Suddenly I could taste him, the first salty offerings that augured his climax. His hands tightened in my hair, his breath coming in ragged bursts now, as his hips pushed forwards. Below I could feel my own hips echoing the thrust. I grabbed at the whore's neck. Deliberately she renewed her hot eager efforts, her saliva trickling down into the thick mat of my pubic hair. I could feel her bringing me on – dragging me, draining me – milking me until finally I could hold back no longer. Above me, as if sensing it, the man shuddered. His thrusts became automatic; he jerked forward. Under my fingers I could feel his balls contract and a millisecond later he filled me up with salty offering, his seed filling my mouth, spilling out on to my chin.

'There was a moment of utter revulsion. I gagged but not before my own climax hit me – red and white lights flickered behind my eyes – the draw of the whore's hot lips against my shaft, the shuddering mind-stopping contraction as I felt my balls give up their creamy load into her hot waiting mouth. I felt her swallow, taking the seed deep inside her, felt her tongue lapping up the drops, and above her I echoed her intimate services on the cock of the blond man.'

In the soft golden light of Alicia's bedroom she glanced up in time to see Catz shudder at the recollection. He seemed to freeze for a split second before he turned towards her; his expression was enough. Alicia allowed the intense erotic images to course through her mind. She felt every sensation by proxy, tasted every drop of their lust. She gasped, reaching up towards him. An electric pulse shook her body. Her breath came in staccato gasps and she desperately fought to regain her composure. Finally she whispered, 'That was wonderful.'

Catz nodded and began to slip off his remaining clothes. She watched him from behind her dark lashes. 'It should be you who is the writer, Catz; you have such a way with words.'

He snorted, pushing down his uniform trousers over the engorged reddened bulk of his cock. Alicia looked at it admiringly and, wetting her finger, reached across the bed to trail saliva across its livid tip.

He glanced across at her as he slipped into the bed, pulling up the thin top sheet over them both.

'Do you want this?' he asked huskily, watching her face.

She smiled. 'Yes,' she said softly, her voice hypnotically

persuasive. 'But not in bed, let me see you. I want to see you. I want to drink you in, Catz – let me admire you.' He slipped with animal grace from the bed and stood beside her. She let her eyes travel over him with proprietorial pride.

He let his fingers move down slowly over the sculptured lines of his body until he grasped his swollen cock. The sensation made him shiver. She smiled teasingly and, leaning forward, prised his fingers away whilst she cupped her tiny hand around its bulk, easing the silken veined skin backwards and forwards, working her fingers along its entire length. He closed his eyes and moaned.

'You are so beautiful,' she murmured appreciatively. 'I want to watch you.'

The curve of his penis lifted eagerly. She giggled appreciatively and wriggled herself up on to her knees.

He stood completely still as she slowly worked her soft hands over his shaft. Her muscles, still alight from her excitement, contracted sharply as she encircled him. She sighed, revelling in the thickness of him, the torrid sensation of his bulk held prisoner by her touch. She drank in his heat and the eager pulse of his captive desire.

Slowly, almost carefully, she began to move her hands against him, letting his movements keep pace with hers. She brushed him with her breasts and smiled as she saw him struggle to keep his desire in check. Trickling saliva over him she rubbed her moist eager fingers along the base of his shaft and shuddered as she felt her own excitement rekindle. His face was enrapt, eyes closed; his breath came in short hot bursts.

In her mind she saw a flash of Francesca; her lips now painted as red as the Rio whore's, her mouth eagerly seeking another, her tongue flicking around open lips, nipples jutting and hard, pushing out from the ruins of a torn blouse.

Alicia's hands speeded up and she could hear Catz breathe deeply, adjusting his movements to match hers. She could feel the hard bite of his pubic bone against her tightened fist. In her frenzied, eager mind Catz became an amalgam of everything she had ever desired; a mosaic of every erotic puzzle she had ever solved. She gasped, bending forwards to brush her breasts against him. He leant forward, his mouth hungrily searching for hers.

She pulled away from him and leant back, her eyes open, eagerly drinking in the expression on his ecstatic face as he sought her out. Pulling him towards her she lifted the hard pink bud of her nipple into his open waiting lips, and instantly she knew he was lost. She tightened her fingers around him, relishing the shuddering violent contractions along the length of his cock. His face contorted into a grimace as she watched the crashing silvery intensity of his orgasm take control of his body.

His silvery warm seed spurted aggressively between her fingers. Above her she heard him moan and gripped him hard, milking the heady contractions of his climax, feeling her rhythmic grip matched and repeated in the final pulsing waves of his orgasm. His lips closed tightly around her hardened nipple, sucking, nipping; she permitted him his pleasure as her hands grasped him harder, pulling him closer to her as she threw back her head and called his name again and again.

# Chapter Four

Francesca opened her eyes. Around her the bedroom was dark and unfamiliar and for a few minutes she was completely disorientated. Desperately she tried to remember where she was; the memories of the afternoon came flooding back in delicious intense detail. Stretching tentatively under the warmth of the bedclothes, her body cried out in complaint. The muscles in her arms and shoulders ached; lower down, her back and buttocks still stung. The hot graphic images of the gallery continued to rush through her mind as she carefully uncurled herself and looked around the room.

Part of her expected, even hoped, to find Catz lying beside her – panther-like – coiled and ready to renew his assault, but the room was empty and the heavy summer air unnaturally still. Pushing back the covers Francesca slipped out of bed, her muscles complaining at every step.

She opened the curtains a little and realised she had no idea what the time was. Time seemed abstract and removed from the vivid tumbling memories which her mind refused to subdue. She shook her head to try and clear it; her neck shrieked.

Outside, the soft golden light of evening kissed the abandoned garden, giving it a warm magical quality.

From beyond the garden wall she could hear the sea sigh as it caressed the beach.

Francesca turned round. In the broad sliver of daylight she could take in the details of the luxurious bedroom where Catz had left her. The walls were panelled like the rest of the house but here they had been painted in dusty faded pinks; beneath her feet was a soft cream carpet scattered with pastel rugs. Beside her, near the window was a *chaise longue*. Someone – Francesca knew it must be Catz – had left a folded bathrobe and towels. She slipped on the robe.

On one side of the bed a door had been left ajar. Behind it she discovered a luxurious bathroom, tiled from floor to ceiling in soft pinks that echoed the bedroom. The floor was black marble, a cool sharp contrast to the warmth of the bedroom carpet, and on one wall were open shelves full of cosmetics and bath oils.

Francesca ran a deep bath and poured in a measure of oil before slipping into the inviting fragrant waters. She moaned gratefully as the deep water embraced her, the heat seeking out the sensitive, pounded areas of her battered body, the soft persuasive warmth kissing and lapping at her swollen sex and bottom. Despite her aching muscles the water renewed the intense images of Catz's attentions and his bitter-sweet assault on her body. From deeper still it drew out the precious dark secret that she had relished his attentions and craved more.

The steam rose in scented clouds around her and she sank back, letting the delicate caress of the water take her. Behind her closed eyes all she could see now was Catz's face. She could imagine his hot eager breath on her shoulders, the brush of his body against her tingling reddened back and his desperate animal screams as he had climaxed, buried deep in the forbidden dark recesses of her eager, compliant body.

The memory of his electrifying, brutal touch made her tremble with delight and she made no attempt to quell it. The tentative embers of excitement renewed themselves and flickered into life, deep in the pit of her belly. Slowly she slid her hands down over her aching breasts, kneading the tender flesh, arousing them with familiar stroking movements. Her soapy hands traced slippery paths of sensation over her nipples, which hardened eagerly under her touch. Catz's face swamped her mind and she did not resist, his features set in a hard unmoving mask, only his glittering, jewel-bright eyes betraying his excitement.

Her hand slid down over the taut aching muscles of her tanned belly, seeking out the soft swollen folds of her sex. One finger pressed down against the sensitive hood of her clitoris; the tiny quicksilver bursts of passion made her gasp and she lifted her hips clear of the water so her dark sex emerged, bubbly and hot, from amongst the oily waves. Her head spun, her body ached but she needed to touch herself, to explore herself, feeling as if in some way Catz had changed her for ever. He had opened a doorway in her mind that she never knew existed.

Her outer lips opened easily beneath her knowing caress and she let her fingers move lower so they slipped into the bruised sanctuary beyond. Her muscles tightened spontaneously around her moist fingers as she concentrated on the familiar sensation. She felt as if she were reclaiming herself, absorbing and accepting the new desires Catz had awakened in her, letting her mind feast on his dark and sensual gift.

As she lay quietly, letting the water support her, she heard the crisp click of the bedroom door outside. Glancing up with a delicious sense of expectation she realised she'd slid the bolt across and was safe within the steamy fragrant waters of her bath. Holding her breath she lay very still, uncertain what to do. She strained to hear some other sound from the room beyond the bathroom, but the only noise she could make out clearly was the soft insistent throb of the pulse in her ears. Slowly she lifted herself out of the bath, wishing that somehow she could hush the noise of the water trickling off her body. Grabbing a towel she ran to the door and wrenched it open.

Outside, the bedroom was empty. The only clue that she had had a visitor was that all the curtains were drawn back, which flooded the large room with soft evening light. Francesca glanced around, part of her hoping that her silent visitor might not have left. With mixed emotions she returned to the bathroom and slipped on the robe, realising as she did so that her own clothes now lay in shreds on the floor of the gallery.

Dry and refreshed, she padded to the door that led into the main house. She turned the handle, wondering for a split second if it might be locked; it swung open freely.

The hallway beyond was deserted. Aware of her vulnerable nakedness beneath the robe Francesca crept across the carpet. The first door she opened slid back to reveal the narrow confines of the lift Alicia had used to get to the gallery. She closed the door quickly, instantly remembering the dark desire in the older woman's eyes, and swung around; further along another door opened on to a landing. With a sense of relief she made her way down the two flights of stairs into the square hallway below. As she stepped silently on to the cold chequered floor Alicia appeared from the shadows. She smiled pleasantly.

'Good evening, Francesca. So there you are. I'd just sent Catz up to let you know dinner is almost ready. I presume you would be happy to join me?'

Francesca could feel the colour rising in her face.

Alicia continued conversationally, 'It looks as if there may be a storm later; the lights in the sitting room keep flickering. Perhaps we'll have a power cut. Mind you, I always think candlelight is so flattering, don't you?' She laughed lightly before turning and indicating for Francesca to follow her. Dumbly Francesca fell into step.

Alicia had changed for dinner and was now wearing a striking cocktail dress in muted rose-coloured silk. Its cut emphasised the delicate sweeping curves of her slim frame and the upswept lines of her small breasts. Her pale hair was caught up into a soft chignon; fleetingly, Francesca wondered if Catz dressed her hair.

Alicia glanced back over her shoulder; in the shadows of the hallway her beauty was breathtaking. She smiled, her violet eyes twinkling diamond bright.

'We're eating in the breakfast room. I hope you don't mind, but the dining room is so far from the kitchen.' She paused and smiled again. 'I loathe lukewarm food, don't you?'

Francesca nodded and pulled her robe a little closer. Alicia, meanwhile, treated her like a welcome guest; as if nothing had happened that should make either of them feel uncomfortable.

At the end of the corridor Alicia opened double doors on to the small elegant breakfast room overlooking the garden. In one wall French windows stood slightly ajar, letting in the soft enticing noises of a fading summer's day. Outside, above the tangle of trees and shrubs, a brittle metallic-grey light in the evening sky confirmed Alicia's prophecy of stormy weather.

Close to the French windows a round table had been laid for two; as if pre-empting the storm, the centre was dominated by an elegant candelabra.

'Please sit down,' said Alicia softly. 'When we've eaten perhaps you would like to spend the rest of the evening with me. I have some matters I would like to discuss with you.' She paused for a second. 'And then Catz will take you home.'

Francesca sat down slowly, rapidly recovering her composure. Taking her lead from Alicia's seemingly unflappable facade she said pleasantly, 'That would be very nice.'

As she spoke, Catz appeared carrying a tray, and in spite of herself she felt the rush of colour return to her face. He stood framed in the doorway for a second until Alicia signalled that he should serve.

Francesca took in every detail of the man who had awakened the dark compelling needs of her body. He had changed into more informal dress, although the effect was just as impressive as before.

His muscular torso was encased in a soft white collarless shirt worn under a black silk waistcoat; the combination highlighted his lightly tanned skin. His shirt sleeves were rolled back to reveal his muscular forearms and the neck of his shirt was open, exposing the soft tantalising mesh of curls that crept up from his broad chest. Below he was wearing thick cream jodhpurs and ankle-length boots that accentuated the athletic musculature of his legs. Francesca swallowed and tried to control the fluttering sense of excitement she felt renewing in her belly. Catz turned towards Alicia who smiled approvingly and, with the merest movement of her hand, gestured for him to serve their meal.

Moving impassively, with the grace of a panther, Catz set a delicate china bowl in front of each of the women. Inside, cradled within leaves of crisp lettuce, lay a selection of tiny, lightly steamed vegetables over which had been trickled a delicious bitter-sweet dressing.

Francesca suddenly realised she was ravenously hungry; the smell of the food made her mouth water, so she picked up a fork. The tiny florets of calabrese and crisp mange-tout tasted like nectar, the miniature carrots as sweet as honey.

Alicia nodded approvingly as she watched Francesca eat, her eyes bright with mischief. 'He is also a superb cook,' she purred, taking a sip of wine from the crystal glass Catz had placed at her fingertips. She glanced up at him and was rewarded with the briefest of smiles.

Francesca looked across at them both, and blushed slightly. Undeterred she speared a tiny plump carrot with her fork.

'A man of many talents,' she replied evenly, managing to control the tremor in her voice before slipping the carrot between her lips.

Alicia laughed aloud and picked up her fork. 'Bravo, Francesca. I have to agree with you. Let Catz pour you some wine, it's excellent. Edgar insisted we always kept a good cellar. You and I have a great deal to talk about and I'd prefer not to mix the serious affair of eating with business matters.'

Francesca looked up at Catz as he filled her glass. As she took it their fingertips brushed fleetingly. The briefest touch was enough to make her shiver. His expression didn't change. Alicia, looking on from behind the rim of her own glass, was unable to disguise the gleam of delight in her eyes as Catz withdrew to bring in the main course.

Later, as the evening darkened, they moved into the sitting room to eat dessert. Catz had prepared tiny sugar pastry baskets filled to the brim with succulent strawberries, their tops sprinkled with crushed brown sugar. Francesca found it hard to reconcile the image of the man whose hands had taken a whip to her exposed vulnerable flesh with the hands that had fashioned such intricate confections.

Finally Alicia lay her plate to one side. 'Now,' she said softly, 'I think we have to get down to business. I would like you to seriously consider accepting the commission to write a book about my husband's life. Edgar was a philanthropist; he did great works for charity. We travelled the world and he was a meticulous diarist; his journals are stored here and in our house in London. They are a complete record of his life and our travels together.'

Francesca was about to protest but Alicia held up her hand to quieten her.

'I appreciate that you have another manuscript to work on but even so I would like you to consider my proposition most carefully. There is another matter -'

She hesitated as Catz appeared with the coffee.

Francesca's eyes were drawn at once towards his outline in the doorway. Catz was stunning. She felt the bubble of excitement rekindle in the pit of her belly as he moved effortlessly across the room. At one level she was angry that the man could invoke such a strong reaction in her. She looked away from him, towards Alicia, and realised that the older woman was watching her reactions with undisguised interest.

'I'd like you to come and work here,' Alicia said softly.

Stunned, Francesca swung round to face her. Catz placed the coffee tray on a side table and stood motionless, with his hands behind his back.

'I'm sorry?' said Francesca hastily. 'Did you say stay here?' Alicia's words fuelled the flush of heat rising from deep inside her that she was fighting so hard to control.

Alicia nodded. 'Of course, it seems to me to be the perfect solution. I would prefer that Edgar's diaries remained within my possession whilst you work on them. Some of the material might be considered – what shall we say – sensitive. So you could complete your other novel here and, as time permits, do some preliminary research for Edgar's story from the source material. Catz can look after us both . . .'

She let the unspoken implication hang between them.

Francesca coughed. 'I'm not certain that would be a good idea,' she blustered. 'There's the cottage . . .'

As she desperately searched for the words to refuse Alicia's offer she could feel Catz's eyes on her. She struggled to maintain her control.

Alicia continued undeterred. 'And there is another matter which I would be grateful if you would help me with.' The older woman paused and signalled Catz to pour the coffee. 'I feel the time is right to sell Edgar's collection of artefacts. It's extremely important to me that their disposal is handled discreetly.'

'I don't understand how that involves me . . .' Francesca began.

Alicia smiled. 'I would like you to act as a go-between, as an agent between myself and the auctioneer. I need someone who would be the soul of discretion, someone who could work on my behalf, ensuring that everything goes smoothly. I would like you to make the arrangements for me and I would pay you very well for your time.'

Francesca protested. 'But Alicia, I've got no experience.'

Alicia nodded. 'I know, but I feel instinctively that you are the one to help me.'

Francesca shook her head. 'I don't know what to say. I have a deadline for the new book.' She glanced back at Catz who met her nervous look with his cool ice-blue eyes. She steadied her voice. 'I'm not sure this is the right place for me to work.'

Alicia laughed. 'Come, come, Francesca, I'm sure we could control Catz sufficiently to allow you to finish your book. Or is it yourself you are afraid of? Remember, you are in control of your own desires.'

Francesca blanched. 'I know, I know,' she whispered. 'Could I have time to think about it? I've rented the cottage for the summer.' Her protestations faded away. She knew that, whatever she said, part of her longed to accept Alicia's proposal.

Alicia shrugged and lifted her hands in resignation. 'There is no compulsion to accept my offer, Francesca. All I ask is that you consider it. We have more than enough space to make an office here for you. The house would be yours to use as you please.'

Francesca fought to quell the answer that pressed up between her lips; fought her desire to accept Alicia's suggestion without question or reservation. Her imagination reeled with intense erotic possibilities. She swallowed, trying to keep her eyes off Catz's muscular torso as he placed the coffee cups on the table beside Alicia.

Beneath the thin material of his shirt she could make out the smooth lines of his muscles, the swelling bulk of his broad shoulders. As he brought her coffee she was careful to avoid his eyes. Instead she was aware of his hypnotic smell, a subtle mixture of fresh, musky male heat and a sharp vanilla and citrus tang of cologne. This close she could pick out the delicate pattern of fine downy hair on his forearms and, beneath, the dark-blue tracery of the veins.

'Would you like milk, sugar?' he asked softly. She could feel her mouth go dry.

'Milk,' she murmured, eyes riveted to the floor.

Hastily she turned to Alicia, fighting to remain in control and at the same time feeling foolish that her desire for this man could render her almost speechless. She coughed to clear her throat and her mind, then took a sip of coffee and turned back to Alicia. When she finally spoke, her voice was low and even, the tone businesslike, almost abrupt.

'I am interested in preparing a book about your husband, Alicia. Though in view of his tastes I think we'd have to be very careful of the material, even the references we include. Let me have a little time to think about it. Could I let you have my decision in a week?'

On the other side of the room Alicia nodded in resignation, sensing she was losing the game she had so skilfully set in motion. 'Of course. Now what about the matter of the auction?'

Francesca shook her head firmly. 'No. No, I really don't think I can help you with that.'

Alicia shrugged. 'Ah well, perhaps another way will present itself. I must insist though that if you take on the book about Edgar, his diaries remain in the house.'

Francesca nodded. 'Fine, once I get the current rewrite finished we'll make a start. After all,' she laughed, her old self reasserting itself with a vengeance, 'the village is only a walk along the cliffs, isn't it?'

Alicia picked up her coffee cup. 'As you wish, but please don't totally dismiss the idea of staying here.'

Francesca smiled, her good humour disguising the uncertainty she felt in spite of her determined words. She knew Catz was looking at her, could feel his eyes on her. She forced herself to smile at Alicia until she heard Catz turn and leave the room.

Alicia leant over towards the fireplace. 'Now Catz has gone,' she said conspiratorially, 'I shall indulge myself.'

As she spoke she produced an ornate cigarette case and lighter from beside the chair. 'Cigarettes do unspeakable things to the complexion and one's health so I restrict myself to just one after dinner. Would you like one?'

Francesca shook her head as Alicia inhaled deeply and blew a plume of silvery-blue smoke from between her beautifully painted lips.

'Would you care to join me on the sofa, Francesca. I'd like to show you some of Edgar's photographs.'

Francesca's expression gave her away.

Alicia threw back her head in delight and laughed. 'Oh, please don't look so apprehensive. Not all Edgar's possessions are so . . .' She lingered over the word. 'So stimulating. Here, come and sit by me in the light. I'm sure you'll find them fascinating.' As she moved, she picked up a leather album from a side table and compliantly Francesca moved beside her.

Alicia turned the first pages and Francesca leant closer, finding herself drawn in by the stark black-and-white imagery. The photographs were fascinating. Edgar was much as Francesca had expected him to be; a tall, cadaverous and balding man whose expensive clothes and elegant surroundings could not quite disguise the sensual self-indulgent look that played around his handsome mouth and eyes.

Alicia turned another page. 'Oh, here we are. This was in an exquisite little restaurant in Paris, around 1967, I think. I'm not sure now if we were on our way to Cannes.'

Francesca leant closer and recognised the distinctive features of a Member of Parliament, wine glass in hand, sitting amongst the smiling group of diners. She looked across at Alicia. 'Is that . . .' she began.

Alicia nodded but held her finger to her lips. 'No names. When you come to prepare the material for the book I'll help you decide what we should include and what to leave out. Edgar was a well-liked man, popular, always involved in charitable work, eager to help with fund-raising. Then, of course, there were his other interests. The famous and infamous faces you will see in these albums and diaries sought him out. Sometimes they wanted help, sometimes they wanted friendship or advice. At other times they wanted something more . . .'

Alicia turned the page and closed the album softly. In the soft light from the table lamps her exquisite face looked as if it had been carved from marble. She turned to Francesca. 'The strange thing is, I loved him, though I was never completely sure of that until he was gone. Sometimes even now I miss him.' Her eyes were bright with tears, giving them a diamond brilliance.

Francesca looked away. 'I think it's time I went home now,' she said softly.

Alicia nodded wordlessly. 'If you ring the bell by the fireplace, Catz will take you,' said Alicia, her voice low and carefully controlled.

In the cool shadowy hall Francesca waited whilst Catz brought the car round to the front of the house. In the warm sitting room with Alicia she had forgotten for a while that she was barefoot, and even the robe had seemed comfortable and adequate. Here, standing in the gloom, the sensation of the cold marble beneath her feet made her shudder and she was aware of her barely covered nakedness.

Headlights through the windows announced Catz's arrival. She hesitated for a few seconds, just long enough for Catz to open the front door for her. As she moved towards him she was surprised that he was now back in the chauffeur's uniform.

He moved quickly to open the back door of the Daimler for her. She picked her way across the gravel, intensely aware of his bright animal eyes on her body. As she climbed into the car his hand lifted for an instant to stroke the long aching muscles of her neck. She shivered and looked up at him. He leant a fraction closer, the smell of his body exciting and hypnotic. He hesitated for a split second and then slowly he ran his tongue across her cheek. She gasped and pulled back from him, but too late to stop his hand sliding stealthily between the thick folds of her towelling robe.

She froze as his fingers moved across her body to cup one of her breasts, his eager fingers seeking out her nipples. A thin moan of excitement trickled from her open lips. His face was expressionless as he let his hand slide away. He took her elbow and helped her gently into the rear seat. As she sat back he let his eyes linger on her exposed legs then travel up over her torso. Finally his eyes settled on hers and under his unguarded examination she could feel her colour rising. Blushing and self-conscious she looked away as he closed the door with a muffled click.

She slipped further back in the seat, feeling dizzy. Heat flushed through her and settled in a warm, glowing sphere in the pit of her belly. Glancing up she could see Catz's broad shoulders in silhouette behind the glass partition and, above, the hard glint of his eyes reflected in the rear-view mirror. His gaze did not falter as he slipped the car into gear and drove out on to the road.

Something about his eyes electrified her; their undisguised animal brilliance with the heady mixture of feigned disinterest and suppressed desire excited her beyond anything she had ever felt before.

She lay back a little and slid a hand across under her robe; beneath her fingers she could feel the soft swelling of her breast and, above, the hard cold outline of her nipple, still erect from Catz's fleeting touch. She let her fingers toy with it, relishing the sensation that rippled down to her belly. Her mouth felt dry; from the front of the car she knew Catz was watching her. She slid down a little lower in the seat, her other hand tugging at the belt; letting the robe slide open. The kiss of cool evening air on her thighs and belly made her shiver while her fingers intensified their attention to her breasts. Slowly she pushed aside the fabric to expose the small uplifted globes to the evening light; her nipples were hard, puckered into dark hard peaks. She glanced up to meet Catz's eyes; something within them could not deny his interest.

One hand slipped lower now, the contrast of her golden, tanned arms sharp and compelling against her paler belly. The moon slid languorously from behind clouds and threw her body into sharp relief. She pushed the robe down over her shoulders so that her whole body was exposed to Catz's cold feral eyes.

She thought she heard his gasp – but perhaps it was an illusion – as her fingers slipped smoothly into the soft folds of her waiting sex. She groaned as her fingertip found the hard engorged bud of her clitoris. She let her fingers slide lower and was startled to find how wet she was – thick fragrant juices trickled on to her exploring fingers, the extent of her excitement tangible and undeniable.

She let her mind wander, let herself rekindle the memory of the intense sensations she had experienced in the library. In her mind she saw Catz's brutal face, felt his fingers on her naked body, felt the exhilarating, terrifying thrust of his sex inside her. Frantically her fingers worked faster, her legs spreading wider to accommodate the hot desperate rhythm of her touch. The sensations seemed to build quickly, spilling and spiralling outwards from under her fingers. The heat grew between her legs, her juices flowing down over her fingers as she moved them between the tight throbbing depths of her sex and the hard eager bud of her clitoris.

Her eyes lifted back to Catz's face. He had slowed the car to a crawl. She could make out the glittering reflection of his eyes caught in the moonlight. He had tilted the mirror to give himself a better view of her and in doing so gave her a fleeting glimpse of his mouth; his tongue, moist and glistening in the moonlight, snaked invitingly over his lips. She groaned in response as she imagined she could feel it lapping at the soft creases of her sex. She thrust her hips forward, lifting them off the seat, and plunged her fingers deep inside. Her desperate throbbing muscles contracted sharply around them as her other hand worked her clitoris relentlessly towards her climax. She lifted one fragrant finger to her lips, then trailed it down to circle her nipples. In front of her in the mirror Catz's eyes seemed to glow with an inner light as he watched her intently.

She longed for Catz to stop the car. She wanted to know she had pushed him beyond the limits, that his desire would suppress his steely self-control. Her body arched upwards, willing him to fill her up. She needed to feel the weight of his body on hers and his savage intense kisses pressed against her bruised and waiting lips. The thought of his brutal mouth and his insistent, persuasive tongue moving across her body was enough to bring the feverish, frantic rhythm to its conclusion; the waves of white heat rolled up through her, her aching body bucked again and again against the insistent stroking and touching of her caresses.

Inside she felt the violent contraction of her muscles as they sucked hungrily at her fingers. She closed her eyes, her breath roaring through her in ragged gasps. As the intensity closed over her, washing away all reason and leaving only pleasure, she cried out his name.

In the mirror – had she opened her eyes – she would have seen the look of delight and desire in his blue eyes and a smile of triumph on his lips.

At the quayside the moonlight tipped the waves of the rolling ocean with silvery light. Francesca's cottage seemed deserted as the Daimler purred to a standstill. Francesca pulled the robe closed over her naked body and glanced up at Catz in the rear-view mirror. His expression was stiff and formal. She retied the belt and waited silently for him to come round to open the door for her. As he stepped from the car another figure moved, staggering out from the shadows. Chris! Francesca gasped.

Catz didn't seem to be aware of his approach. Silently he opened the side door and extended his hand for Francesca to help her from the car. She could feel her colour draining as Chris stepped forward into the moonlight.

'Where the bloody hell have you been?' Chris snapped belligerently, ignoring Catz completely. 'I've been looking for you all day.'

Francesca's first instinct was to slip back inside the car, but Catz gently held her steady. She looked at him gratefully and was surprised to see a look of concern in his eyes. He glanced across at Chris who swayed a little and then staggered towards them.

'Well? I asked you a question. Where in God's name have you been?' Chris hissed venomously.

Closer now, Francesca could smell alcohol on his breath. She stepped away from Catz and the car towards the cottage. Suddenly she realised, almost frantically, that she had left her bag in the gallery at the villa. She looked back at Catz in desperation. From the driver's compartment he produced her shoulder bag and handed it to her.

She whispered her thanks and moved towards the door. As she passed, Catz said softly, 'Would you like me to deal with him?'

Francesca shook her head firmly. 'No, I'll be all

right. I think it would be better if you left,' and began to rummage in her bag for the keys to the cottage.

Chris lurched towards her, grabbing at her arm. Suddenly he stopped, his face contorted into a dark furious mask as he realised she was wearing a bathrobe.

'And what the hell has happened to your clothes?' he growled. As he swayed closer Francesca could see Catz to one side of her, his eyes alive and bright.

She turned to Catz and said softly, 'You'd better go, Catz. He's had a bit too much to drink, that's all. Please leave, I can handle him.'

Catz nodded but he didn't make any attempt to move. Francesca waved him away, knowing that his presence would make Chris more angry not less so. Catz shrugged and climbed back into the Daimler, his eyes still on Chris and Francesca as they stood under the eaves of the cottage.

Chris rolled unsteadily in front of her, his expression betraying a confused mixture of emotions. 'What in God's name are you playing at, Fran? Where have you been? I don't understand this.' His voice broke into a thin whine.

Francesca pushed past him. 'You don't have to understand, Chris. It's got nothing to do with you. You ought to go home, you're drunk. Let me call you a cab.'

Chris snorted furiously and grabbed her arms. 'What do you mean, nothing to do with me? Of course it's got something to do with me. You're my – my . . .'

Francesca pushed him away and threw open the door of the cottage. 'I'm not your anything, Chris. I thought you were my friend but it seems I was wrong.' She slung her handbag on to the stairs and snapped on the hall light.

'I was worried about you. I've looked everywhere . . .' he began, following her into the house, head down on his chest.

In the light of the hall Francesca could see how dishevelled and tired he looked. Instead of fear or anger she now felt pity. He looked wretched and she had to admit that he probably had had cause for concern.

'Oh, Chris,' she said softly. As she turned towards him the belt on her robe slipped and the front opened. Chris instantly stepped back, eyes ablaze. When he looked up, Francesca felt a shiver of fear run down her spine. Desperately she looked past him into the dark; there was no sign of the Daimler or Catz.

Her nakedness seemed to have sobered Chris instantly. He moved towards her, face white, jaw tight.

'What have you been doing, you little whore?' His voice sounded like splintering glass, his features contorted into a mask of fury.

Francesca pulled the robe tight around her. 'I think you'd better leave now, Chris, and come back when you're sober. Then I'll explain.'

'Explain!' he spat back at her. 'I don't think I need any explanations; what's been going on here is perfectly bloody obvious, even to a stupid sod like me. You've used me, used me to get you down here, used me to get this cottage, while I, like an idiot, help you move in. You're all the same . . .'

Francesca shook her head, 'Chris. Chris, for good-ness' sake listen to yourself. This is silly; I'm free to do what I want, I don't have to answer to you and I haven't used you.'

As he looked back up at her she saw something else in his eyes, a dark dangerous gleam of obsession. She backed away from him on to the stairs, afraid now.

'I love you,' he said slowly, quietly emphasising every syllable. 'I always planned we should be together here, you and me. I've waited and planned for this, Fran. Trust me. I've waited for you for years. I've always loved you.' He looked up at her. 'And now you do this to me.' Suddenly the anger snapped back; blind dangerous fury. His voice rose. 'You filthy little slut.'

He drew his hand back; she didn't have time to duck as he slapped her hard across the face. She screamed, as much from shock as pain. She felt the bright metallic taste of blood in her mouth and staggered back on to the stairs. Her robe fell open as she stumbled back against the treads. Eyeing her nakedness beneath him, Chris's eyes narrowed to thin black slits.

'I'll show you what whores are for,' he hissed and fell forward on to her. She fought against him as his insistent lips forced down on hers, his beer-sodden tongue forcing its way between her lips. His knee lifted between her thighs, forcing them apart, and one hand clawed aggressively towards her sex. She whimpered as his other hand snatched at her breasts, grabbing and pulling at the tender flesh. She struggled, pushing herself against him in an effort to force him off her.

'Please,' she pleaded. 'Please stop, Chris.' But her protestations were lost under the foul-smelling pressure of his wet mouth. She clawed aggressively at his jacket. Her hips wriggled under him but this seemed to make him more determined.

In her mind she heard Alicia's cool, even voice. 'I want you to be free,' said the older woman softly, her violet eyes alight and intriguing.

Suddenly Francesca was furious; Chris's slobbering obsessive desire kindled an intense white-hot fury in her belly. She pushed him away and to her amazement her anger gave her a brittle unnatural strength. 'Get off me!' she screamed at him furiously, all thoughts of compliance or submission lost and gone as her anger grew.

Shocked by the venom in her voice Chris drew back. Suddenly all the bluster and fury had drained from him and he looked as she had seen him in the hall light, pathetic and wretched. 'I'm so sorry. I didn't mean to hurt you,' Chris began, tears welling up in his eyes.

Francesca pulled her robe tight around her.

'Please believe me, I didn't mean to . . . I'm so sorry,' he sobbed, backing away.

'Not good enough,' she said coldly. 'No man has the right to hit a woman. You don't own me, Chris. I promised you nothing – how dare you behave like this?' Her words were ice-cold, her tone even and unshaken.

Chris seemed to shrink back under her gaze. 'But I love you,' he whimpered.

Francesca shook her head and moved towards the

door. 'No, you don't,' she said softly, 'you want to possess me, to own me – that's something totally different. That isn't love, Chris, that's a prison. Now get out of here.' She held the door open for him.

He moved slowly, shoulders hunched. 'I'm so sorry,' he said again. 'I didn't mean to hurt you. Let me ring you tomorrow. Please, Fran. I only tried to help you, you owe me that. . .'

Francesca caught his eye. 'No, Chris,' she said evenly. 'Whatever you believed we had is over, do you understand? I want you out of my life, I don't owe you anything.'

Chris's answer was a thin pathetic sob as he stumbled out on to the dark quay.

Francesca closed the door softly behind him and slid the bolt across. Her anger drained away and she began to shake. Tears bubbled up and threatened to engulf her. Pushing them down under control, she went to the kitchen; with unsteady hands she made herself a mug of tea. Outside, the moon painted the water with a broad silver brush. Cradling her tea, she picked up the phone and rang Alicia Moffat.

# Chapter Five

The next morning Francesca stood by the handrail of the quay. A gentle breeze ruffled her hair, its cool fingers stroking the bruises around her mouth. In the doorway of the cottage behind her stood the few possessions she intended to take to the villa.

Though she seemed still and peaceful her mind was racing; part of her was anxious that Chris, full of remorse, might appear to beg her forgiveness and persuade her to stay with him. She knew that there was no way she wanted the desperate obsessive love he could offer her. The other part of her, the newly born dark half, was alive with the anticipation of spending time at the villa with Alicia and Catz.

Behind her she heard the distinctive low purr of the Daimler and turned; Catz looked steadily at her from behind the wheel.

Francesca could feel her control crumbling; the intense mixed emotions took her by surprise. She began to tremble and tears, unbidden and unexpected, tumbled down her face.

Catz walked towards her across the quay. She swallowed hard, trying to regain her control. His large hand lifted gently to her face and cupped her chin. She leant into his touch as his eyes lingered momentarily on her bruised mouth, and without thinking she stepped towards him, letting him take her in his strong arms. His reaction was to embrace her gently, encircling and comforting her as if she were a child.

He guided her slowly to the Daimler and helped her into the passenger seat. She felt foolish and afraid. She hadn't realised how vulnerable Chris had left her feeling. Catz quietly collected her possessions from the porch of the cottage. When they were all packed in the boot he came around to the passenger compartment. His voice was low and gentle. 'Is that everything?'

She nodded dumbly. He didn't move. She felt his eyes travelling over her. To her surprise, amongst the trembling uncertainty and sense of violation that she felt at Chris's betrayal, she also felt an intense flutter of desire for Catz. The sensation grew and pushed aside her confusion. She felt her colour returning and lifted her eyes to meet his; deep within his icy-blue gaze she could detect concern and, deeper still, his desire for her. She shuddered and smiled, to be rewarded by the merest fleeting smile in return. He leant forwards, and for an instant she thought he might kiss her; but instead he pulled a soft cashmere blanket from the seat and wrapped it around her legs. 'We'll go, then,' he said softly and she nodded.

*

Alicia was waiting for them in the sitting room. Her face was tight with concern, and as Francesca came in Alicia got to her feet and embraced the younger woman tenderly.

'Are you all right?' she asked softly, holding Francesca at arm's length to examine her face.

Francesca nodded, angry at herself that she felt her tears returning. Alicia sat her down whilst Catz disappeared into the dark shadows of the house.

'I've had Catz prepare a suite for you on the first floor; I'm sure you'll be comfortable there. We've organised a desk in the dressing room next door to it so you'll be able to work. Catz will take your things upstairs and you must tell me if there is anything else you need. I'd like you to treat the villa as your home for as long as you're here.'

Francesca nodded gratefully.

Alicia leant closer. 'And I think now is a good time for you to reconsider my suggestion that you organise the auction of Edgar's collection.'

Francesca shook her head, 'I don't understand . . .' she began.

Alicia silenced her with a wave of her hand. 'The auctioneer I intend to use, Gerald Foxley, is an old friend of mine. His main offices are in London. We have a large town house in Kensington and a considerable part of Edgar's collection is housed in a top-floor gallery there. Now might be an appropriate time for you to consider taking up my offer. You could travel down today on the train, stay there for a while. While you're there you could meet with Gerald and set the wheels in motion.' She paused.

Francesca, I wouldn't have asked you to help me if I didn't think you were capable of doing the job. Besides, if you accept, it would mean you were out of the area for a few days. Perhaps, under the circumstances, you might enjoy a break.'

Francesca stood up and walked towards the large picture window overlooking the garden. Beyond she had a perfect view down towards the sea wall where she and Chris had made love. Now it seemed as if it was someone else who had made love to her in the afternoon sunshine; it was almost impossible to reconcile the tender hands of her summer lover with the drunken brutal man of the night before. 'I never suspected that Chris was so obsessive,' she began.

Behind her Alicia said nothing.

'I should have read the signs. I suppose I wasn't really looking; it all seemed so perfect, the cottage, the new book. He was so kind to me and so supportive after Paul died. He was always there, fighting my battles for me or sometimes just being a shoulder to cry on.' She hesitated. 'All the signs were there now I look back. I should have realised that it was part of his plan. I feel such a fool.'

Alicia moved to stand beside her. 'Think about my offer, Francesca,' she said softly. 'It will give you a break, a change of scene and time to think. Besides that, I *do* need the job done.'

Francesca considered for a moment before turning back to Alicia. If she stayed, Chris would try to find her. He'd invested too much in the relationship to let it just fade away. She needed time to decide how she would deal with him when they met again. 'Yes,' she said slowly, 'yes I'll do it.' Her voice was even and under control.

Alicia smiled. 'I'm so glad. I'll have Catz organise it for you. Now, let me show you to your room. I'm sure you'd like to get settled in.'

Francesca's new home was a comfortable first-floor suite overlooking the rear of the house. It consisted of a bedroom with small bathroom, and a dressing room that had been hastily converted into a makeshift office. Beyond that was an elegant sitting room set out with comfortable armchairs and occasional tables. Alicia left Francesca alone to settle in and unpack.

Francesca carried the box with her laptop into the dressing room. Against one wall was a desk and chair with a lamp; beside it a mesh grating amongst the woodwork created a pool of light in the otherwise dark room. Francesca glanced through it and smiled. The mesh panel was part of a door that opened up into the gallery. From the dressing room it would be possible to watch the activities in the gallery unobserved. Francesca allowed herself just the merest peek before beginning to unpack.

The adjoining bedroom was dominated by an enormous ornate mirror that reflected the bed and tables to either side. Francesca regarded her reflection coolly; there was little to show from her ordeal of the previous night except for a slight dark stain of bruising around her mouth.

Next to the bedroom the sitting room was small but comfortable. Francesca arranged a few of her favourite books on one of the tables and noticed with pleasure that someone had put a large crystal bowl of white roses on the table nearest the fireplace. As she was about to turn away her eyes were drawn from the roses to a wooden plinth standing in a pool of sunlight near the window.

On the plinth was a small marble sculpture, no more than a few inches high; she took a step closer. The soft morning sunlight enhanced the statue's beauty, its shadows and highlights making it seem almost alive; two slender women lay side by side, their bodies entangled in a tantalising caress; every delicate curve and feature had been captured by the sculptor as they moved together in a silent dance of all-consuming passion. Francesca stepped closer still, feeling her pulse quicken. Their naked bodies were draped in exquisitely carved tumbling curls of hair entwined with ivy leaves; one woman's head was tilted back as she abandoned herself to the waves of ecstasy, her lips slightly open, eyes closed. Her ample rounded breasts rested lightly on those of her lover beneath, whose long fingers were buried deep inside the woman's open sex.

Francesca could almost feel the silvery glistening moisture as it trickled over the woman's fingers; could smell the faint perfume of the ocean and detect the subtle heat of their excited bodies as they moved against one another. She looked away, wondering whether it had been Catz or his mistress who had chosen this delicate but erotic focal point for her room.

As she turned, there was a soft knock at the door. She moved across the room, glancing back at the sun-kissed figures. Catz stood in the doorway, a slight smile playing around his lips. She wondered if her excitement was obvious to him. Catz looked beyond her towards the plinth; unconsciously Francesca followed his gaze and felt a little electric pulse of excitement as she looked back and caught his eye.

'Alicia would like to see you in the sitting room when you are unpacked,' he said quietly.

Francesca nodded. 'Thank you. Would you tell her I'll be down in a few minutes.'

Catz turned away slowly but not before he let his eyes wander down to her breasts. Francesca felt her nipples harden in response, pressing up against the thin fabric of her summer blouse. She looked up at him dumbly, knowing that she couldn't hope to conceal the pleasure he awoke in her.

He moved away, and she murmured softly, 'Catz?'

He glanced back and smiled. His ice-cold eyes held the promise of more pleasure than she had ever dreamed of.

Slowly she closed the door and leant against the cold panels. She felt dizzy with desire and longing. It was as if Catz had turned on a wellspring of possibilities that she had no desire or power to control. Her heart beat loudly in her ears. She took a deep breath and let her eyes move slowly around the rooms that would be her new home.

Francesca arrived in London late the same day. Alicia had suggested that the sooner she left, the less difficult it would be for her, and Francesca had agreed. She had hoped that Catz might come with her but knew his first responsibility was to Alicia and the villa.

The train journey gave her a chance to think over the events of the past two days. Allicia had offered her an opportunity to experiment with a life she never knew existed outside her darkest fantasies. At the station she had said goodbye to Catz, longing for the days to pass quickly so she could return to his erotic ministrations. The prospect of exploring Edgar's London gallery alone did not excite her.

A black cab delivered her to the prestigious London house, where she was met by Alicia's concierge. The elderly woman had removed the dust sheets from the main sitting room and made up a bed for her in one of the smaller bedrooms on the first floor. In the kitchen she'd prepared a cold supper and bottle of wine for Francesca. She expressed her thanks and ate her meal alone in the enormous echoing kitchen after the old woman had left.

The house was huge. Once the concierge had gone Francesca felt desperately isolated and alone despite the luxurious surroundings. She began to wonder if her rapid departure to London had been a mistake. Part of her had wanted to stay so she could sort out the situation with Chris. There was so much she had left unsaid that would have rid her of him.

She cleared the plates into the sink and picked up her bag. Inside were the keys that Alicia had given her to open the top-floor gallery and also the study where Edgar's diaries were kept.

Glancing at the clock, she decided that exploring the gallery would have to wait until the morning. She would take a look at Edgar's journals instead and hope that they would quell the uneasy loneliness she felt. Walking through the house she doubted it; her footsteps sounded loud and uncanny in the great vaulted hallway. Above her the darkened chandelier glistened in the hall lights. Slowly she climbed the stairs.

Edgar's study was on the first floor. As Francesca turned the key, the sound of the tumblers falling in the lock seemed unnaturally loud in the silence.

Inside, the room was tastefully decorated in a colonial masculine style. Hanging around the walls were framed photographs of Edgar and Alicia with different distinguished-looking people at charity galas and others in exotic foreign locations; many of their faces were immediately recognisable.

Here and there awards and letters of thanks decorated the side tables and bureaux. The slightest hint of cigar smoke still lingered in the air as if the room's occupant had just stepped outside. Beside the hearth a leather Chesterfield was turned to face the empty grate and the chimney breast was flanked by two large glass cabinets containing row after row of bound journals.

Francesca poured herself a drink from the bottles arranged on a tray beside the chair and selected a diary at random.

Inside, the handwriting was small, cramped, almost childish, but the contents were not. Francesca read the opening paragraph and then turned on a table lamp, all thoughts of an early night vanishing as she read on . . .

'Caroline and her cronies had organised a party for the trade delegation from England at Vernon's hunting lodge this evening. She was hoping to give the stuffed shirts a taste of life in the African bush.

'Alicia looked stunning; I personally oversaw her dressing tonight and helped her with the corset I love her to wear. The shiny black silk nips a little into her cool pale flesh and in my mind perfects her already delightful figure. In the heat her skin glistened like quicksilver as I laced it a little tighter. She told me she loves the sense of constriction and the bright little sparks in her eyes confirmed her words. Before she slipped on her evening gown I painted her nipples carmine red. They hardened deliciously under my attentions. All evening over dinner I imagined them pressing against her silk evening dress leaving little excited kisses on the taut fabric.

'During dinner I saw Vernon admiring her. He's always struck me as a good-looking man in a sort of cruel way – his narrow little mouth betrays him. I could see during the course of the evening that their attraction was mutual;

the teasing way Alicia tipped her head in his direction, the faint flush in her cheeks as he joked with her.

'When the ladies withdrew for coffee I followed Alicia on to the veranda, where she had gone to cool off, and suggested she slip off her panties – a little trophy for our good friend Vernon. The evening was unnaturally still with barely a breath of air. From outside in the velvet-black darkness came the relentless noises of the African night and, beyond, in the sky the electric promise of a coming storm.

'Alicia isn't keen on the heat. A light flush had risen over her shoulders and neck. She looked divine and I was tempted to return and call Vernon outside to join us and invite him to take her there and then. I imagined seeing her elegant skirt lifted, legs apart as the famous hunter buried himself deep inside her. When I told her she laughed and suggested that there were others amongst our party who might be as eager to watch as I was.

'I laughed too and said I would have a word with Caroline when the stuffed shirts had retired for the night. I stepped forward and lifted her soft skirt up to waist height. The sight below was delectable; her shapely legs encased in black silk, white thighs plump and mouthwatering crossed by tight suspenders and, above, the outline of her quim pressing against the thin fabric of her French drawers. She leant back a little so that I could savour the view. Her hands lifted to the waistband of her underwear and she slipped the material down over her hips and the mound of her sex. My God, I could smell her fragrance even from there; that delicious hypnotic aroma of woman.

'Behind us, above the babble of voices from inside the lodge, I heard the quiet click of the screen door as it closed. Alicia's eyes did not leave mine as she allowed the thin fabric of her pants to snake down over her legs. Elegantly she stepped out of them and leant back again so that she was exposed to our unknown observer. Since coming to Kenya I have kept her shaved – the heavy lips of her sex are exposed and vulnerable, like the delicate petals of some exotic orchid. Peeping between the heavy folds I could see the tight moist bud of her pleasure and could feel the heat pulsing up through me. Then Vernon spoke up; his voice was thick.

'"I came outside to look at the view," he said, almost as an apology. "It never ceases to entrance me."

'I wondered if his nerve would fail and he'd scuttle back to the ladies, whose voices I could hear from the room behind us. Instead I felt him step up behind me to observe the view more closely and was rewarded by his soft desperate groan. I looked at Alicia; a fine beading of sweat had formed on her top lip. I could see her nipples, her tightened painted nipples, hardening against the soft fabric of her evening dress. Her eyes had darkened to pinpricks of excitement.

'"Perhaps," I said lightly, "you would prefer to do more than just look."

'Vernon was so close to me I could hear him swallow. He began to bluster – as men often do when confronted with their wildest dreams – so I let Alicia hold her skirt, and I took Vernon's arm and guided him towards the object of his desire. I am sure he had never seen a grown woman shaved before; his eyes didn't leave her heavenly pink mound and I swear the man was drooling. I moved behind Alicia and slipped the straps of her evening dress down. The little corset she was wearing strapped only her waist and ribs, leaving her breasts pouting forward. Unrestricted now they spilled out, their tight buds still a little reddened from their earlier colouring – my only regret is that I did not have time to paint them again before Vernon had a chance to see them.

'He moved like a man mesmerised towards her and I caught hold of her skirt and wrists so she was entirely his, to do with as he pleased. His cruel little mouth hardened as he saw her vulnerability, though below my fingers I could feel her excitement rising, her pulse beating like a drum. He brushed a finger over her mound and down into the tight wet depths beyond. I felt her shudder in anticipation. He was torn between his choice of a beginning – I could see he longed to touch her painted breasts – but he also wanted to lap at her sweating and naked sex; or perhaps he wanted to dispense with both of these and force his manhood cruelly into her delicate fragrant depths.

'In the moonlight I could make out the gratifying bulge in the front of his jodhpurs and could smell his excitement. Finally he sank to his knees in front of her and lapped like a kitten at the bud of pleasure nestling between her swollen outer lips. She let out a whimper of pleasure as the tip of his tongue brushed against her hardened clitoris.

'I let go of Alicia's wrists, though still held her skirt

in a rough bundle, and used my two fingers to draw her outer lips further apart so he could truly enjoy her. His eyes were closed, his expression ecstatic, enraptured. Alicia pressed her body back against me, writhing with delight under Vernon's ministrations. Oh, the delight of it! She shuddered and I could see her moisture spreading over Vernon's face as his tongue ploughed the furrow between her outer lips. I longed to see him inside her, wanted to watch him press home into the tight swollen folds of her sex, and I was not disappointed. He stood up, oblivious now of me behind her or the noises of his guests – so close that you could almost hear their breathing – and unbuckled his belt.

'His erect manhood was a marvel; circumcised and meaty its engorged purple head jutted eagerly towards us. I encouraged Alicia to lie back against me so that I could take her weight. I held her thighs open and guided Vernon into her – he was oblivious of my assistance or my touch – so keen was he to feel his manhood grinding inside her. He let out a gasp as he entered her heat and at once began to force himself deep into her. Glancing down I could see the silken moist junction of their bodies, the swell of her lips embracing his manhood and the smell of her heat mingled with his ripe animal scent as he pushed into her again and again. His eyes were open but unseeing as he thrust harder and harder, feeling the exotic bite of her naked pubic bone against the deep hairy nest at the base of his manhood. She trembled against me, her nipples reddening and swollen as Vernon thrust into her.

'Oh, the expression on his face – the exhilaration, the passion. At the very last moment, when I could see he was almost at the point of no return, he withdrew from the swollen silky-pink lips and fastened his cruel little mouth around one of her nipples, as with a great shuddering moan, he spurted his warm seed over Alicia's belly and my hands. She quivered as his offering splashed over her and leant back harder into my body, her breaths coming in tiny tight gasps.

'In the brief silent moments that followed I felt a curious annoyance at his denying Alicia her pleasure. Through her dress I could feel her quivering intensify, humming; so close to her own climax. But I didn't need to worry. Vernon, a gentleman to the last, sank once again to his knees before Alicia and returned his attentions to her aching desperate body. His tongue followed the hypnotic course between her exposed pleasure bud and the fragrant lower folds. He lapped greedily, eagerly; almost desperately. As he worked on her I slipped a finger around from the rear and slid it deep inside her. I felt her muscles tighten around it eagerly in response to my gentle thrusts whilst Vernon tongued aggressively at the silken open folds of her quim. She felt divine, her juices like warm spun silk. His enquiring excited tongue added an extra dimension to my probing as it brushed my fingers buried deep between her lips. I felt her tighten still further as her hips thrust sharply forward towards Vernon's open mouth. The rhythmic contractions and her gentle breathless moaning sent me into ecstasies of delight.

'She bucked, and grabbed the back of Vernon's head to ensure he did not leave her before her climax had been fulfilled. At last as the final contractions subsided she pushed him away. Vernon seemed to cling for a moment to her exposed body before finally sliding to the floor at her feet. I carefully wiped my darling wife and adjusted her dress. She turned to me, eyes bright and satiated. Delicately she leant forward and kissed me tenderly on the cheek. Oh, Alicia, my beloved.'

In the study of Alicia's London house Francesca could feel the flush in her cheeks. Beside her, her drink stood untouched. She glanced back at the even, rounded writing of Edgar's journal in astonishment. As she picked up the glass she wasn't at all surprised to see her hand shaking. Almost reluctantly she closed the pages of the diary and picked another from the shelves, her eyes bright with anticipation. Opening a page at random she curled herself deeper into the armchair and began to read . . .

'I have been privileged to witness a delightful entertainment this evening which added a certain sparkle to an otherwise very mediocre supper party. New York can be so dull at this time of the year unless one is particularly inventive. Alicia has been in a flurry of excitement since seeing our host's little diversion and I look forward to hearing her own account of the events at some later date.

'We had been invited to the ambassador's home

for supper. A dull chap – or at least I always thought so until this evening. The supper was indifferent – poorly prepared, badly served – though the company was convivial enough. Afterwards, when the ladies had withdrawn, our host suggested he might be able to compensate for the rather indifferent fare with something a little more to our mutual tastes. I wasn't interested at first; he's a chap who struck me, until this evening, as the type who thought a good game of poker a little risqué. Over the port he began to talk about an interesting fantasy his wife had always entertained.

'My ears pricked up – his wife is a large robust woman with ample breasts and great voluptuous thighs – a little too heavy for my taste but nevertheless wonderfully attractive in a Junoesque way. She has always struck me as a little overwhelming for the ambassador, who, despite his elevated status, is a small and rather insignificant little man.

'As he discussed his wife's predilection, a plan evolved between us. We would tell the ladies (Alicia excluded) that we had been called to an emergency meeting at the consulate and the evening would have to come to an abrupt close. Taxis and staff cars would ferry the ladies home and leave us alone with the ambassador's wife and mine. There were seven couples present – myself, the ambassador and five other gentlemen and their wives. One – a rather red-faced and officious chap – declined the ambassador's invitation to join us but promised to keep our intentions secret from his wife and the other ladies.

'There was almost an air of high theatre as we

reassembled in the billiard room when the others had left. The lights had been dimmed, leaving only a couple of lamps on side tables throwing the table into sharp relief. Into the pool of light stepped the ambassador's wife; she looked a little nervous so one of the younger chaps handed her a large brandy which she drank as if it were water. Beside me Alicia asked me what was going on. Of course I couldn't tell her, I wanted her to enjoy the scene unfolding without any preconceptions of its outcome.

'The ambassador's wife began to undo her evening dress; she fumbled nervously, so I suggested that Alicia help her. She smiled at me, believing she had discovered the answer to her earlier question. She stepped forward into the lamplight. I was gratified to see how many pairs of eyes looked at her appreciatively. Her delicate fingers made short work of the other woman's dress fastening. The ambassador's wife smiled at her gratefully and then slithered from her cocktail dress – the unveiling was breathtaking.

'Beneath the elegant dress the woman was wearing a gaudy green silk corset, buckled and strung tightly around her ample frame. She wore suspenders and delicate black lace stockings with nothing over them, so that the scintillating mound of her sex was exposed. Her large breasts were barely confined by the intricate lacy trimming of the corset and her huge dark nipples pressed eagerly forwards against their inadequate restraint. Her areolae were as big as saucers and the nipples themselves were erect and excited, jutting provocatively towards her entranced audience. Her waist was narrow in comparison to the delicious expanse of flesh above and below. It swooped down under the tight restraint of the corset toward broad capacious hips and heavy thighs.

'Though large, in her state of partial undress she was magnificent. What made her beauty all the more memorable was the breathtaking contrast of her creamy-white flesh to the vibrant copper of her hair. Around her sex tight copper curls spread out in a broad triangle reaching as far as her thighs. With one movement of her tiny fluttering hands she loosed the intricate bun on her head and her thick curly auburn hair tumbled loose over her broad shoulders. My God, that woman was a celebration of female flesh if ever there was one. The observers, to a man, gasped at her stunning eroticism.

'I handed Alicia a large paisley handkerchief and indicated that she should blindfold our host's wife. This she did willingly though she still had not comprehended our intention.

'Now the ambassador stepped forward and with great tenderness assisted his good lady on to the billiard table. At first she resisted him a little; I'm sure it was just a little nervous tension, as she certainly needed no encouragement once the exhibition was in full swing.

'The hostess knelt on the table, and the gentlemen now drew straws. I declined to join them – my preference being to watch – and so for my part I held the straws to ensure fair play. The gentlemen had discussed at some length over their port and cigars what was to follow. I guided Alicia to my side so that she could get a close view of the proceedings.

The first gentleman to shed his evening clothes and ascend the table worked in the civil service; a wonderful charming fellow destined, I'm certain, for great things in the future. He knelt before our hostess. It was obvious she had heard him climb on to the table but she still jumped as his hands encircled her heavy breasts. His eager fingers folded back the last of the lace on her corset so their ample proportions were on full view. He cupped them lovingly before leaning forward to take one of the great nipples in his mouth. The lady shivered with delight and his hands moved lower to cup the broad lips of her quim, one speculative finger slipping into the warm fragrant sheath of her depths. She groaned excitedly and spread her creamy thighs to give him greater access then threw back her head in delight as he found her pleasure bud. As he probed her she dropped her backside instinctively to expose her open wetness to his searching fingers. To our delight she now crawled forwards towards him and he lay back to allow her to explore his body. His manhood was already hard and ready and everyone could see her pleasure as her plump little hands circled the base of his engorged shaft. Legs akimbo, he didn't resist her as she slipped further forwards, her magnificent breasts brushing his chest, until finally she slipped his arched red member into her waiting quim.

'I guided Alicia around the table so that we could watch from behind the coupled pair. Our hostess, still blindfolded, was up on her hands and knees now drawing the man into her. The delicate creaminess of her behind with its brush of coppery-coloured hair was in stark contrast to the thick reddened shaft of the man beneath her. Her breasts swayed delicately with the rhythm of their movement. I lifted my hands to rest them on Alicia's neck and was delighted to feel the excited pulse beneath my fingers.

'The second participant of our engaging hostess's largesse was almost undressed and rapidly climbing on to the table. He took up a position in front of the lady, straddling our friend below her. The man's cock was rather thin, though with a distinct upwards tilt to it. With great civility he rested one hand on the back of her neck when he had made himself comfortable, and she eagerly leant forwards to find the bulk of his manhood. With relish she allowed his member to slip between her painted bow-shaped lips. Her guest shuddered and closed his eyes as the warm sensation engulfed him. The ambassador looked at me for approval and I nodded my applause. His wife was truly magnificent. 'He now slipped out of his formal attire and climbed up to the rear of his good lady. I heard Alicia gasp in anticipation of his entry. With one broad hand he smeared some kind of lubricant over his manhood. I moved a little so that I could see the moment of penetration. Alicia, flushed, with her pupils dilated, followed me eagerly though she found it hard to disguise her shock. The ambassador spread the heavy white cheeks of his wife's buttocks. Beneath him the first gentleman had slowed his movements to a halt and remained still whilst the ambassador slipped one oiled finger into the tight button of his wife's backside. The hostess gasped, her breasts rippling at the sensation, and then obligingly she lowered herself to permit her husband easier access. Withdrawing his finger the ambassador re-oiled his manhood and with great deliberation allowed it to make its dark and secret journey into the forbidden recesses of his wife's body. I could see between her legs that the moisture from her sex had trickled down over the shaft of the man beneath. Her heavy breasts were flushed with excitement and as the ambassador pressed home his attack she threw back her head and growled like a wild beast.

'The ambassador, kneeling, wrapped his arms around the narrow waist of his wife taking as much of her considerable weight as he could, whilst the gentleman from the civil service did the same below (though not before guiding one of the lady's engorged nipples into his waiting mouth). The kneeling man took his share, although his face suggested he was not far from the moment of release. The two final gentlemen, eager now to have their portion of pleasure, practically leapt on to the table once the ambassador's wife was able to free her hands thanks to the support of her other three lovers. Kneeling to either side of her they permitted the lady to take a cock in each hand,

'The scenario was complete. It had the look of one of the statues in my collection from the far east, now given life and movement. The glow from the table lamps cast intense pools of light and shade over the performance, giving it an abstract and magical quality.

'The rhythm of the ambassador's thrusting was taken as the beat for the others and they continued to move ever more excitedly. Beside me Alicia couldn't take her eyes off the scene. Every man's face was contorted in an effort to control his excitement, every movement and thrust seemed to be echoed a second later in each of them. The noise of their delight – their excitement and their journey towards release – filled the smoky room until it seemed as if they were all parts of the same great passionate beast.

'The ambassador's wife thrust, sucked and stroked with a singlemindedness that quite overcame me and it was her instinctive animal thrusts of climax, not those of her lovers, which signalled the end of the passionate beast's life. As she bucked, with thin mewling growls of satisfaction trickling from around the man's cock, her lovers lost control.

'Each now bayed after their own goal, thrusting deeper, pushing harder. Backs arched, sweating in profusion, they each began the sharp downward spiral towards oblivion. The gentleman with his manhood sucked deep into his hostess's mouth was the first. He opened his eyes, bright with concentration and delight; clenching his buttocks he lunged forward, a banshee shriek of pleasure spilling from his lips as he reached the moment of climax. His silver seed trickled over the soft reddened lips of the ambassador's wife and the others were now truly lost.

'Beneath her the civil servant bucked dramatically and plunged his member home. The thrust threatened to unseat the ambassador but he clung on, fighting towards the last intense seconds and then could hold no longer. His face contorted into a tight grimace of pleasure and he groaned as his climax overwhelmed him. The two gentlemen to the right and left were seconds behind, their passion spilling out between the eager fingers of their hostess.

'Satiated and exhausted the men slowly slipped from the woman's body. She let herself down on to all fours. A magnificent sight – her body hot and flushed, trembling with the final flurry of her excitement – each man in turn climbed down from the table whilst Alicia hurried forward to remove our hostess's blindfold. Exposed, her eyes were bright and excited. She glanced around the room delighted and eager to search out the faces of her lovers. The men seemed engrossed in dressing, which was a pity as I felt the lady deserved a hearty round of applause.

'The ambassador handed his wife a cloth before helping her down from the table. The lady seemed remarkably composed and within seconds had re-established order. Dressed, though with her hair still down, she checked all her gentlemen guests were respectable before ringing for brandy and cigars. The brandy was a wonderful vintage though the cigars were a little dismal. . .'

Francesca was about to return the diary to the shelves when a photograph slipped from inside. It showed Alicia, younger but still as stunning, leaning against a street sign in a small American town. She looked glorious, her delicate complexion shaded by a cowboy hat. Below it her eyes were bright with love and mischief as she posed for the snap. Francesca slipped the photograph back in where it had fallen from and began to read again. The date on the entry was a few weeks later . . .

'Dull dull dull. I had not intended we should travel so far into the heartland of this hot and dusty and uncivilised country but Hank (our host for this part of our mission) insisted we should go and spend some time with him on his ranch. In some ways it reminds me of Africa; the broad expanses of grassland, the horizon glittering in a heat haze away in the far distance. Alicia loathes it – Hank is a bore – but I have promised to try to find her some little diversion that may amuse her.'

Francesca let her eyes move down – past the accounts of trail rides and trips but on to the plain for picnics – to the following page . . .

'I have taken more than a little time during our stay here to let Hank know that my interests do not lie purely with horseflesh and cattle. This afternoon, as we were riding back from seeing some calves being branded, he suggested, rather dismissively – perhaps in case he might offend me – that I might like to spend the evening with him at the local bordello. My expression must have betrayed my enthusiasm, because in the next breath he began waxing lyrical about the beauty of the girls and their cleanliness.

'As we rode along a little further I tactfully broached the subject of Alicia's joining us. I had expected him to be a little nonplussed, even shocked, but his reaction surprised me. He had decided at some stage during our stay that Alicia was probably not my wife, but, given the disparity of our ages, a mistress I was passing off as my wife, and he heartily embraced the idea that she might, in his word, "benefit" from a night on the town.

'The bordello itself, I'm afraid, was a cliché; little froufrou bows here and there, lots of lace and the heady smell of cheap perfume and cigar smoke. When we arrived, the bar was being tended by a rather muscular young woman dressed in a faded cotton body suit, cut off at mid-thigh and trimmed with a single band of cotton lace. Her bleached blonde hair was caught up on top of her head in an untidy bun, giving her a slovenly and unintelligent appearance, though when we ordered a drink I could see her casting an experienced eye over us.

'Hank, eager to be away, introduced us to the madam, a plump motherly woman in her early fifties. She winked at me whilst she arranged for Hank to visit his regular sweetheart and returned to our table as soon as the aging cowboy was settled. I sent Alicia to replenish our glasses whilst I quickly explained what I had in mind for her. The madam grinned and said it would present no problems.

'Once in a little rather garish bedroom on the first floor, I prepared Alicia; taking a tip from our ambassador friend from New York I blindfolded her to add another dimension to our lovemaking. She shuddered beneath my fingers as I carefully unbuttoned her dress to mid-waist and slipped the material down over her shoulders. Beneath she was wearing a white silk camisole top, and below a matching pair of French drawers. I slipped her dress down over her ankles; in the heat I could smell the slightest hint of perspiration on her, warm and sensuous against the contrast of her perfume. I could sense the tight little buzz of excitement under her skin as I sat her down on the edge of the bed and sat myself back in an armchair to wait for the events to unfold.

'A second or two later the door opened and the girl from the bar entered. I should have guessed her tastes when I first saw her. The outline of her nipples pressing against the little body suit she wore betrayed her excitement as she regarded the blindfolded figure of my wife. Even from where I sat I could smell the heady sexual perfume of her body; she glanced at me and sneered, which sent a tiny tingling bead of excitement down my spine. She circled around Alicia like a cat, watching, weighing her up, as Alicia – blindfolded – trembled with expectation.

'The woman snapped sharply, "Put your hands above your head." Her accent was divine, rolling up from the depths of her rounded belly. Alicia jumped and then complied. The whore moved closer and lightly stroked one of Alicia's nipples. She let out a tiny, thin whimper, her mouth fell open and, below, her nipple hardened lushly under the thin silk. The whore leant closer and sucked it into her mouth through the fabric, her tongue lapping and eager, whilst her hand pulled the curve of Alicia's breast closer to her. Alicia whimpered as the woman moved her attentions to the other breast. The effect was spectacular; the whore's wet lips had made the material almost transparent and against the saturated fabric Alicia's nipples showed their excitement in taut dark circles.

'The whore stepped back and slid from her body suit. Beneath it she was stunning; long muscly legs, a thick waist and, above, the heavy sway of her magnificent breasts. Her nipples were large, dark. I swallowed as she turned towards me; between her legs was a great tangled mat of jet-black hair that totally obscured her sex and rose in a thin hairy line to her navel.

'Roughly she pushed Alicia back on to the bed and straddled her thighs, dragging at the delicate silk of her drawers. Alicia bucked against her but did not resist as the woman ripped them down over her hips. Now the whore's dark sex lowered slowly on to the soft curves of Alicia's mound, brushing her lightly before grinding against her. Alicia let out a little shriek, silenced almost instantly by the whore's red lips closing over her open mouth. Her large capable hands pushed Alicia's camisole up to her shoulders and I was enchanted as the whore's heavy breasts with her tight dark nipples brushed aggressively against those of my wife.

'The image was stunning. Now she began to work against her, mouth to mouth, sex to sex, her pushes and her grindings making Alicia gasp. I thought this alone might bring the matter to a conclusion but the whore had other ideas. She turned and I could see, with growing excitement, what she had in mind.

'Alicia's legs hung down over the edge of the bed, her sex lifted, the delicious mound straining upwards. The whore turned full circle so that now her face was level with my wife's exposed sex and her own hung inches above Alicia's face. I had to move and watch. The lips of the whore's sex where enormous, pendulous, whilst within they throbbed with a scarlet intensity that I have never seen in my life. Fraction by fraction she lowered herself. I knew Alicia must be able to smell her, and instinctively she rolled and tossed her head away from the inevitability of their meeting. Below, the whore's fingers spread Alicia's sex and I gasped as her pink tongue pushed out between her painted lips and slipped inside. In the instant her tongue entered Alicia the whore's hips thrust backward, placing her clitoris against Alicia's lips.

'I heard myself groan in satisfaction as the woman above began to lap and move against my wife below. At first I could sense Alicia's reluctance and revulsion and then she started to respond to the surge of pleasure from the warm folds, shimmering brightly beneath the whore's lips. I saw her tongue lift— lift just a fraction from between her lips – towards her rider's quim above and quite suddenly she began to lap at it, her tongue seeking out the deep fragrant pleats and folds. The whore moaned appreciatively and renewed her attentions to Alicia.

'My God, what a sight – the whore's quim, throbbing amongst those great dark curls, her crimson lips swelling and darkening even as I watched, whilst beneath her my beloved Alicia rolled and bucked madly. Her hands lifted now to embrace the whore and to seek out the heavy gyrating bulk of her pendulous breasts.

'Their climax was seconds away; around them the air crackled and sparked with their growing excitement as if they rode on the breath of a storm. Suddenly I saw Alicia thrust her hips up, her quim intent on seeking out her lover's tongue. From her mouth, pressed hard against the folds of the whore, I heard a thin intense shriek of pleasure. The whore, in response, plunged her tongue harder in Alicia's waiting lips and roared with satisfaction as Alicia's brought her to the fringes of paradise. Satiated they slipped down on to each other, a hot, erotic liaison, both trembling wildly in the aftermath of their mutual passion.

'Later in the bar below . . .'

Francesca, her hands trembling, closed the diary and poured herself another drink. The house seemed so still and so empty after the intense noises of passion within her mind. She felt desperately dizzy with an aching need that refused to leave. Glancing around the room she wondered what other extremes of passions this house had witnessed during Edgar's lifetime.

The diaries had left her hot and unsatisfied but she also knew then that she would never be able to write a book about Edgar's life. The glass-fronted cabinets were crammed with leather-bound diaries, each meticulously filled in his small rounded hand. What biography could possibly convey the man accurately when so much would have to be excluded? Edgar's passion for the erotic, for the bizarre, for the intense pleasures of voyeurism, made up so large a part of his life that any biography written without including them would make him appear two-dimensional – a cipher of a man. She turned the pages again; they were littered with the names of the rich and famous. The book could never be written – even so long after his death.

She replaced the books carefully and locked the cabinet, her hand still betraying the slightest tremble. It was with a sense of regret that she closed and locked the study door. Making her way along the dim corridors, she wondered what other secrets the house held in store for her.

Her room on the first floor was comfortable and warm. Exhausted she slipped off her clothes and slipped between the crisp linen sheets. In her sleepy mind she conjured up the image of Catz, his rugged face and cruel blue eyes, his exquisite body now jumbled and intertwined with the accounts she had read in Edgar's diaries. She quivered and wished that he was with her. Her hands moved slowly across her aching unsatisfied body, but before she could bring herself to the climax that her body craved she had slipped into a deep dream-filled sleep. Beside the bed lay the keys Alicia had given her; tomorrow she would begin her exploration of the gallery.

# Chapter Six

Francesca's tumbling erotic dreams were interrupted by the harsh clanging of a doorbell. Sleepily she looked around the bedroom and realised it was morning and that she was in Edgar's London house. Slipping out of bed she pulled on her robe, glanced in the mirror and grimaced; she certainly looked in no fit state to receive visitors. She tied the robe a little tighter and ran her fingers through her hair, trying to tidy it before hurrying downstairs. The bell rang again. In the hallway below her the concierge was scurrying across the parquet floor to answer the door; gratefully Francesca slipped back to her room to get dressed.

When Francesca came downstairs a few minutes later she could hear the low hum of voices coming from the sitting room; the concierge met her in the hallway carrying a tray and said quietly, 'It's Mr Foxley and his assistant, Miss.'

Francesca thanked her. She checked her appearance briefly in the hall mirror before going in to introduce herself. The bruises had started to fade around her mouth and despite her late night she looked fresh and alert.

As she stepped into the sitting room, Gerald Foxley got to his feet and self-consciously ran his fingers through his unruly thatch of gingery hair, straightened his tie and then came towards her with his hand extended in greeting. Francesca took it; his touch was dry and smooth beneath her fingers. He was dressed in an expensive pinstriped suit which gave his rather narrow frame a sophisticated businesslike air despite the rapid nervous adjustments to his appearance. Beside him, still sitting in one of the armchairs, his assistant now rose to greet Francesca. Melissa Andrews, a striking blonde with languid blue eyes, murmured hello in a soft, low voice before extending one perfectly manicured hand.

Francesca invited them to sit and then waited until the concierge had served the coffee before speaking again. 'Have you been in contact with Alicia?' she asked, to open their conversation.

Gerald nodded. 'Oh, absolutely. She rang me yesterday and explained that she finally wanted to dispose of her husband's collection of artefacts and memorabilia. She seems quite determined, so that's why we've called today. Alicia says you will be acting as her agent. I hope you don't mind that we didn't ring first?' His voice was thin and cultured with an enthusiastic boyish lilt to it, his sentences coming in breathy staccato bursts.

Francesca smiled and then continued, 'Not at all. I wonder, Gerald, have you any idea of the nature of the collection?'

Gerald sipped his coffee and smiled pleasantly. 'I've heard of it, of course. It's quite famous, you know, or should I say infamous.' He laughed nervously. 'Over the years I've seen one or two of the more interesting pieces – my father was one of Edgar Moffat's closest friends. Occasionally Edgar bought something that needed some attention, restoration, that kind of thing, and my father organised it for him. On other occasions my father acted as his agent at auctions.'

Francesca nodded. 'Then you appreciate that the sale has to be arranged with the utmost discretion?'

Gerald laughed. 'Of course. Rest assured, the matter is already in hand. Edgar Moffat's collection is well-known amongst connoisseurs and collectors of erotica. The sale will excite a great deal of interest of the most discreet and intense kind. Buyers of this sort of material all value their privacy, but will still fight tooth and nail for some of the more exotic pieces in Edgar's catalogue.'

Melissa listened intently. It was obvious from her face that she had never seen any of the artefacts and her curiosity was aroused. Francesca glanced across at her; Melissa coloured slightly and looked away.

Gerald followed Francesca's eyes and continued in answer to her unspoken question. 'I'd like to add that Melissa is one of my most trusted members of staff. I hoped that you might be able to arrange for her to work on the cataloguing of the items in London whilst I busy myself contacting the potential buyers.'

Francesca nodded. 'Certainly, but if the collection here is as large as the one at the villa it'll be a mammoth task for one person on their own.' She glanced back at Melissa. 'Would you mind if I gave you a hand?'

'That sounds like a wonderful idea,' said Gerald before Melissa had a chance to answer. 'Now, I wonder if we might be permitted to take a look at the collection? I've never actually been up there.'

Francesca nodded and led them upstairs. She was grateful that the concierge appeared to restrict her attentions to the lower floors. Passing the door of the study, Francesca wondered if Gerald had ever had the opportunity to dip into Edgar's journals. Looking back at his rather boyish and insipid face she doubted it. Behind them Melissa followed, quietly carrying a clipboard, though Francesca noticed that her eyes took in every detail of the house's expensive and beautiful fixtures and fittings.

In the sitting room Francesca had wondered if Melissa's function was purely decorative. In her narrow high heels and short, well-cut navy suit she had the look of someone's expensive plaything. But first impressions can be deceptive and now Francesca could see the younger woman was shrewder than she had first thought.

The main door to the gallery was at the top of a flight of stairs. Francesca slipped the key into the lock, wondering what would lie behind the subdued elegant panelling.

Pushing the doors open she had to stop herself from gasping in surprise; the gallery was almost an exact replica of the gallery at the villa although here, on one wall, hung an enormous mirror which made the room look far larger than it actually was.

She turned back to Melissa and Gerald. Carefully controlling the tremor in her voice, she said, 'Here we are, Edgar's London collection.'

But Melissa had already slipped past her and was looking into the first display cabinet. Francesca saw her freeze for an instant before turning back towards them, her face quite pale.

Francesca smiled and then turned to Gerald. 'I'm afraid I haven't had a chance to look over the things here yet. Alicia says there is a small office at the far end of the gallery where we can work.'

Gerald nodded and then began to walk along the displays. He seemed unmoved by the exquisite pieces that stood on plinths and behind protective glass. Melissa, by contrast, had turned her attentions back to the first display cabinet and seemed rooted to the spot.

Gerald walked back briskly. 'Well,' he said calmly, 'I think if you don't mind I'll leave you ladies to it. Melissa knows what needs to be done. I've arranged for some photographic equipment to be delivered later today, so once you have the items catalogued we can select one or two pieces to illustrate the nature and quality of the collection. All right, Melissa?'

When Melissa turned back Francesca was astounded to see bright pinpricks of excitement in her eyes. She seemed to be almost breathless as she nodded dumbly and then, composing herself, added quickly, 'Certainly, Gerald. That will be fine.'

Francesca showed Gerald to the door. He took her hand and smiled pleasantly. 'It's been a pleasure to meet you. If you ring Alicia, please let her know I foresee no problems. Everything is in hand.'

Francesca thanked him and was about to slip back upstairs when the concierge appeared to let her know she was leaving for the day. She said she had arranged a cold buffet in the dining room for them when they wanted lunch. Francesca smiled and thanked her. The woman had explained when Francesca arrived that she only came in occasionally to air the house and prepare any rooms as required, but normally lived out.

Alone in the main house now Francesca went back to her room to have a quick shower and change. After half an hour or so she slipped back downstairs to make Melissa and herself some coffee before returning to the gallery. On the tray she also took a notebook and pen – best to look businesslike, she thought wryly – particularly as Edgar's precious collection was likely to leave them both feeling a little hot under the collar.

She pushed open the gallery door with her foot and was surprised to see Melissa standing almost exactly as she had left her. Hearing the door open, Melissa turned. Her face was pale, her blue eyes had darkened to stormy grey and, despite her attempts, there was no way she could disguise her arousal. Francesca put the tray down on the nearest display case.

'Have you seen these things?' Melissa murmured softly.

Francesca shook her head. 'No, not these, but

there are more in the country house.' She hesitated, remembering the effect Edgar's statue had had on her. An image of Catz appeared in her mind and she wondered how he would have reacted to Melissa's barely concealed arousal.

She said evenly, trying to mimic his calm invitation to her, 'There is everything you could ever want here, and more. Every pleasure, every sensation – nothing here is forbidden.'

Melissa turned back to the display case and Francesca joined her to see what had excited and entranced the blonde woman.

Inside, carefully mounted on a wooden base, was a long fragmented strip of papyrus. Despite its obvious age and disrepair its effect was galvanising, the colours and the figures still as bright and enticing as when it was first painted.

The scene was of three women drawn in the Egyptian style. One woman was lying across a table or low bed, her golden skin highlighted here and there with discreet touches of gold leaf. Straddling her face was another younger girl with tiny uptilted breasts; her hand had slid down into the soft dark mound of her sex, her fingers holding open her dark outer lips to allow the woman beneath her to insert her tongue. The third woman stood between the prone woman's legs; in her hand she cradled a thick black dildo which she was skilfully inserting into the woman's eager, waiting body. Around the dildo the lips of her sex were exaggerated, drawn larger than life, and here and there tiny droplets of glistening moisture had been painted in. The woman with the dildo was leaning forward, her expression blissful and enrapt as her tongue eagerly sought out the tight erect nipples of the young girl in front of her. Every muscle, every sinew, every sensation of the triangle of passion seemed to have been captured and recorded.

Despite herself Francesca could feel the moist heat growing between her legs. The ancient scroll was alive with the sounds and smells of exquisite forbidden pleasures. Slowly she turned to Melissa, knowing that she wouldn't be able to disguise her own excitement. Melissa's hand snaked up to the top of the display cabinet and Francesca gasped; in her tightly clenched fist she held an exact replica of the black dildo so exquisitely painted on the parchment.

Melissa said softly, 'I tried to tear my eyes away from this picture. I thought I'd look at something else but the images kept bubbling back up in my mind and then I saw this in a display case.' Her voice failed her and Francesca glanced down. Through the tight fabric of Melissa's suit she could see the faintest outline of her nipples as they pressed excitedly against the material.

Melissa ran her tongue around her painted lips and swallowed hard. 'I have always wondered,' she began, 'what it would be like to make love to a woman.' Her eyes were almost black now, her face flushed and glowing. 'I've dreamed about it . . .'

Francesca swallowed as Melissa closed her eyes and unbuttoned her jacket before letting it slip to the floor.

Beneath it she wore only the tiniest of black lace bras that pushed her heavy breasts forwards. Melissa lifted a hand excitedly to her own nipples and let her long painted fingernails toy with the dark hardened buds. Her other hand, which still gripped the dildo, trembled with excitement as she moved its cold unwieldy bulk to lie between the deep crease of her cleavage. Her tongue peeked from between her reddened lips and with a little shuddering moan she lapped at the end of the heavy carved phallus.

Francesca felt an overwhelming sense of panic; her belly griped as she watched the woman work the shaft further into her waiting mouth. The picture of her painted lips around the dark wood was hypnotic. Melissa's other hand toyed with the erect, excited hardness of her darkening nipples. Slowly, almost imperceptibly, she let her hand slide down to the side fastening of her zip and struggled to free it. In spite of herself Francesca moved forwards, caught hold of the little catch and pushed it down smoothly.

Melissa snaked free and pushed her skirt down over her gently rounded hips. Francesca gasped; under her skirt Melissa was wearing a tiny black suspender belt and knickers that matched the bra, and below that delicate flesh-coloured stockings. The erotic effect was breathtaking as, above, Melissa's lips continued their journey around the broad shaft of the ornate phallus.

Francesca felt the moisture gathering in the soft folds of her own sex, felt warm fingers of desire flush through her and knew that part of her longed to experience the sensations of her hands on Melissa's lithe excited body She swallowed hard, trying to push the desire back into the deep recesses of her mind.

Mesmerised, she stepped closer, her senses alight as she breathed in the soft aroma of Melissa's perfume and the undertones of her sweet body smell. Feeling her so close Melissa lifted a hand towards Francesca and caressed the soft arc of her throat and neck. Francesca moaned at the delicate contact, the conflict raging in her mind as she leant forward further so her lips brushed the other woman's cheek.

The sensation was electric, so soft, so delicate. Melissa slipped the dildo from her mouth and placed it carefully on top of the display cabinet. Her eyes opened slowly as if from sleep. Lightly her hands lifted to the buttons of Francesca's blouse and began to undo them.

Francesca, caught in a paradox of excitement and revulsion, lifted her hands to stroke Melissa's narrow shoulders, quivering at the tight pulse of excitement she felt beneath her fingertips. Instinctively she pushed down the shoulder straps of Melissa's bra, her hands moving across to cup the heavy arc of her breasts. She took their weight, marvelling at their delicate softness and the way she could detect the slightest tremor of Melissa's excitement. Above her, Melissa shuddered deliciously at her touch and now in turn cupped the small tingling orbs she found hidden beneath the soft folds of Francesca's summer blouse. She leant forward, pushing the fabric aside and licked at Francesca's tiny tight nipples. Francesca sighed as Melissa sucked the tight little bud into her wet mouth, her tongue working in enthusiastically. As her lips closed contentedly around its hard outline she pushed Francesca's blouse back off her shoulders, and in response Francesca let her hands slip around and unclasp Melissa's bra, allowing her heavy breasts their freedom.

For an instant both women drew back and looked at one another. Between them the electric hum of desire was almost tangible. Francesca slipped her soft summer skirt down over her hips and let it drop to the floor, revealing the creamy silk triangle of her knickers. Melissa sighed appreciatively and stepped forwards to take Francesca in her arms.

There was a moment, the merest split second, in which Francesca held back and then she felt the tantalising brush of Melissa's erect nipples against her own. Then she knew she wanted more than anything to experience the touch and the feel of this woman and the pleasures they could share.

She pulled Melissa towards her, letting the warmth of Melissa's body engulf her. Her small hands moved across the delicate curve of her back, relishing the soft almost liquid pressure of Melissa's heavy breasts against her own. Melissa's face turned towards her, her hot mouth burning out a lipstick-tinted trail across Francesca's neck and face until she could resist the woman's desire no longer and pressed her lips against Melissa's open mouth. The taste and texture of the other woman's lips was entrancing, delightful; her soft kisses a stunning contrast to those of men she had kissed. Her saliva was as sweet as honey, her tongue a soft enquiring presence in her own as it gently lapped and caressed her.

Francesca felt a desperate rippling shudder course through her. Eagerly she slipped her hand up to Melissa's heavy flushed breasts, her fingers stroking and caressing the taut nipples. She was rewarded by the sound of Melissa's excited animal whimpering as the other woman's hands slipped lower to the waistband of Francesca's pants.

Francesca, despite her desire and longing, still felt a little trickle of anxiety. Part of her – a distant part that she was fighting to subdue – was horrified as Melissa's hand snaked its way between the thin fabric of her panties and the soft downy warmth of her belly. She let out a tiny cry as the other woman's hand brushed the soft hair of her mound and then gasped as Melissa moved still lower and with knowing, skilled fingers parted the moist lips of her sex. Beneath her fingers the hardened, engorged bud of her clitoris strained and ached for Melissa's touch. Delicately she began a gentle circular movement around its sensitive hood. Francesca could barely control the excitement growing inside her; Melissa's subtle understanding of her body's needs was breathtaking and at some level terrifying – it was almost as if she were making love to herself – so delicate and perceptive was Melissa's touch. Melissa's moist fingers slipped back further, reaching into the tight hot confines of her body, and Francesca felt herself opening willingly under the other woman's exploration.

Inspired by the sensations and her longing to share

the subtle heady caresses with Melissa she moved her own hands down towards the dark outline of Melissa's mound where it pressed against the shimmering fabric of her panties. Cupping its delicate contours from the outside Francesca was surprised by the heat and the moisture she could feel. Slowly – a little nervously – she slipped her hand inside the waistband of Melissa's knickers. The blonde woman pushed eagerly towards her, her legs opening under Francesca's tentative exploration, and her mouth and tongue renewed their hot intense search.

Melissa's hair was flattened against the thin wall of her panties and felt silky smooth. Hypnotised by the feel of it Francesca moved further down; the rounded damp folds opened obediently under her caresses, seeming to almost draw back at her touch to reveal the harder more urgent press of her clitoris. Fleetingly Francesca let a finger slide over its sensitive hood and was rewarded again by a soft mewling whimper of excitement bubbling up from deep inside Melissa's throat.

Deeper still now, Francesca revelled in the delicacy of the folded moist lips of Melissa's sex; Edgar had been right, it truly felt like an exotic flower, an orchid, with its subtle contours and silky enticing surface. The beauty of it surprised her. Well acquainted with her own body, she couldn't reconcile the strange feelings of familiarity and strangeness that Melissa's body awoke in her. As she touched she could almost feel the effects of her caress deep inside her own body; she shivered.

Melissa's mouth slid away from Francesca's and traced a hot salty path down towards Francesca's breasts. Her lips nipped and suckled, her tongue circled eagerly around the buds, whilst her fingers plunged deeper and deeper inside Francesca's desperate body.

Francesca struggled to keep her excitement in check so that she could echo her attentions on Melissa. Slowly Melissa drew back, looking up at Francesca with those bright sharp eyes. Both of her hands now lifted to Francesca's hips and pulled down the fabric of her knickers, exposing her totally. Francesca gasped as the woman pulled more insistently so they both sank to their knees amongst the tangle of their discarded clothes. Slipping clear of Francesca's eager fingers Melissa slipped off her own knickers, leaving only the cold crisp lines of the suspender belt, her sex framed by the straps.

Melissa's mound was sparsely covered in fine blonde hair which only partially hid the deep crease of her sex. A tiny bead of moisture clung to the hair and sparkled enticingly. With gentle hands she lay Francesca down, pulling a skirt out from under them to pillow her head. Francesca waited with bated breath for their lovemaking to resume; she reached out to Melissa who smiled gently, her eyes still sleepy.

Melissa gently resisted her advances. Instead she began a soft assault of her own, her tongue resuming its path down over Francesca's nipples, her fingers slipping back into the receptive and eager depths of her body. Softly her thumb brushed against the erect bud of

Francesca's clitoris and she arched her back instinctively to allow the woman greater freedom, her thighs falling open in willing surrender to the advances she was certain were coming. Melissa's tongue eased lower, lapping around and defining the shadowed curves beneath her breasts, lifting to outline the receptive folds of her inner arm. Her tongue moved away, trailing lower, circling her navel, dipping into its sensitive creases before swooping to lap along the suntanned bowl between her hip-bones.

As she worked, Melissa began to subtly change position from kneeling between Francesca's legs to lying alongside her. Now Francesca could make out the golden touched folds of her sex, smell the delicate musky odour of her excitement and knew – knew deep inside – that wherever Melissa led she would gratefully and eagerly follow.

The first tentative touch of Melissa's tongue when it came was as shocking as it was intense. Her tongue barely brushed the outer lips but enough to drive Francesca close to the edge of the void; her hips thrust forward automatically to greet the next experimental probing. In return her own arms linked around Melissa's thighs and she found herself pulling Melissa's body closer to her. The smell of her body was at once both deeply exciting and repelling, her senses reeled at the confusion as she opened her mouth and took the first soft brushing lick at Melissa's sex. The confusion did not leave her as the first salty taste of the woman's juices crept across her tongue. Melissa's hips moved to encourage her and Francesca let the tip of her tongue seek out the hard pulsing bud of her clitoris.

Below her Melissa moaned and then echoed the touch. Locked in a dance of passion, each woman licked and kissed and probed in turn, each caress increasing their confidence and their certainty. Francesca could feel the tight glorious glow of her orgasm building inside her. She felt the muscles in her thighs contract, the muscles of her belly echo the contraction and she heard herself begin to groan as the crystal glittering moment came closer and closer. To her surprise, despite feeling the same excitement echoed in Melissa's hot thrusting body, the blonde woman pulled away.

As Francesca was about to look down, Melissa suddenly knelt upright and slipped her leg over Francesca's so she straddled her face. The exposure was startling; her exterior lips hung apart revealing the soft wet folds of their secret dark inner contours, whilst above, over the sensitive bridge of flesh, Francesca could clearly see the tightly closed button of her bottom. Her hungry musky smell was tantalising.

It suddenly flashed through Francesca's mind that Melissa was intent on emulating the image on the ancient scroll. Almost in the instant that she thought it she felt the brush of something cool against her legs. Glancing down between Melissa's thighs she saw the dark shape of the dildo cupped lovingly in the blonde woman's palm. Francesca gasped and stiffened. Melissa, as if sensing her fear, began to stroke Francesca's breasts and circled the heated, excited lips of her sex as she skilfully inserted the cold bulk of the smooth antique phallus between them. Her fingers moved lower to hold her open, smoothing and easing its chilling entry.

In spite of her fear Francesca's excited muscles, so close to release, tightened sharply around the cold contours of the smooth phallus; she felt them draw it into her gratefully. The chill of it sliding against her sensitive swollen lips made her shudder in a tangled web of emotions. As she began to relax Melissa leant forward and began to kiss again at Francesca's sex. Francesca bucked up to meet her, impaling herself on the hard dark coolness of the ancient pleasure device. Melissa began a steady and seemingly unstoppable rhythm between tongue and phallus, her lips drawing – sucking – heady circles around the sensitive tip of her clitoris. Francesca's hips began to move automatically in time with them both.

In response Melissa dropped her hips, tilting them to put her own exposed sex within reach. Without hesitation Francesca began to lap at it, pushing aside all the confusing emotions. Her tongue sought out the depths of her body before rising to find the hard ridge of Melissa's clitoris. Now they began to move against each other as if synchronised, tongue, fingers, lips and the dark bulk of the smooth dark phallus; a spiral dance of pleasure that drove them both towards their mutual orgasm.

Overcoming every shred of reluctance Francesca reached up to fondle Melissa's heavy engorged nipples and pulled her down further on to her waiting tongue.

Below she felt the vibrations of Melissa's desperate moan against the hard biting bone of her pubis. The phallus pushed deeper inside her, filling her, stretching her wide under its relentless thrust as she felt its cold head pressing hard against her womb. White-hot waves pressed closer, the sensations more intense, rippling, roaring and then crashing through her as her inner muscles clutched desperately at the hard unyielding bulk of the dildo.

Above her Melissa bucked and forced herself downwards. Instantly they were both lost in a sea of mutual all-engulfing pleasure. Melissa sobbed with excitement whilst below her Francesca's mouth was filled with the heady sweet juices of her orgasm.

Exhausted, Melissa rolled off Francesca and lay still beside her, her chest heaving with emotion and exertion. Francesca closed her eyes, as the last few intense ripples of pleasure juddered through her. She heard Melissa move, and gasped as the blonde woman gently slipped the dildo out from inside her, her muscles aching to retain it.

The silence of the gallery was broken only by the intense, gentle sounds of the women's breathing. Finally Francesca opened her eyes and looked across at her beautiful blonde lover. Melissa smiled and leant forwards to kiss Francesca on her lips, still fragrant and moist from Melissa's juices. The kiss was soft, gentle, a kiss of thanks and trust between new lovers. Francesca smiled too and embraced Melissa.

*

When Gerald Foxley arrived at the London house a few days later it was pouring with rain. He always found the smell of summer rain on hot tarmac and concrete invigorating. Climbing from the cab he shook out the umbrella he always carried, hurried up the front steps of Alicia's house and rang the bell. After a few seconds the concierge opened it and explained that the ladies were already working upstairs in the gallery. He smiled. He'd been right to entrust this rather delicate mission to Melissa; she had a real talent for the unusual and always rose to a challenge. Momentarily he thought about her soft inviting curves and the delicate cast of her sensuous lips. He shuddered and hastily pushed the image from his mind.

He also had good news for Francesca. First indications suggested that the potential buyers would be only too pleased to finally get a chance to snaffle up a little of Edgar Moffat's exotic collection.

Slipping off his sodden raincoat he handed it to the concierge, who announced that she would be most grateful if he could tell Francesca that she was now leaving for the day. Gerald nodded, though declined her offer to take his umbrella; over the years he'd lost too many to risk leaving this one – a particular favourite – in Alicia's hall-stand.

He climbed the stairs slowly, taking time to admire the collection of antiques and paintings that graced the landing and stairwell. A particularly elegant side table caught his eye, almost certainly Chippendale. He sighed; it was unfortunate that Alicia wasn't thinking of auctioning the entire contents of the house. Collectors could seldom confine themselves to just one area and Edgar's taste in furniture and art works would net them all a fortune if they ever came to auction.

On the landing of the second floor he could make out the subdued voices of Francesca and Melissa. The doors to the gallery were slightly ajar and through the narrow opening he could see the women were engaged in arranging a particularly interesting sculpture against a creamy-white sheet. Melissa was peering through the viewfinder of a camera on a tripod, trying to make sure the image was sharp and well-defined.

She stepped back and beckoned to Francesca to take a look. Gerald, peering through the half-open door, thought they looked particularly enchanting; one blonde, one brunette, and casually dressed in simple summer dresses. He noticed the soft tendrils of their hair as they leant together over the viewfinder, picked out in the light from the studio lamps; he swallowed hard. The lights also revealed the delicate outline of their bodies silhouetted through the cotton fabric.

He stepped in through the door and called his greeting. Both women looked up at once and he was surprised to see both were devoid of make-up. They looked young, almost girlish. He tried to contain the little ripple of desire that passed through him, disguising it with a smile.

'Morning ladies, how's it going?' he said cheerily, placing his umbrella on the nearest display case.

Francesca smiled. 'Fine. We've catalogued nearly

everything, though I think you ought to give Melissa overtime rates, Gerald. We've had to work very late.'

Did he detect a mischievous look between them? He thought so, but by the time he looked again it was gone. He rubbed his hands.

'Wonderful. It sounds as if we're well on schedule. There has been a great deal of interest in the auction. I'm setting the date fairly soon. Not rushing things, you understand, but one of our big American contacts is planning a trip to Europe in the next couple of weeks, so we can't let the chance of that slip through our fingers, can we?'

He glanced up; the look was there again, playing around Melissa's full lips, something teasing and delightful in Francesca's eyes. He glanced down to see if he'd left his flies undone. Reassured, he looked back at them; the women had a kind of bloom about them, a smooth contentment that almost defied description.

Finally, rather uneasily he coughed and said, 'Well, I'm delighted that you and Melissa are getting along so well. Perhaps you ought to consider a job with us when Alicia's commission is finished.'

To his surprise Francesca grinned and turned away. Struggling to compose herself she turned back quickly. 'Sorry Gerald, it's just the atmosphere up here; it's difficult to always remain serious when there are so many strange and unusual things around you.'

Gerald glanced down at the statue they had been arranging on the cream sheet and had to agree. An Eastern piece cast in mottled bronze, it depicted a plump elderly man strapped tightly over a barrel, his buttocks naked and, between his legs Gerald could clearly make out the rounded exposed bulk of his testicles. Standing behind the supplicant was a small Oriental man in a coolie hat who was preparing to administer a sound flogging with a short length of bamboo.

Gerald swallowed hard and nodded. 'Er, I see what you mean.' He indicated their rather casual dress. 'I suppose it's more comfortable to work up here in something casual, more relaxed . . .' The sentence was meant to disguise his sense of excitement at the erotic *frisson* that he got from the little statue; instead, to his horror, Melissa grinned at him and leant provocatively against the tripod. In the harsh glare of the spotlight he could clearly make out the delicate arc of her sumptuous uptilted breasts.

'It gets very hot up here by late afternoon,' she purred mischievously, glancing across at Francesca. Francesca gave her a sharp look as if to reprimand her and Melissa rapidly composed herself and moved over to one of the display cabinets. Casually she picked up a clipboard and began to look over its contents.

'I've completed the preliminary listings. Edgar Moffat was particularly meticulous about dating his pieces; recording place of origin, where he bought them, how much he paid and, where possible, the maker,' she said.

Gerald nodded appreciatively. Mystified by her earlier behaviour, he decided to act as if nothing had happened. 'Wonderful, I hope the same is true of his collection at the villa, though I don't suppose we have any reason to suspect he hasn't been as thorough there. I hope you'll be able to help us there too, Francesca?'

Francesca nodded. 'No problem. I'm based there for a little while until I've completed the book I'm working on.'

Gerald beamed, 'Oh, you are an author. Would I have read anything of yours?'

More relaxed now, the mysterious tantalising secret between the two women seemed to fade into the background as they chatted. Gerald was rather taken by the slim lightly tanned author. Her handsome intelligent face offered a nice contrast to the sculptural and more traditional beauty of Melissa. Finally their conversation returned to the collection.

Once the cataloguing was complete in London, Gerald suggested they all met up again at the coast to continue the work there. The exhibits would then have to be packed, labelled and shipped down to London for the sale. Melissa nodded but added it might be a good idea if she went back to the office before going down to the villa, to begin typing up the catalogue herself. The fewer people who knew about the delicate nature of Edgar's collection the better. Not only that but they would have to be extremely careful who developed the photographs they had taken. Better to find a private studio used to handling unusual and sensitive material. Delighted with the progress of the cataloguing and a little excited by the new mysterious intimacy between his assistant and Alicia's friend, Gerald jogged cheerily down the stairs. He tried to keep his own particular predilections hidden from even his closest friends and most definitely from his employees, however trusted. His tastes were very similar to Edgar's, though he didn't restrict himself exclusively to voyeurism. There were one or two exclusive activities that he permitted himself; he'd spoken earlier in the day to one of his close contacts in Germany and looked forward to renewing their acquaintance. It had been too long since they had met.

At the front door he retrieved his raincoat, his eager mind rerunning his last encounter with his German associate. With his hand on the doorknob he suddenly remembered he had left his umbrella upstairs. He opened the door, thinking he could always collect it later. Outside, the rain tipped down, lashing up against the pavement; better to collect it now. He closed the door and made his way back upstairs.

As he reached the second floor he was about to call out but something in the tone of the women's voices from the gallery made the words catch in his throat. A sixth sense made him slow his pace. Quietly he crept towards the partially open door and almost betrayed his presence at once by letting out a gasp of surprise.

In the brilliant light of the photographic spotlight Francesca was eagerly pulling Melissa's dress down over her shoulders. She was naked beneath; her heavy breasts jutted forward, nipples engorged. Grinning she wriggled provocatively, letting the thin cotton shift drop to the floor. Francesca smiled approvingly and leant forward to kiss her full on the mouth, their tongues brushed fleetingly before their lips met in a brief passionate embrace. Melissa's hand lifted to the buttons on Francesca's dress; her hands moved quickly and confidently over the fastenings, pushing the fabric back over her narrow shoulders. Seconds later Francesca let the shift fall to the floor; beneath it she was naked.

The two stood face to face, barely a breath apart. Their nipples brushed lightly against each other as they moved even closer. Where they met their breasts pressed together, forming an erotic curving liaison.

Gerald gasped in spite of himself. Their firm smooth bodies glistened under the lights; each muscle, every curve, every hair picked out under the unforgiving eye of the lamp. Even under its impartial glare they were beautiful, breathtaking. Melissa leant back a little, gathering up Francesca's little pert breasts in her hands, and her lips lowered to seek out the sleek uptilted nipples. Her tongue caressed them, nibbling and sucking them into her open mouth.

Francesca's hands moved lower still, seeking out the blonde-kissed folds of Melissa's sex. Gerald could feel the intense stirring in his groin and the press of his cock hardening against the expensive material of his suit. He tried to control the pressure building up deep inside him.

'My God,' he hissed, unable to tear his eyes away from the scenario in the gallery. Melissa was sinking to her knees, her hands opening Francesca's sex wide to accept the tender ministrations of her tongue. The glistening silver moisture on her lips sparkled like diamonds under the harsh light. The darker woman shuddered and threw back her head, her long neck forming a straining arch, her hands reached up to encircle her own breasts, her fingers stroking and teasing her nipples.

Gerald crept closer, his longing almost all-engulfing. In his mind he imagined his joining them, drinking up their juices, slipping into their compliant eager depths, his body hovering between the smooth temptation of their sex and curve of their breasts, buried deep in one, lapping at the other. Perhaps as he impaled one the other would lap at their junction, her tongue moving-seamlessly between quim and cock.

The thought made him shudder, his erection pressed harder, his aching emphasising his desperate, almost overwhelming, need for release. He imagined the subtle blending of their intimate perfumes on his fingers and tongue and then watched mesmerised as in the gallery beyond his reach they both sank slowly to the floor. Their hands, lips and tongue feasted on the other's sensitive exciting plains and hills, their fingers sought out the tight buds of their sex, fingers moving effortlessly between clitoris and the deeper wetter folds. Melissa raised herself and spread the fragrant juice of their bodies over her nipples where they hung like shimmering gossamer threads.

Heads and tongues and mouths moved in perfect orchestration; lapping, sucking, nipping, probing deep, brushing furtively, kissing eagerly. Both women seemed totally immersed in their mutual journey of discovery.

From where he stood he could see the heavy lips of their open sexes, juices and saliva trickling in an intoxicating brew, the images burnt into his feverish mind.

Finally, when Gerald – close to the point of no return himself – thought their entrancing display was at its climax Francesca slipped a hand under the white back-cloth and produced an ebony dildo. Gerald gulped, trying to keep his anticipation under control as with skilled and knowing fingers Francesca opened the lips of her willing companion's mound and slipped the phallus deep inside her. Melissa arched her hips upwards to allow Francesca's easier deeper entry . . .

Gerald felt a tidal wave of excitement engulf him. In the brilliantly lit gallery the women moved against each other, breast to breast, mouth to mouth, Francesca plunging the cold phallus deeper into Melissa's eager body.

Suddenly Melissa bucked against her, clasping Francesca tightly to her whilst her fingers continued their own rhythmic stroke. of Francesca's sex. Francesca threw back her head, eyes alight, skin flushed and glowing, calling out in ecstasy as the fierce heat of their mutual climax washed down over them both, shuddering through their breasts, bellies, over their thighs.

Gerald turned away, unable to absorb another detail. Desperately he pulled his cock from his trousers and, dragging a handkerchief from his top pocket, ejaculated violently into it. The waves of his climax throbbed throughout him, his breath desperate. His ragged gasps threatened to betray him; sliding his exhausted member hastily back into his underpants he turned, red-faced and sweating, and practically ran down the stairs.

In the gallery Francesca caught a glimpse of movement behind the door and leapt to her feet. She ran, naked, out on to the landing and peered over the banisters in time to see Gerald Foxley's retreating figure bounding down the stairs. Smiling, she turned and went back to the gallery. Inside the door, Melissa, still naked and covered in the lightest gloss of perspiration, was peering down the viewfinder of the camera.

She looked up at the sound of Francesca's approach.

'Visitors?' she whispered softly as she pressed the shutter release.

'Gerald,' said Francesca, smiling as she looked around for the next piece they needed to photograph.

Downstairs on the pavement Gerald hurried across the road to find a cab, his mind reeling from the events he had just witnessed. Before returning for his umbrella he had been toying with the idea of letting the two women handle the cataloguing of the artefacts at the villa on their own. Now he fully intended to be there with them; the thought made him shudder. When finally a cab drew up he stepped inside, still deep in thought and totally oblivious to the fact he was now soaked through to the skin.

# Chapter Seven

Melissa stretched like an exotic cat amongst the tangle of sheets on Francesca's bed, her tousled blonde hair giving her a vulnerable childlike appearance. From the bathroom Francesca watched her reflection in the mirror. She smiled; whilst her experiences in Edgar's London house with Melissa were not ones she would have sought out, the thrill of them had been beyond any of her darkest fantasies. The days and nights spent with the other woman and their long explorations through the heights of passion were times she would remember for the rest of her life.

Melissa slipped from the bed and came to join her in the bathroom; she was dressed provocatively in a white cotton shirt which barely covered the soft curve of her buttocks. From beneath the thin fabric the dark outline of her nipples was clearly visible.

Francesca splashed her face with cold water and reached for the towel. Behind her on the door she'd hung her outfit ready for the trip back to the villa.

Melissa crept close up behind her and gently slipped her arms around Francesca's waist.

They grinned at each other in the mirror.

'Only a few days and we'll be together again,' she said tenderly.

Melissa nodded and then buried her face in Francesca's neck, her lips pressing against the soft curve of her flesh. 'It won't take me too long to get the details typed up. Once they're on the computer I can add the rest when we've finished the cataloguing,' she said between soft dry kisses.

Her hands lifted stealthily to caress Francesca's nipples which hardened instantly under her touch. Melissa laughed and then snuggled closer, brushing the soft hair of her sex against Francesca's bare buttocks.

Francesca couldn't resist giggling at the soft tickling caress, feeling the first stirrings of excitement between her legs as one of Melissa's hands slipped lower. The stroke of the other woman's fingertips, feather-light against Francesca's belly, made her shiver. In spite of herself she felt her legs open in response to her caress and gasped as Melissa slid her fingers lower, slipping effortlessly between the dark folds of her outer lips. Melissa's fingernail brushed lightly across her clitoris, Francesca groaned frantically and grabbed Melissa's wrist, trying to wriggle away.

'Not now. If we're not careful, I'll miss my train.'

Melissa purred seductively. Though her wrist was held tight in Francesca's hand, her long fingers moved teasingly, making Francesca grab at her again and this time holding her tighter. One finger still moved relentlessly against the hardening ridge of her clitoris.

'Would that be such a dreadful thing?' Melissa whispered, trying to prise all her fingers free.

Francesca snorted, then said more gently, 'It would be lovely, glorious, but I've rung Alicia and asked if Catz can meet me at the station.'

As she spoke his name the memory of his face and body filled her mind and fleetingly she imagined the three of them engaged in a passionate embrace. The idea made her quiver with delight. Melissa, sensing Francesca's growing excitement, though not realising it was the memory of Catz that produced it, moved her fingers in a slick slow arc over Francesca's rapidly moistening sex and slipped a finger inside her. Franceses threw back her head, pushing down hard against Melissa's fingers.

'Please,' she whispered half-heartedly, fighting her own desire as much as Melissa's touch. 'I really do have to go.'

Melissa reluctantly – conceding defeat – stepped away but only removed her fingers slowly, teasingly. Francesca groaned and slithered away.

'I'll miss you,' she said softly, reaching up to stroke Melissa's face.

The blonde woman leant into her caress. 'Me too but it won't be too long before I get down to the villa; a couple of days at the most.'

Francesca turned and slipped on her blouse. 'You'd better ring Gerald and let him know we've finished here.'

Melissa grinned. 'I rang last night. He said he won't be in the office for the rest of the week.'

'Why not? I thought he was hot on the trail of prospective buyers?'

'All he needs is a phone. No. I'd say, knowing Gerald, he's already down at the villa. After spotting us in the gallery I'm surprised he didn't pay us another visit here. I suppose he thinks there'll be more of the same once we both get to the coast.'

Francesca spun round and embraced Melissa warmly, her lips seeking out the blonde woman's mouth. 'Well I'm hoping much the same thing myself, so don't be too long with the typing!'

The journey back to the villa seemed to take for ever. The cab ride across London was nerve-racking as the driver careered in and out of the traffic to get Francesca there on time. The railway station was dusty and claustrophobic with passengers pressing forward to find a seat on the train and, in comparison to the crystal silence of the Kensington house, the echoing noise of the station seemed overwhelming. Francesca hurried aboard and found herself a seat by the window. Once the train drew out of the station she sat back and let the rhythmic movement of the carriages lull her into a state close to sleep. Outside the dusty windows the tightly packed houses of London changed slowly into the sprawl of suburbia and beyond that into the open green spaces of rural England.

Though her stay in London had been a success

Francesca couldn't help wondering what her reception would be like when she arrived back at the villa. And then there was Chris. She realised with surprise that, until she'd climbed aboard the train, she'd barely thought of him since that disastrous night at the cottage. Despite the nature of their parting she felt she hadn't seen the last of him.

The memories of Catz got sharper and clearer as the train passed familiar landmarks. In London she had begun to wonder if their encounter had been as exciting, even as real, as she imagined, but as the train pulled into the little rural station and she spotted his familiar outline amongst the waiting passengers she knew her encounters with him had only just begun.

Stepping from the train she was pleased to see him turn and walk stiffly towards her, though she was astonished to realise how arousing and exciting his presence made her feel. A fluttering glittering plume of anticipation spun up through her belly and she felt herself tremble as he came closer.

He didn't speak as he approached her, his rugged face unreadable as he bent to pick up her luggage. Silently she fell into step behind him, a fluttering pulse beating in her throat.

In the car park she recognised the familiar lines of the vintage Daimler and walked towards it. At the passenger door he hesitated, his hand resting lightly on the door handle; slowly he turned. 'You know Gerald Foxley is staying with us,' he said flatly.

The sound of his dark cold voice set every nerve

ending alight. Francesca could feel her colour rising, a sensual intense heat gripping her. She nodded but still he didn't open the door. Instead his eyes lingered on her face as if absorbing every facet of her and she knew then that Gerald Foxley had told Alicia every tantalising detail of her exploits in the gallery with Melissa.

Catz did not move; instead he allowed his eyes to sweep across her body, resting momentarily on her breasts outlined by her summer blouse. The effect was instantaneous; she felt a warm flood of moisture between her legs, and her nipples – hard and desperate – betrayed her as they pressed frantically against the thin fabric. She swallowed hard, feeling dizzy and vulnerable.

His hand moved to undo the door and then took hers to guide her into the car. As their fingers touched she saw the briefest smile on his lips and any resistance to her desire for him was lost.

Breathlessly she whispered, 'Come to me, Catz – tonight. Please.' Even as she spoke the words she cursed herself. Was her need so desperate that she had to beg? she thought furiously.

He said nothing, turning instead to stow her luggage in the boot. She felt foolish, embarrassed, and during the drive back to the villa refused to meet his eyes in the rear-view mirror.

At the villa Alicia was waiting for her in the sitting room. As Francesca walked into the room Alicia got to her feet and embraced her fondly. To her surprise

Francesca realised she was genuinely pleased to see her. Alicia looked stunning, simply dressed, in a tunic of soft green silk that seemed to bring out the exotic richness of her eyes. Perfectly in control as always, and with enviable poise, she reintroduced Francesca to her other house guest: Gerald Foxley.

Francesca had seen Alicia's skill at hiding her excitement and arousal after her encounter with Catz. Alicia was well-used to appearing as if nothing had happened or would happen. Not so Gerald Foxley, who stood behind Alicia in the sitting room and was barely able to keep his eyes off Francesca. Every look betrayed his desire and as he shook her hand in greeting she could feel the slight tremble of his excitement beneath her fingers.

While Alicia made polite conversation Francesca could feel Gerald's eyes moving slowly over her body. She then watched as his attention was drawn again and again to the large picture window that dominated the sitting room. Glancing at his glittering eyes Francesca knew, without a doubt, that Alicia had told him about her afternoon in the garden with Chris.

Gerald and Alicia talked business over tea whilst Francesca, suddenly feeling distant and sleepy, listened with half an ear. In her mind she marvelled at how familiar and comfortable Alicia's home felt to her; even Catz bringing in the tray could not dislodge the feeling of having returned to somewhere she wanted to be. As he poured her tea she let her eyes linger over his sleek animal beauty. The stirring and the longing was there inside her, even the tiny sharp thrill of fear that his closeness brought out in her, but she was at ease with it, accepting – even relishing – the dark temptations he offered her.

After tea Alicia suggested they break until dinner. Relieved to be excused, Francesca headed to her room; the travelling had left her feeling tired and grimy. Once inside her suite she slipped off her clothes and lay down on the bed. Sleep soon claimed her as her mind replayed the fantasy scenes with Catz and Melissa that she had considered in the bathroom in London.

On the same floor, Gerald Foxley was reading through the list of possible buyers he had contacted about the auction. The first response had delighted him; very few people had declined the invitation. Better still – and he smiled as he thought it – Alicia had seemed enchanted by his story about discovering Melissa and Francesca in the gallery together. He hadn't failed to notice the twinkling flame of excitement in her eyes as she had carefully extracted every last succulent detail from him. It hadn't worried him at all that she had insisted on Catz listening in, too. Catz, he thought, was an intimidating looking fellow but there was something about him too that was tantalising, almost hypnotic.

Alicia had pointed out to him that the villa had been designed for pleasure of many kinds, and that if he wanted she had no objections to the gallery being used for its intended purpose. Her only proviso was that he couldn't use coercion.

'Freedom, Gerald, freedom to choose' had been her actual words. Gerald swallowed hard; he didn't think he would have to coerce either of the two women and hadn't resisted when Alicia suggested she take him on a guided tour of the house.

First of all she'd shown him the gallery. It had been interesting, even stimulating, but something else had excited him more. In a small room on the same floor as his own there was a large two-way mirror that overlooked the bed in Francesca's room. As he had stood in the dark little room with Alicia he had felt dizzy at the possibilities the room offered him, and in his mind he imagined Francesca and Melissa seeking each other and performing unknowingly for his delight and pleasure.

He shuffled the papers and put them down on the desk. Perhaps if they showed no objections he might even join them. In his mind he replayed the scene under the bright light of the photographic lamps; the delicate curve of their bodies, the delightful conjunction of their breasts as they had pressed closer to each other. The memories made him quiver and he felt the familiar tightening at his groin. Suddenly the papers in front of him seemed dull and uninteresting. The prospect of his stunning blonde assistant with her tongue lapping at the compliant body of Alicia's house guest pressed out almost all other thoughts. He swallowed hard and put his jacket back on.

With the stealth of a tiger he set out across the landing towards the door of the small room, intending to mentally play out his fantasy before the event. As he opened the door he was both surprised and delighted to see Francesca lying naked on the bed. The dark-haired woman was relaxed, teetering on the very edge of sleep. Silently he slipped into the room and made himself comfortable to observe her. Francesca's legs were slightly apart, her eyes closed. He pulled his chair closer to the glass and watched excitedly as she moved her hands slowly down over the soft inviting curves of her own body. One finger slipped into the dark folds of her sex as behind closed eyes her dreams caught hold.

In the ground-floor library Alicia read through the menu Catz had planned for dinner. A little light on her desk flashed discreetly; it was tripped by the opening of the room behind the mirror. Smiling, she hoped that Gerald found the view to his liking.

Dinner that evening was a formal affair in the large dining room at the front of the house. Francesca had chosen to wear a soft black sheath of a dress that moulded perfectly to her slim body. She admired herself in the mirror, running her hands over the smooth lines of her breasts and hips. Her hair was arranged into a loose knot; stray tendrils framed her small face, giving her a vulnerable, sensual look.

She posed, stretching languorously to show her body off to its best advantage, little knowing that behind the glass Gerald Foxley watched with a growing sense of expectation.

\*

Dinner was served by candlelight. Alicia sat at the head of the table, dressed in a simple silver shift, her pale hair caught up in a matching bandeau. Gerald, to her right, was in black tie, whilst to her left Francesca looked enchanting in the elegant black ensemble. Catz moved silently around the table serving, pouring wine, attending wordlessly to their every need.

Francesca caught his eyes resting on her and she returned his admiring glance openly. Beside her, Alicia smiled and turned towards Gerald whose eyes also seemed to return repeatedly to the shapely outline of the younger woman.

'Gerald, I'm feeling quite neglected,' she said teasingly. 'Tell me, what do you think of the wine?'

The conversation was light, convivial. Alicia, a perfect hostess, encouraged Gerald to relax and tell them stories of his various exploits at auctions throughout the world, including some bizarre tales he'd heard from his father. She teased Francesca into telling them about her latest book and contributed stories of her travels with Edgar. As a hostess she could not be faulted, and she watched with a delicious sense of expectation as her guests drank more wine and visibly eased in each other's company. The tension, the suggestion of something more, was ever present, but now it was veneered with relaxed good humour and bright laughter.

Alicia glanced at Catz and was rewarded with a conspiratorial wink. She smiled. She'd always thought winking showed extremely bad taste but on Catz's rugged and brutal face it had a certain erotic quality that could not be ignored. She glanced at Francesca, sipping at her glass and listening intently to a story of lost lots, misunderstood phrases and the vagaries of buying goods in the Far East. Francesca roared with laughter at Gerald's self-deprecating humour,

The woman had surprised her. Alicia hadn't realised while watching her in the garden that Francesca's passion was so close to the surface, so easy to awaken. She sipped her wine thoughtfully; there was a certain pleasure in still being surprised at her age, and Gerald's account of Francesca's exploits with Melissa had captivated her. She wondered fleetingly how long it would be before Melissa joined their little party.

After coffee the conversation returned to the impending auction. Alicia pouted in displeasure.

'Do we have to talk business? Let me show you Edgar's art collection. Gerald, I'm sure it will be of great interest to you; we have some delightful early English watercolours here, and several wonderful canvases from the Scottish school.'

It was almost midnight when Francesca finally, wearily, climbed the stairs to her rooms. She felt tired but exhilarated at the prospect of Catz's visit. During dinner she had seen him watching her, his eyes moving across her body, catching her eye; the cool sparkle of his interest had excited her. During dinner she had been absolutely convinced he would come to her room. Now as she opened the door she wasn't so certain. The wine and food had left her feeling relaxed and heady and she wondered if perhaps she had overestimated the strength of his desire.

She turned on the table lamp in the bedroom and slipped her evening dress down over her shoulders; beneath she was wearing a sleek black teddy, and matching black stockings held up with a narrow band of elasticated lace. She rather liked the delicate sense of restriction they gave her. If Catz didn't come it was his loss, she thought, twirling around to admire herself. The reflection smiled back appreciatively – in her high patent shoes she looked wonderful.

'You look very beautiful this evening.' Catz's voice from the shadows of the bathroom made her jump. She swung around and in the light from the bedside lamp could make out the sharp pinpricks of light reflected in his eyes.

She backed away from the open door and swallowed. 'I didn't see you there,' she mumbled nervously, suddenly feeling a genuine tremor of fear. The fantasy of Catz's presence in her room and the reality of it were worlds apart.

He stepped out into the light. He was dressed casually in a white shirt – with sleeves rolled back – tucked loosely into a pair of jodhpurs. She swallowed hard; he was beautiful. His cold brutal eyes moved over her, lingering over her delicate curves, taking in the details of her undress. She shivered and stepped away from him.

I thought you wanted me,' he purred softly.

Her mouth was dry, unable to find the words to answer him.

Catz shrugged and moved towards the door. 'Or was I wrong? Perhaps you prefer more tender meat these days?' He brushed slowly past her, the smell of him hypnotic, exciting – the tight swell of his muscles, the way he moved. Francesca turned and put her hand on his shoulder.

'Don't go,' she murmured. 'I want you to stay.'

The effect of her words was immediate. He swung round and encircled her neck with his hands, pulling her towards him. His hard lips sought out her mouth, his hot wet tongue forcing its way brutally between her half-dosed lips. She gasped at the speed of his assault and at the same time let out a little desperate groan of excitement. This was all she had dreamed of; to feel him against her again, to feel his heat, to experience his strange, compelling eroticism.

His tongue sought out hers; she shivered and moved against him. His hand slipped on to her shoulders and his fingers slid beneath the shoestring straps of her teddy; she shuddered at his touch. He pulled back a little and looked into her eyes. She felt as if he could see every dark dream, every unspoken desire; she wanted to close her eyes against him but found it impossible. Part of her wanted him to share every secret sensation she had ever longed to experience.

Catz's fingers slipped out from under her shoulder-straps and down to the soft, smooth rounded lines of her buttocks. His hands rubbed the thin silk of her teddy against her sensitive skin and pulled her hips sharply towards him. She could feel the exhilarating brush of his hardening cock against her belly. His excitement thrilled her; she could feel her own excitement rising to match it and the beginning of the soft moist flow between her legs. She brought her hands round to cup his bulk but he pushed her hands away roughly, his eyes narrowing to thin dark slits.

His hands slid down over her thighs seeking out the fastening between her legs that held her teddy closed. She knew she was wet and longed for him to free her sex, to push his cock deep inside her, to take her, to love her. Instinctively she thrust forward to meet his fingers; the snaps opened under his touch and she felt one cool exploratory finger run along the hot delicate fold of her outer lips. She gasped, pushing hard against his touch.

He pulled away, pushing up the fabric of the teddy so her sex was totally exposed. Gently he turned her towards the mirror so she could see herself. She gasped – the lips of the sex hung open, pink and moist, betraying their need for pleasure. Catz stood behind her and slipped the shoulder-straps of her teddy down; his eyes held hers in the mirror, the soft fabric slithered down over the small orbs of her breasts. Not only did she feel the delicate caress of its fall but she watched in the reflection. Her nipples had darkened, gathering into tight excited peaks.

Catz's hands slid down to cup them, rolling their hardness between his fingers. The picture of her desire, framed in the mirror's shimmering silver, was electric.

She could see the dark dilated pupils of her eyes flickering with a hungry flame of need; she could see the slight heady flush over her body. She whimpered and pushed her buttocks back against his thighs. In the mirror she saw Catz's sly smile as his fingers slid down to her sex, spreading the heavy outer lips to expose the soft folds within; her clitoris, engorged and tender, pressed forward to try to meet his eager fingers. She stared into the mirror, watching Catz's fingers move over her, feeling the sensation, following the path of his caresses with her eyes; the combination was stunning in its intensity.

In the mirror, reflected like cold blue flames, Catz's eyes sparkled with desire – this wasn't an end to their game but just the beginning. His fingers slipped inside her; she felt her muscles close tightly around them. His thumb lifted to brush her clitoris; she moaned and watched the reddened lips of her reflection open breathlessly as, below, her gaping moist sex thrust forwards to draw his fingers further into her.

Slowly he withdrew his fingers and lifted the fragrant moisture to her nipples, drawing tight silver lines around them. From above she could smell the heavy musk of her excitement and again pushed back against the dark hard pressure of his erection. He resisted her though his lips now pressed against her shoulder, their wetness and the tight tiny caresses of his tongue making her shudder. She leant against him, drowning in the heat of his body against her naked flesh.

Slowly now his hands lifted and he guided her

backwards; a part of her resisted, longing instead to watch herself, as her excitement grew, in front of the mirror. Catz sat down on the ottoman at the foot of the bed, his hands sliding down to her hips. She leant against him allowing him to guide her around until she stood beside him. His fingers brushed against her sex; she moaned and leant into his touch. He looked up at her, his eyes intense.

'Bend over,' he said coldly. 'Gerald tells me you've been a naughty girl.'

Part of her wanted to laugh at the game they were playing, but another part relished the idea of this poignant little punishment. She looked down at him, her eyes dark. 'The only thing that was naughty about it, Catz, was that you weren't there to share it,' she murmured throatily. Wordlessly he lifted his hand to the small of her back, guiding her forwards until she rested across his knees.

She resisted a little, afraid that she wouldn't be able to tell him she wanted this to continue if he asked her again. The hard muscles of his thighs pressed up against her belly and ribs. She felt heady and hot.

Glancing up she could see them framed in the mirror: her, laying across his lap, breasts and buttocks exposed; above her, Catz's unreadable face staring back at her. The feelings of exposure and expectation were almost overwhelming; she choked back a little sob.

His fingers moved over her buttocks, softly stroking, seeking out the wet and expectant folds of her sex; she relaxed under his touch as one finger slipped into her.

She eased herself back against him, opening willingly under his caresses. His finger slipped out and his hands moved away. She didn't move, her breath light and expectant . . .

In the reflection she saw his hand lift and for an instant was fascinated as it swung back in a broad arc. It seemed abstract, almost distant, and then she felt the white-hot sensation as his hand stung the soft cheeks of her bottom. The feelings snapped her mind back from the reflection to reality. She squealed out in surprise and pain, feeling the heat spread through her. His hand lifted again and she braced herself for the contact. The sensation was a heady mixture of pain and pleasure. Her bottom stung and tingled but between her legs the glow of excitement rose relentlessly. Now, with a rhythm established, he smacked her again and again. She moaned against his stinging touch, arching her back instinctively against the sensation of his hand, in doing so exposing her damp folds and tight dark bud behind.

She whimpered; his other hand slipped around to cup her breasts, his fingers seeking out the delicate sensitive buds of her nipples. He pressed and rubbed them, the tenderness a startling contrast to the smacking he was administering behind. Every smack sent a shudder of pleasure and pain through her; each time his hand touched her, her hips bucked while beneath her belly she could feel the hard and insistent press of his erection.

The combination made her frantic with desire. Finally, when she thought that he would never stop, he straightened his legs and she slithered unceremoniously on to the floor.

She crept up on to her knees, feeling a strange sense of exhilaration, and at the same time felt apprehensive at what Catz had planned for her. The cheeks of her bottom felt as if they were alight whilst between her legs a more intense inferno blazed brightly.

Catz looked at her impassively, his cold expression at odds with the excitement of his cock pressing against the tight fabric of his jodhpurs. 'Do you want more?' he asked softly. The choice is yours.'

Francesca nodded, feeling herself blush as the electric longing deep in her gut cried out for satisfaction.

Catz shook his head. 'You know that's not enough; I need to hear you say it. You have to ask, Francesea. You have to tell me you want what I can give you.'

Francesca felt her colour intensify. He was offering her a way out, a choice; there was never any compulsion. Wasn't that what Alicia had told her? She looked up at him, her eyes bright with desire and excitement; she swallowed hard. 'I want you, Catz,' she said softly, letting her eyes travel over his muscular shoulders and down his suntanned arms.

'Look at me as you say it,' he said evenly.

She resisted him, looking down instead at the engorged, hardened outline of his cock forcing itself up against his belly.

His hand cupped her chin and purred. 'Look at me, Francesca. Tell me you want me.'

She looked into his eyes; they had an intimidating

brilliance that unnerved her. He was temptation; he was desire.

Slowly but distinctly she whispered, 'I want you. I want everything you can give me.' As she spoke she knew that she meant it; she wanted him and his subtle dark understanding of her needs more than anything. 'I want you to touch me, I want you to teach me, I want everything . . .'

Catz nodded and trailed his fingers along the curve of her throat, his merest touch making her quiver as every nerve ending glowed white-hot. He drew a tantalising line up under her chin, skirting her lips, his eyes never leaving hers. She shuddered.

'Get on your hands and knees,' he said softly. 'On the ottoman so that we can see you.'

Francesca looked up at him and then silently complied. She knelt facing him, eyes bright, unable to disguise her eagerness. She felt excited at her unquestioning desire to obey him, to accept his every command.

Catz leant down and lightly pressed his mouth to hers. His lips were wet and she opened her mouth willingly under the slow sensual enquiry of his tongue. One hand lifted to cup her breasts, his fingers circling her nipples; she whimpered at the gentleness of his caresses. He stepped away from her and slowly undid the buttons of his jodhpurs. She gasped as his hands moved lower, freeing the engorged reddened bulk of his cock. His other hand slipped something from his pocket.

She looked up at him, waiting, the sense of expectation growing with every second. He moved closer and let the moist tip of his erection brush across her lips. She lifted one hand to touch him; he moved back a little further, making her wait, making her longing so intense that she thought she might faint.

'Please, Catz,' she whispered. 'Please.'

He held her gaze, eyes mesmerising. She could feel a sprinkling of perspiration lifting on her top lip, could feel a deep trembling in the pit of her belly. In front of her, so close, he waited.

Gently he slipped a condom over the great curve of his cock and then, without hesitating, stepped forward. Desperate for him now, she grasped him to her and guided his shaft into her waiting mouth. The sensation made her shudder, the sleek engorged bulk of him filled her up; she closed her lips tightly around the end, sucking and teasing with her tongue, whilst her hands stroked back along the length of him, seeking out the tender delicate weight of his balls. As her fingers stroked down over them he shuddered and ran his hands up over her neck, locking them in her hair before pulling her eager lips further on to him.

Behind them in the shadows the bedroom door opened silently.

Gerald Foxley had sat enrapt behind the mirror in the dark warm confines of the observation room, watching Catz's tender assault on Francesca's body. He had almost been able to smell the woman's excitement as Catz had encouraged her closer to her reflection. He'd wanted to reach out through the glass and slide his fingers into her enchanting dark depths as Catz had spread the lips of her sex. He could almost feel the scintillating bite of her muscles against the other man's exploring fingers. Her dark throbbing nipples had hypnotised him. He could imagine them hardening in his mouth, her body bucking and arching against him and the smacking; Gerald shuddered at the memory of it. The image of her swaying breasts, her hips lifted to receive her punishment. The way her belly had curved as she held herself ready in anticipation of the next blow. He swallowed hard, his mouth watering at the prospect of her compliant, submissive body.

Her willing submission to Catz had made him tremble. He'd relished the expression on her face – the ecstasy – as Catz had administered a sound spanking. She had practically begged him when he'd finished to continue, begged him to take her higher and further . . .

Gerald had watched mesmerised as Francesca had arranged herself on the ottoman for Catz's pleasure and gasped as she had guided his cock into her waiting mouth. As she began to suck at the other man Gerald could resist no longer. Seeing the way her belly had dropped instinctively to draw in Catz's phallus, Gerald slipped from his hiding place and hurried across the landing.

As he opened the door he saw Francesca jump a little but Catz's hand moved across her body to steady her, stroking at her neck, teasing at her breasts. As he crossed the room Gerald slipped out of his evening clothes, his nervous fingers fumbling with the buttons and zip. In front of him he could see the curve of Catz's body as he contracted his firm buttocks, thrusting gently into Francesca's waiting mouth. Catz seemed almost oblivious of him as Francesca worked at his shaft.

He moved quietly around them. From the rear Francesca looked delectable; her hips had dropped a little to expose the soft inner lips of her sex framed by dark hair; the tight bud of her forbidden closure seemed to contract rhythmically as she sucked Catz into her. Above the broad swell of her hips her body narrowed sharply before widening again at her shoulders. She looked beautiful – a classic erotic hourglass. Tangled amongst the soft tendrils of her dark hair Catz's hand twisted and moved as he encouraged Francesca to explore him further.

Gerald speculatively ran his hands over her rounded thighs; she felt warm and deliciously slick under his fingers. For an instant he felt her freeze, her surprise and fear tangible and exhilarating. He leant closer to watch Catz stroke her, soothe her, petting her like a cat, and beneath his fingers Gerald watched entranced as Francesca began to relax.

He stepped closer to her; from the nest of gingery hair at his groin his slim cock jutted forward, and the very tip of it brushed the back of her thighs. Gerald shuddered excitedly and gritted his teeth. Francesca's instinctive reaction to his touch was to thrust back towards him, opening eagerly under his gaze.

He slipped one tentative finger into the swollen confines of her sex. The heat of it took his breath away; her muscles grasped at him, seeming to suck his finger deeper. He slipped another in and she moaned gratefully, the noise trickling from her mouth as it lapped around the bulk of Catz's member.

Catz glanced across at him, his eyes highlighted by icy glints of excitement, and he lifted a hand to Gerald's shoulders, his soft caress not quite hiding his strength. Gerald leant gratefully into his rugged masculine touch, savouring it against his cool pale skin. Catz's other hand moved away and he slipped a condom from his pocket. Gerald felt nonplussed and could feel the redness flush through his face. Catz smiled at him and unpeeled the packet.

Gerald swallowed hard, feeling uneasy and self-conscious as he moved closer to Catz, sidestepping the inviting scenario of Francesca's pulsating open body. With a gentle deft movement Catz unrolled the sheath along the length of Gerald's shaft. As he reached the soft junction where Gerald's erection met the delicate gathered swelling of his balls Catz ran a finger across the puckering. Gerald gasped at his caress, feeling the delicate skin tighten and ripple. Catz's fingers lifted again to Gerald's shoulder and with the gentlest of movements he guided the other man back behind Francesca.

Gerald was almost overcome with excitement. He could feel the deep straining sensation building in the pit of his belly, feel the throb of the pulse in his throat.

He was almost lost as he slid the smoothly covered curve of his shaft into Francesca's sex and was instantly rewarded by her grinding her buttocks hard backwards.

Enthusiastically he grabbed her hips, pulling her back sharply; her wetness enclosed him, sucking him into the moist sanctuary of her body. Under his fingers he felt her shudder, felt the tight grasp of her muscles around him as she began to move rhythmically back and forth against him. It was as if his mind travelled deep inside her, his every sense, every feeling echoing through his cock before coursing into his feverish excited mind.

In front of him Catz had thrown his head back, relishing the eager attentions of Francesca's mouth and fingers. Gerald could see a silvery trickle of sweat forming in the pit of the other man's throat. Gerald plunged deeper as Francesca's sex seemed to open further under his thrusts. He pushed again and again into her, making her moan, her cries stifled by Catz's stiff excited phallus sucked deep into her mouth.

In front of him he heard Catz whimper; he glanced across to the mirror and knew all was lost. The triangle of straining and frenzied bodies, glowing and thrusting towards release, was captured inside the cool glass, giving Gerald a scintillating perspective. Francesca's breasts hung down, swaying in rhythm with Gerald's thrusts; her hips rose and fell against him. Crystals of perspiration along her spine glittered jewel-bright in the soft light from the lamps. Clinging around her belly were the damp gathered folds of her teddy, painting a startling contrast to her slick skin. Her neck was straining forward to take Catz deep into her mouth whilst one hand was lifted to caress him and cradle the heavy bulk of his balls.

Catz's reflection was arching back, hands kneading Francesca's shoulders as he pushed headlong towards his own climax. Behind Francesca, Gerald watched himself, his eyes bright, pupils dilated as he plunged his moist curving shaft again and again into the tremulous eager depths of Francesca's waiting sex.

Seeing the scenario unfold was too much for him. Gasping he looked away and felt the unstoppable white-hot contractions as the first of his seed spurted through him. Facing Gerald, still arched and desperately straining against Francesca's lips and fingers, Catz, unable to hold back any longer, bucked and called out as his own orgasm crashed over them all, the ecstasy of it contorting his face into a tight grimace. Gerald felt the last contractions of his own climax echoing those of his companion.

Exhausted, Gerald slid to the floor, trembling with excitement as above him Catz slipped from Francesca's mouth. Francesca rolled over, her slim body covered in the most delicate gloss of perspiration. She lay back on the bed, legs open, shaking violently. Gerald watched entranced as Catz moved towards her and knelt lovingly between her legs. Gently Catz pulled her shaking legs up over his shoulders. Francesca moaned as if to deny him as Catz plunged his tongue into her – the woman's hips thrust upwards to meet him. Gerald, unable to resist, clambered to his feet and eagerly watched the last delicious moments of their liaison as Catz skilfully brought Francesca to the point of orgasm. His fingers slipped inside her, where a few minutes earlier Gerald had buried his cock entirely, and his tongue sought out the hard swollen ridge of her clitoris. Under his ministrations Francesca moaned and whined with pleasure as Catz circled her hard engorged bud again and again. Her hips thrust up to meet his kisses, spreading herself wide to absorb every electric sensation. She gave herself to Catz totally, lifting her hands to hold her sex open for his tongue. Gerald watched hypnotised, seeing the intricate tracery of the man's skilled eager tongue against Francesca's body. Suddenly she let out a tiny intense shuddering cry and her body stiffened as Catz took her beyond the white-hot pulsing-point of ecstasy. Gerald, stunned by the display, sunk to his knees and sobbed with pleasure.

# Chapter Eight

When Francesca came downstairs the next morning, Gerald was waiting for her in the hall. As he stepped out from the shadows he grinned at her, his face red and flushed. Nervously he began to tidy himself, straightening his tie, running his fingers through his thinning hair. She smiled and stepped to one side, and at the same time he moved in front of her, blocking her way to the breakfast room. He reddened again and mumbled an apology. She looked at him.

'I don't know what to say to you,' he muttered, his eyes alight with a mixture of embarrassment and barely concealed lust. His face was slick with a fine gloss of sweat.

Francesca smiled pleasantly. '"Good morning" would be nice, Gerald, and don't skulk about in the shadows. It's very unnerving being pounced on.'

The auctioneer blustered, 'Oh, oh I am so sorry. I wasn't skulking . . .' His face was crimson.

Francesca laughed gently. 'Gerald, please try to relax.

Let's both take a tip from Alicia and behave as though we last met at a sedate garden party. Now, please let me through. I'm absolutely starving.'

Gerald leapt to one side as if he'd been shot. Francesca couldn't resist another smile. The auctioneer followed in her wake.

In the breakfast room at the end of the hall Alicia was already seated at the round table sipping a cup of tea. She looked glorious, dressed in a pale peach kimono and almost devoid of make-up. She looked up as they came in and lifted her cup in salute. 'Good morning, Francesca, Gerald. I hope you both had a good night,' she said mischievously before indicating that they should join her at the table.

Francesca smiled and sat down beside her. 'Wonderful thank you, Alicia. I slept like a baby.'

They both now looked at Gerald whose immediate reaction was to blush. He pulled out a chair, sat down uneasily and began to fiddle with his napkin.

Alicia poured the tea and said nothing, though her face could barely contain her amusement.

When they were settled, Alicia asked them their plans for the day. Francesca hesitated; she knew she should make a start on her novel which was lying neglected in the dressing room, but part of her wanted to begin a preliminary exploration of the gallery. She was about to speak when Gerald interrupted her train of thought.

'Actually, I'm thinking about popping back down to London,' he said quickly. There was the slightest tremor in his voice as he continued, 'I thought I'd nip into the office and see how things were going with the arrangements. I can't leave all the practicalities to the staff.'

Alicia nodded politely. 'An absolutely splendid idea, Gerald.' She paused theatrically and then added, 'I wonder whether you might like to invite Melissa to come back with you if she's finished her typing. We've all heard so much about her.'

Gerald choked on his tea and Francesca couldn't help smiling. She leant across the table and handed him a napkin.

'Went down the wrong way,' Gerald snorted, fighting to regain his composure.

Alicia smiled sympathetically but continued, 'Gerald, do get a grip, dear, we're all adults here. Now shall I ring the bell for breakfast or will you?' Gerald, still mopping at his shirt-front, stumbled to his feet and pulled the cord near the door. A second or two later Catz appeared at the door with a tray.

Gerald left almost immediately after they had eaten. He was furious with himself for being unable to keep his emotions under control, particularly when Alicia had mentioned Melissa. It had seemed as if the older woman had been reading his thoughts.

As he'd waited for Francesca to come down for breakfast he'd been running the possibilities through his mind. He had imagined the two women working on his compliant eager body, perhaps even tying him up first. He shivered – the possibilities were almost endless.

First he would encourage them to put on a little display; memories of the London gallery supplied the material as he fantasised about Francesca bending over to lap at the sex of his attractive blonde assistant. He would want to be close enough to them so he could watch her tongue slide in and out of the soft moist folds of Melissa's sex before she slipped the black wooden phallus into position, buried to the hilt in the blonde woman's aching, arching body. He shuddered. Perhaps he would take it from Francesca's hands and push it home himself, sliding it between Melissa's tight inviting lips. She would squeal and wriggle against him, her hips lifting to let him slide the dark shape in and out of its slick fragrant sheath.

They would be excited, eager for his body; he would deny them, let them wait for his attentions. He would bring Melissa to the edge of the abyss. His fingers would stroke the dark, enclosed and mysterious depths of Melissa's sex, letting the moisture pool and trickle around the thick wooden shaft. Melissa would cry out, arching her rounded thighs up against his thrustings. He would watch, encouraging them higher. Francesca would move fluidly to straddle her companion, lowering her own open eager body on to the tongue of her friend below. They would lap and suck, fingers and tongues caressing, teasing. He would be able to walk around them watching the union of their bodies, smelling their hot fragrant odours as they moved closer to the instant of release. On all fours Francesca's sex would hang open as it had the night before, her inner lips swollen in anticipation. Gerald shivered at the recollection.

When both women were in the delicate sweaty state he had seen them in London – so close to orgasm, teetering on the brink – he would stop them, pull their delicious hot bodies apart and insist they turn their attentions to him. He would be all powerful, all commanding, and they would be desperate to obey his every whim. He shuddered and let the images take him.

Melissa's soft feminine curves would straddle his chest; facing him she would crawl backwards, rubbing her heavy breasts along his body until she rested between his thighs. Her sex would trail fragrant wet kisses along the smooth lines of his lean body. She would let her moist sex rest against his belly before slipping lower to kneel between his legs and beg him to allow her to suck his throbbing desperate cock into her waiting mouth. Meanwhile above them, Francesca would creep closer, all her smiles and laughter gone. He would be able to smell her exotic heady aroma, the scent of her excitement, and would straddle his face so he could replay the lessons he had learnt from Catz. The other man's name added a dozen other variations.

So by the time Francesca had appeared on the stairs that morning he'd realised how he'd already thought himself into a desperate frenzy, and the reality of the attractive, seemingly unmoved woman walking towards him had almost been too much. He had felt the insistent press of his cock against the cotton of his briefs. He'd accidentally blocked her path, uneasy, nervous because she looked as if she had been totally untouched by the events of the previous night. She had stepped lightly down the stairs dressed in a light floral dress that showed every curve of her ripe and sensual body, her dark hair tied in a loose plait. Her casual manner had made him tremble.

Now, as he eased himself behind the wheel of his car, he tried to press the dark possibilities back under some sort of control. His reward was to see the bright teasing face of Francesca at breakfast. He would make her understand what he wanted, she would be eager to comply. She didn't know that he'd seen the exciting delicious way she had submitted to Catz the night before.

Reddening, he put the car in gear and pulled out of the drive. He would have the two women together and he would relish them both. The thought took on a life of its own and, in spite of his resolutions, the hot fragrant images flooded back through his mind and remained with him all the way to London.

Francesca went back to her rooms. The interior looked deceptively tidy; no signs remained of her encounter with Catz and Gerald. She picked up the crumpled black evening dress and slipped it into the wardrobe. Restlessly she moved around her suite touching what were becoming familiar objects; in the window the delicate sculpture of the two women making love reminded her of Melissa. Remembering their teasing of Gerald over breakfast, she realised she was looking forward to seeing her blonde companion again. Outside the windows the sky cleared and a brilliant shaft of sunlight picked out the tiny perfectly carved features of the women's faces. Their lips were parted in a sigh of passion, a tiny soundless record of their physical love. Francesca turned away and shook her head to clear her mind; she'd got work to do and her agent wouldn't take unrequited lust as an excuse for her manuscript being late. Slipping on a cardigan she went into the dressing room to begin work on the book.

By mid-morning it was obvious that no matter how hard she tried she couldn't concentrate on the rewrite. Beside her desk was the enticing mesh panel, a constant reminder of the gallery beyond. She groaned and bent back over the keyboard, tapping furiously, trying to concentrate on the chapter in front of her.

Rereading her notes the book no longer made sense. The story seemed to have nothing to do with her. It was as if someone else had written it; the characters came from the life she had stepped away from. Lying beside the keyboard were the dog-eared pages of notes that had been written whilst she'd been waiting for Chris to call for her. Even his name no longer conjured up a face. The only images that returned again and again were the distinctive features of Catz.

She glanced up at the mesh grille and angrily threw her pen across the room. If the call of the gallery was that strong perhaps she should begin the cataloguing on her own; even if she couldn't, she knew there was no way she was able to concentrate on the book.

Picking up a notepad she opened the small concealed door in the dressing-room wall. The gallery beyond was silent, washed with the subdued golden light of the summer sun. She walked slowly along the display cases, her eyes drawn unconsciously to the wrist-cuffs set up high on the wall. She swallowed, feeling her colour rising and walked back to the head of the spiral staircase. Being back in front of the statue of the dark woman and her attentive master brought the memories of Catz even closer. She stood still in front of its dark sensuous lines wondering if she would ever be able to catalogue the items. The statue echoed her passion, the oriental woman's eyes intense and mocking.

The impressions in her memory, even the quality of the light, made it impossible for her to look at anything without remembering Catz stealthily moving towards her, his eyes bright, his muscles tensed as he prepared to spring at her.

She took a deep breath and said quietly, 'This is ridiculous.'

In the silence her voice echoed around the panelled walls. 'What is?' asked a familiar voice.

Francesca swung around. Alicia was standing by the door of the lift, now dressed in an elegant blue suit.

Francesca shrugged and held up her hands in mock surrender. 'It's no good. I can't concentrate this morning,' she said, walking towards Alicia. 'I've been trying to work on the rewrite of my novel but it's impossible, so I thought I'd come in here and make a start on the cataloguing for Melissa.'

Alicia nodded. 'And is your concentration any better now that you're in here?'

Francesca laughed and shook her head. 'No – not at all. If anything it's worse. Tell me, do these things affect you?'

Alicia laughed. 'I think one would have to be dead for them not to have an effect,' she said, looking around, 'though eventually you do get used to them, accept them as part of your life. Rather like familiar old friends.'

She pointed towards the statue of the dark woman near the staircase. 'We bought that in Thailand. Edgar was out there with some sort of government trade mission. I remember we found it in a street market; carefully turned to face the front, I might add. Edgar couldn't resist it. Afterwards we went to a whore-house and had to leave it in the foyer – the madam tried to persuade Edgar to sell it to her, said that it might drum up trade.' She smiled and then turned back to Francesca. 'Tell me, did you enjoy your evening with Gerald?'

Francesca felt herself flush lightly. 'Yes,' she began slowly, 'I think I did, but it was Catz I wanted. Gerald would have had no idea on his own.'

Alicia smiled and stroked the heavy buttocks of the statue. 'Catz always has an idea, Francesca; he is a wicked tantalising addiction. As for Gerald? Well, he's a good man but not at ease with himself or what he desires. He wants to be free, to know more, but he traps himself with his fears.' She paused thoughtfully. 'Let me show you my favourite piece. It's over here.'

Francesca followed Alicia across the gallery; in a small frame on the wall was a delicate watercolour of a girl stretched across a day bed. Her lithe body was draped in a sheer, almost transparent white cloth which revealed every curve; beneath the carefully arranged folds the tiny pink buds of her nipples pushed up; every breathtaking detail of her erotic beauty was lovingly captured by the artist. Below, amongst the gathers of her wrap, it was possible to make out the deep shadowy crease of her lightly haired sex.

Alicia turned back to Francesca. 'Do you recognise the model?' she said softly.

Francesca moved closer and smiled. 'It's you.'

The figure's identity was impossible to mistake. The girl's youthful bloom could not disguise the distinctive outlines of Alicia's bone structure, the familiar tilt of her chin nor the bright diamond depths of her violet eyes.

Alicia lifted a finger to touch the frame. 'It was me. I had been married to Edgar for three years when this was painted. He commissioned it as an anniversary present. This watercolour was one of the artist's preliminary sketches, but Edgar was so entranced by it that he insisted on buying it. I'm glad he did now; the oil painting wasn't so fresh or lifelike. I felt this one captured me better.'

She turned back to Francesca. 'The artist who painted this was my first real lover; of course Edgar instigated it, though I had no idea at the time. I was consumed by guilt at my betrayal of our vows. The artist was called Janus; he was looking for a patron and stumbled across Edgar at a gallery in London. The two of them were inseparable for years, though I don't think their relationship was strictly confined to the arts.' She paused as her mind travelled back over the years to the sunlight studio and to recollections of her lover.

'He was beautiful.' She laughed. 'Edgar used to say Janus had the face of an angel and the mind of the devil. I suppose it's a cliché but it described him perfectly. He set out to seduce me on Edgar's instructions, little knowing that his every caress, his every sweet word was being observed and relished. Poor man, he set out consumed with an almost ungovernable lust to possess my body and ended up falling in love with me. There is a great irony in that. From controller to controlled, from taker to taken; poor Janus.'

Francesca looked closer. The artist had captured Alicia's youth and lovingly portrayed her striking, almost virginal beauty. His intense passion was captured in every brush stroke. Unable to disguise his desire or his longing, the picture had the poignancy of a love-letter; an eloquent supplication to an exquisite woman, both desired and worshipped.

Francesca turned away. 'It really is beautiful. Surely you're not going to let this go in the auction?'

Alicia shrugged. 'I'm not sure. In some ways it would be easier if everything was gone. It is all too full of the past; too many memories, too many secrets.' She paused and let her fingers trail across the glass. 'Too many years. It's time for me to move on.'

Francesca smiled, trying to understand Alicia's reasoning and the emotion that spurred her to consider selling the collection. 'Perhaps you're right,' she said softly. What became of the artist?'

Alicia's face flushed. 'I would like to say that he recovered from his infatuation with me and went on to be rich and happy. I'd like to say he escaped Edgar's clutches and went on to marry a fat wife and live off his talent, with a clutch of angelic children in the suburbs. But he didn't; he was too fragile, too ephemeral. As he got older he began to believe he would never be as good as the established artists he admired; he thought his work was not taken seriously. Poor sad Janus was a very muddled and very vulnerable man. While Edgar and I were away in Switzerland skiing he hanged himself in the summer house of our home in France.' Alicia's eyes were bright with tears as she turned back into the gallery. There was a moment when everything was still and silent between them, almost as if time had stopped. Then Alicia smiled. 'But that is all in the past now,' she said with unconvincing heartiness. 'Let's look at some of the other pieces; every one has a history, a memory.' She turned and walked briskly back along the gallery. Francesca followed her thoughtfully. 'Alicia,' she said quietly. 'I have to tell you that I think writing a book about Edgar is going to be impossible.'

Alicia turned back to face her, her violet eyes still bright. She seemed about to protest and then her eyes began to move slowly around the artefacts and paintings. Finally she shrugged. 'Perhaps you're right. After all, without all this, what sort of portrait of him could you convey? Without his tantalising vices he would be hollow, even dull. Oh well.' Her tone was resigned.

'Let's not dwell on that now. Come, let me show you some of the things we brought back from India.'

The objects in the gallery took on a new perspective with Alicia as a guide. Francesca took notes, thinking that perhaps Melissa could include some of the details in the catalogue, though in her mind she also wondered whether at some stage in her life she might be able to write the book that the collection deserved.

Alicia paused by a sculpture of a young man carved from marble. Kneeling at his feet in an act of worship, another older man took the youth's carved phallus between eager lips, his eyes closed in ecstasy. Above him the young man's eyes were open, gazing into the distance, one perfectly carved hand resting amongst the curls on his lover's head. Alicia lifted her hand to stroke the boy's cold, unmoving face.

'We bought this in Florence while we were there on holiday. I believe that the artist was trying to copy the sculpture of David. See the way the young man's face shines with an almost angelic quality . . .' She hesitated and then said quietly, 'I would like to watch you with Catz.'

Francesca could feel the heat flush through her and slowly placed the notepad she was carrying on a display cabinet, afraid to speak in case her excitement betrayed her.

Alicia continued in a voice barely above a whisper. 'I long to watch you with him. I've barely thought of anything else since we first met, since the day he showed you the gallery. My dreams are full of the two of you touching, kissing. I want to see his hands on your body, to watch as he . . .'

Francesca turned, her face alight with arousal. Breathlessly she ran from the gallery. Behind her Alicia moved more slowly, her violet eyes glowing with an intense and unspeakable desire. She picked up Francesca's notepad and walked towards the lift, the tiniest flutter of a pulse rising in the hollow of her throat.

Francesca ran down the spiral staircase, afraid to stop, her pulse beating out a tattoo in her ears. She wrenched open the door at the bottom and sped into the dark corridor beyond, her heels beating out a frantic rhythm on the marble tiles. She had to find Catz – she needed him. The exhibits had aroused her and Alicia's words had brought her need to a crescendo. The kitchen was empty; she called his name frantically, tearing open the doors along the corridor until finally she reached the hall. Throwing open the front door she was confronted by the object of her desire standing in the driveway calmly washing the Daimler.

He looked up as the door opened and his eyes narrowed as he instantly recognised the expression on her face – the reason for her breathlessness – and then he smiled.

'Catz,' she whispered and closed the door. He moved slowly towards her, skirting around the car. She stepped out from the shadow of the porch into the sunlight, her shoes crackling on the uneven gravel.

Ahead of her he moved closer and with a deft flick of the wrist turned the hose on her. She screamed at the shock; the cold water stung her, making her gasp, rooting her to the spot. Every sense reeled as the brittle coldness flooded through her. She cried out again and ran towards him, furious, breathless and desperate for his body.

Her thin summer dress clung to her, revealing every curve, every subtle plain. As she drew level with him he threw the hose down and grabbed her roughly, his mouth seeking out hers. She ran into his waiting arms, returned his kiss feverishly, pulling him close to her. She forced her tongue between his teeth and into the moist confines of his mouth, seeking out his tongue and the delicate sensitive ridge of his palate.

His hands lifted from her arms and caught hold of her dress; she felt his hands close around the sodden fabric. She pushed herself against him and was rewarded by the desperate animal eagerness of his fingers as they ripped at the thin cotton. Her scream of desire was stifled by his lips as his fingers tore away the buttons, pulling aside the fabric to expose her tight frozen breasts. Beneath the material her nipples hardened with cold and excitement. His lips left hers to suck one into his hot mouth, his tongue and teeth rising against it. One hand slid lower down over her hips, dragging up the sodden folds of her skirt, his fingers angrily seeking out the clinging material of her knickers. She gasped as his fingers hooked inside the waistband and with one stroke he tore them away. The material bit into her frozen flesh; she squealed as his fingers returned and he splayed her open, exposing her soft vulnerable lips to his frantic probing fingers.

The paradox of her attraction to Catz flooded her consciousness; the fear and the intense extremes of passion mingled into a heady cocktail. She moved closer to him, revelling in the dark sensations he awakened in her, breathing in the smell of his heat and her desire. She ran her fingers through his short hair and eagerly thrust her hips forward to meet his invasive fingers. He plunged deeper into her, bruising and crushing the soft folds. She responded by pulling his head closer to her so more of her breast was sucked into his 'waiting mouth.

He pulled back against her fingers and looked at her, his eyes dark and threatening. His fingers slipped from her body and roughly he twisted her round in his arms so she faced the house; above them in the landing window Francesca could see the pale stark outline of Alicia's face pressed close to the glass.

Behind her now, Catz turned his attentions to Francesca's neck whilst his hands cradled her exposed breasts, his fingers rough and unstoppable. She leant back against him, resting her weight on his chest, trying to draw in the warmth from his body as his aggressive mouth sucked and bit along the muscles of her shoulders. One hand slipped lower to drag up the sodden mass of her skirt, revealing her open swollen sex, the lips gaping in expectation of his assault.

His fingers opened up her lips, brushing against the aching bud of her excitement. She moaned and opened her legs wider for him. His touch was red-hot in contrast to the chill of her wet cold body. His fingers moved down, opening her wider still and then hesitated for an instant before plunging back into her fragrant depths. The brutality of his touch made her scream out in frenzy; she wanted him more than anything she had ever wanted before and tried to turn back into his arms. He resisted her; instead he began to stroke and rub her breasts with one hand whilst below, beneath the tangled bundle of her skirt, his fingers plunged deeper and deeper. She whimpered as the soft pad of his thumb brushed back and forth against the hard ridge of her clitoris.

She began to feel her passion growing, desperate ripples of pleasure flooding through her as his thumb and fingers moved relentlessly against her. On her back, through the ruined mess of her dress, she could feel the intense press of Catz's erection against her. She moaned and pushed back harder against him, grinding her wet buttocks into the muscular curve of his body. She felt him shudder and she pushed harder, trying to move him, trying to convey her overwhelming need to feel his excitement; his reaction was to bite her hard. She squealed and bucked forward, impaling herself further on his invasive fingers.

He let go of her breast, letting it slide from between his fingers, and lifted his hand to her shoulders. Slowly he began to peel the sodden ruins of her dress down over her body; the material clung stubbornly to her frozen skin. He jerked it away and she heard it rip under his touch. He pulled his fingers out from inside her and dragged the dress down over her hips. She was naked, frozen, exposed to Catz's desperate attentions and above, in the dark window, the eager violet eyes of Alicia Moffat.

The sodden wreck of her dress clung to her legs. Catz knelt and pulled it down further, his fingers lingering over the shivering downy outline of her thighs and calves as he pushed it down to the gravel. She stepped out of it and for an instant was free of his hands. Eagerly she turned away from the window and back to face him. Her sex was level with his face. He looked up at her and she could detect, deep in the storm of his eyes, the bright flames of excitement.

He caught hold of her hips and turned her again. Francesca knew that this was so Alicia could see them both as his tongue began its exploration of her body. The realisation sent a little quiver down her spine. He leant forward; she shuddered in anticipation and closed her eyes as he kissed the wet shiny hair at the junction above her outer lips. His delicacy surprised her, his first hesitant kiss was light, a tentative loving caress. She glanced down as his tongue slipped from between his lips and traced a silvery narrow line down between the crease, the very tip brushing the sensitive hood of her clitoris. She gasped at the intense fleeting sensation. His fingers lifted to push the heavy lips apart; his tongue circled her, brushing soft feathery kisses against the most sensitive part of her body. She groaned, feeling herself relax under his subtle caress. Her legs opened to him and she felt a tiny tight tremble down her spine.

His kisses moved lower, seeking out the tiny sensitive folds of her inner lips. He let his tongue play along their length until finally they parted under his gentle insistence and he slipped his tongue inside her. Bright twinkling crystals of excitement fluttered through her. His tongue slipped deeper and she could feel the sensations growing, whispering through her body, sparkling up through her belly. She lay back on to his caresses, giving him every access, offering her body to him, gratefully, willingly, and relishing her act of surrender.

Catz's fingers moved to join his tongue, their ministrations as gentle and enticing as those of his tongue. She whimpered as he began to circle her clitoris with his mouth whilst his fingers took the place of his tongue deep inside her. Every aspect of her consciousness seemed to be seated in her sex, every feeling, every thought stimulated by Catz's caresses.

She could feel the intensity growing, knew that the spiral was soaring towards its conclusion. She slid her hands into his hair, pulling him on to her. His lips began to suck at her and she knew she was almost lost; her muscles began to contract rhythmically around his fingers and she lay back to drink in the last intense seconds. Almost at the very peak of her desire Catz pulled away. She moaned and looked down at him; his bright eyes looked back and he rose to take her hand.

Throatily he murmured, 'Come with me, Francesca, let me take you to paradise . . .'

She moved towards him wordlessly; he pressed her

fingers to his lips and kissed them as he led her to the car. Amongst the muddle of gravel and weeds he knelt again and slipped off her sandals, his fingers lingering over the soft curves of her instep; she trembled. With great gentleness he lifted her on to the bonnet of the Daimler. She lay back, relishing the heat of the metal against her back. Under his gaze her body opened for him, her nakedness and vulnerability accentuated by the glistening black paintwork of the car beneath her body.

She closed her eyes against the harsh sunlight as if her vision might rob her of the intensity of sensation, knowing too that above her at the landing window Alicia was drinking in every detail, every nuance of her willing and eager submission. Her legs slid easily across the paintwork until they lay either side of the engine cover – she was totally and gloriously exposed for them both.

Even behind closed eyes she could see the light change as Catz came towards her, blockng out the sunlight. She heard the delicate muffled sounds of his clothes falling from his body and the soft purr of his excited breaths. His hands lifted to her hips, pulling her forward to meet him, and she shuddered as she felt the first intoxicating caress of his cock brushing against her inner thighs.

Moving closer he put the very tip between her inner lips; she could feel the heat of him, and longed to feel him slide it home. She swallowed as he slowly entered her, his penetration delicate and controlled. The sensation was almost overwhelming as he filled her; her muscles gripped him hungrily, pulling his engorged phallus tightly into the eager depths of her aching body. She lifted her hips towards him and slowly he pressed home his throbbing bulk.

With her pelvis tipped back against the sensual contours of the car's bonnet his every stroke brushed against her erect glowing clitoris, bringing the intense lingering spiral of her excitement closer and closer to the moment of release. He began to move faster now, his hips and belly moving against her, his hands dragging her further on to him. She could hold back no longer, the crystals of sensation shattered, filling her with a brilliant engulfing light. Great shuddering waves rolled over her and she bucked against him as her climax crashed to its brilliant conclusion. She gasped, breathless and satisfied, and tried to move out from under the subtle crush of his body.

Crying out, desperate now, she tried to roll from under him, trying to stop the brushing teasing stroke of his body against her clitoris; the sensations were too fierce, too intense, threatening to drown her. Relentlessly he pressed on, his narrow hips and belly rubbing against her, the bite of his pubic bone agonising as he pushed her out beyond the realms of any pleasure she had ever experienced.

She screamed out; the sensations were too cruel, too all-engulfing, and then just when she thought she might pass out she felt something stronger, something hypnotically compelling. On the other side of her passion – out beyond the white-hot intensity of her climax – approaching like a row of crashing breakers came a flood of new sensations; indescribable, unstoppable, they flooded through her bringing her again and again to the heights of ecstasy.

In the moments when she believed her body could take no more she felt Catz buck against her, his hips moving instinctively as he reached his own earth-shattering climax. He pressed himself deep into her, his breath roaring in her ears. She was astonished to feel her own body responding to the muscular contractions of his cock buried deep within her. The searing white-hot waves closed over her again, pulling her down to the brink of unconsciousness as their strength sucked every last breath from her exhausted and sweating body.

In the window above them Alicia tried to control her breathing. The passions enacted below her had brought a slick gloss of perspiration to her face, and a crashing excited rhythm to her pulse as it thundered in her ears. Catz's magnificent body pushed again and again into Francesca's body, his every stroke matched by the excited upward thrust of Francesca's hips.

Beneath him the younger woman's eyes were closed, her face contorted into a sob of ecstasy. Around them the sunlight threw every curve, every line, into the sharpest relief. Alicia could almost smell them and in her mind felt she could nearly reach out and touch them as they writhed in the last shuddering moments of their passion.

She watched bewitched as Catz threw back his head, unstoppable, his cock buried deep within Francesca's compliant body. Below him the younger woman bucked again and clutched at Catz's broad muscular back in the last frenzied sensations of her own climax.

Finally they lay still. Seconds passed, the two lovers lay on top of each other, the only movement their laboured desperate breaths. Alicia shuddered and moved her eyes across their slick sweat-covered bodies. Eyes closed, they could almost have been asleep.

Moments later Catz sat up, slipping his exhausted member from Francesca's body. Alicia saw her quiver at the loss and smiled to herself. Catz leant forward and kissed the bud of her clitoris where it peeked between her wet and swollen lips and then bent to scoop up his discarded clothes.

Alicia turned and made her way back to her bedroom, her excitement resonating just beneath her skin. At the dressing-room door she slid out of her day dress and slipped on the silk robe she used as a dressing-gown. Within seconds she heard Catz's footfalls on the landing and moved across into the bedroom.

He threw the door open and stood in the doorway, magnificent in his nakedness. Alicia shivered. His ice-blue eyes were cloudy, satiated.

She smiled at him and purred. 'You were glorious, Catz. It was everything I could have ever hoped for and more.'

Catz stepped into the room, letting the bundle of clothes slip to the floor. He looked at her robe and a narrow smile played across his lips. 'I'm glad you enjoyed it,' he said throatily. 'I aim to please.'

Alicia laughed and stepped towards him, the light in her eyes hypnotic and compelling. 'I never doubted it,' she whispered and sank slowly to the floor in front of him. Catz stood still but couldn't control the gasp that escaped from between his lips as she took his exhausted flaccid cock in her mouth. He groaned and tried to writhe away from her touch, her caress too soon after the intense pleasures of Francesca's body. She looked up at him. His eyes were closed and he was shivering. She slipped back on to her heels, her expression amused and delighted.

'So,' she said softly, 'we've finally met our match, have we, Catz?'

The man opened his eyes and laughed. 'There was never one made,' he said softly.

She stepped back towards the bed, her eyes bright and mischievous. 'I believe you,' she purred and opened the soft folds of her robe; she was naked beneath. Moaning softly Catz dropped to his knees and crawled towards her, the tip of his tongue just visible between the red outline of his lips.

Below them in the drive Francesca was collecting together the shreds of her sodden dress, her mind full and her body totally exhausted. Between her legs her sex throbbed painfully; she slipped on her sandals and made her way back into the villa.

# Chapter Nine

Francesca ran herself a hot bath and spent the rest of the day in her room dozing lightly. She felt exhausted, her body aching and frozen to the marrow from Catz's lovemaking and the sharp bitter cold of the water. As the evening light crept into the bedroom, Catz knocked on her door to announce that dinner would be served in fifteen minutes. She wondered whether she would be able to face Alicia. Stiffly she crawled off the bed and looked into the mirror. Her hair was a tangled mess and nothing could disguise the startling redness of her tender lips. She showered, sharp fingers of water finding every tender, aching muscle.

Downstairs she found Alicia waiting for her in the breakfast room. The older woman had poured herself an aperitif and was standing by the open French windows. She turned at the sound of Francesca's arrival.

'Good evening, my dear,' she said softly, lifting her glass in a toast of greeting. 'Why don't you join me in a little glass of something delicious.'

Francesca laughed in spite of her discomfort and went across to a tray of bottles on the sideboard. 'I don't mind if I do.'

Alicia smiled evenly, her eyes unreadable.

Francesca poured herself a glass of wine and turned to Alicia. 'You know, Alicia, you astound me. Are you always so composed in the aftermath of your little adventures?'

Alicia shrugged. 'No, not always, but I have learnt to brush over my own – what shall we call it – excitement, interest, whatever. Firstly, with Edgar it was inappropriate. If we'd had a particularly tantalising evening it was hardly considered good form to chat about it over breakfast with one's house guests. Later I discovered that other people are embarrassed by their own desires and experiences, and since then – well, what's done is done, however exciting or wonderful it was.' She paused and sipped from her glass. 'Come and look at the garden. I love it now that nature's taken over.'

They stood shoulder to shoulder in the doorway; outside, the garden tumbled and rolled silently towards the sea. Here and there the ivy had broken through the sea wall. Alicia pointed it out. 'One day, the garden will break free and spill over on to the cliff path; maybe if I'm lucky I'll live to see it. Edgar would be furious; he so liked to be in control.' She turned. 'Shall we sit now? Catz will be here in a second. Oh, and could you get the candelabra. I think tonight we ought to look at each other in a more flattering light.'

Francesca laughed and lifted the heavy silver

candelabra from the sideboard and set it in the centre of the table. Alicia pulled the doors closed and lit the candles. They looked at each other through the flames and smiled. Alicia pulled out her chair. 'Come and sit down, dear,' she said softly. 'You look exhausted.'

Francesca sat down as Catz came in with their first course. He looked lovingly at each of them and then at the candles.

'Had I known you ladies wanted a romantic candlelit dinner I would have arranged it,' he said lightly, placing the plates in front of each of them. Arranged in tiny porcelain dishes was a selection of seafoods, each beautifully prepared.

Alicia smiled. 'Oh, Catz, my favourite – *fruits de mer*. How splendid! Let's break open a bottle of something glorious, Francesca. We need to steel ourselves for the arrival of Gerald and Melissa.'

Francesca looked at her questioningly as Alicia picked up her fork and skewered a plump pink prawn.

'Don't worry,' she said, popping it into her mouth. 'They won't be here until tomorrow; Gerald rang this afternoon. More than enough time for us to prepare ourselves.'

Francesca felt herself flush and Alicia laughed.

'Come, come, dear. We must show them how to behave in the face of temptation.'

She glanced across at Catz and waved him away. 'Catz, don't hover. Go and find something wonderful in the cellar.'

\*

That night, after a delicious supper, Francesca went to bed early, feeling grateful for the chance to sleep, her body still aching and weary. The next morning the sky was bright and clear with a promise of a glorious day to come. She woke early, feeling refreshed. After breakfast with Alicia she decided that the book held no appeal and she knew if she sat for too long looking at the manuscript, the temptation of the gallery would be too much. Slipping on a pair of shorts and T-shirt, she picked up a towel and headed out through the cool shadows of the house and into the garden beyond.

Beyond the cliff wall, a narrow path led down to the beach below. The tide had just turned, leaving a great strip of virgin beach, a moist necklace of weeds and pebbles marking the kiss of high water. Francesca slipped off her sandals and, draping the towel round her neck, set off for a walk, the sun and sea air an exhilarating contrast to the cool mysterious shadows of the villa.

By mid-morning she had settled herself amongst a scattered outcrop of rocks, laid out her towel and was blissfully soaking up the heat of the summer sun.

'Robinson Crusoe, I presume.' A soft feminine voice broke into her dozing dreams.

Francesca grinned and sat up, holding her hand to her face to block the bright sunlight. Struggling along the sand towards her was Melissa, waving brightly. Francesca laughed and waved back. 'You're not exactly dressed for beachcombing, or do you normally come on to the beach in a business suit?'

Melissa laughed and threw her high heels and

briefcase down into the sand beside Francesca's towel before sitting down. 'Alicia told me you'd be down here. It's beautiful, isn't it? I can understand why you wanted to get back.'

Francesca nodded. 'Blissful. How have you been?'

The blonde woman smiled. 'I missed you,' she said quietly. 'Oh, and I've finally met the mysterious Catz up at the villa.' She shivered. 'He's a cool customer, isn't he? There's something about his eyes.'

Francesca laughed. 'That's almost exactly what I said to Alicia when we first met. Believe me, there's a lot more to him than his eyes.' She thought back to their lovemaking of the day before; he had shown her places she never knew existed. The recollection sent a tingle of excitement down her spine. Melissa moved closer.

'I can see his appeal,' she purred, lifting her hand to Francesca's face. Her lips moved closer and brushed delicately against the soft contours of Francesca's lips. For a second there seemed to be only the two of them in the whole universe. Francesca slid a hand around Melissa's back and pulled her closer; between her lips she felt the gentle enquiring touch of Melissa's tongue. The blonde woman quivered beneath her fingertips and let out a soft compelling sigh.

'Ahoy there, ladies.' Gerald's voice echoed along the empty beach like a foghorn. Francesca pulled away regretfully, seeing the grey misty light of desire momentarily flicker in the other woman's eyes.

'Over here, Gerald,' she called, her eyes not leaving Melissa's face. A few seconds later, Gerald appeared around the outcrop, his ginger complexion flushing red in the heat.

Francesca couldn't resist a smile. He grinned. 'Thought I'd find you both here he said, folding himself on to a shady rock. 'I was rather hoping you would help Melissa with the rest of the cataloguing.'

Francesca nodded. 'I've already said I'd help, Gerald. I wasn't sure what time you'd arrive; are you hoping to make a start today?'

Gerald nodded. 'I'm afraid so; after lunch probably.' His eyes moved across her body, drinking in the details of her skimpy beach outfit.

Francesca pulled herself to her feet. 'Okay, well we'd better get back so I can have a chance to shower and change before lunch.'

Gerald's face couldn't quite hide his disappointment.

At the house, Alicia was waiting for them in the sitting room. Francesca hurried upstairs to change before Catz served them lunch in the dining room.

Over the meal, Gerald laid out his plans for the auction and for transporting the contents of the villa gallery. Businesslike and very much in his element, Francesca thought that Gerald seemed a very different man to the one who had shared her body with Catz. After some discussion, they decided to leave the cataloguing until the next day. They agreed to spend the afternoon in preliminary examination of the artefacts, also checking that Gerald's records were as thorough at the villa as they were for the London collection.

In the daylight, the atmosphere in the gallery was convivial and light. Alicia gave Melissa and Gerald a guided tour of the exhibits, whilst behind them Francesca watched quietly. She could sense the items that excited Melissa, watching the unmistakable flush of excitement flood through her blonde friend. In front of them, seemingly oblivious, Alicia explained in a calm dispassionate voice where the items had been bought or bartered and gave snippets of their history. Gerald and Melissa hung on her every word.

It was late afternoon by the time their tour was complete, and the subtle change of light seemed to affect them all. Beneath the sound of Alicia's calm voice, a new delicate tension began to grow, a faint fluttering electric hum that captivated each of them.

Finally Alicia suggested they meet up again over dinner. Francesca was the first to slip away, almost unnoticed, through the little hidden door into the dressing room beyond.

She dressed with care, choosing a soft pale-blue evening dress that she had bought on a whim. The material was clinging, skilfully tailored to highlight her narrow waist and small rounded breasts. The delicate colour highlighted the deep blue of her eyes and complemented her light tan. She pulled back her hair in two combs, framing her small features with a curtain of dark shiny hair.

There was a tight undercurrent of expectation during dinner. Melissa looked breathtaking in a red silk cocktail dress, Gerald elegant in black tie whilst Alicia surpassed them all in a cream silk full-length gown that gave her the look of a glamorous film siren. The conversation was light, but between the words the promise of the night ahead crackled like a summer storm. Outside the windows, as if echoing the electricity in the air between the diners, the grey metallic edge of a storm prematurely darkened the evening sky.

During dessert, Alicia dropped casually into the conversation that Melissa and Francesca's rooms were next door to each other. Nobody commented but everyone understood the unspoken implication. Over coffee and liqueurs in the sitting room, Alicia showed them photographs from her collection but nothing could dispel the tension in the air. Outside, the first brilliant finger of lightning split the night sky.

In the village pub near the quayside, Chris Pearce was consoling himself with another pint of local brew. The last week or so had been a blur of alcoholic indulgence. He glanced up into the mirror above the bar and heavy bloodshot eyes returned his stare. He couldn't understand what had gone so desperately wrong between Fran and himself. As he thought about her, the image of her delicate handsome face flooded his mind. He had been so certain of her, so desperate to . . . to what? He sensed he had been deceived by her but wasn't sure why or how. He snorted and ordered another beer. He felt betrayed and bitter.

The barman looked at him sympathetically, and said,

'Are you sure you want another one, mate? It seems to me you've had quite enough.'

Chris snorted again and slid his glass across the bar. 'Not enough. I can still remember why I'm drinking. Just get me another, will you? If I wanted your advice, I'd ask for it.'

The man tucked Chris's empty glass under the pump. 'Woman trouble?' he asked philosophically. 'They always get you, mate, every time.'

Chris pulled a face. 'You're right there – bloody little tramp. You know, I gave her everything she wanted . . .'

As he spoke, he thought of his visit to her cottage. He had driven there on the morning after he'd caught Francesca climbing out of the old car. He tried not to think about the things that had happened after they had gone into the cottage. It had come as a shock to find the cottage locked and deserted; his guilt and regret at behaving badly had rapidly turned to anger. The image of the vintage car suddenly emerged in his beer-sodden brain – the car and the man in the uniform.

He turned back to the barman. 'Say, can you tell me something? A few days ago I saw a funny-looking car around the quay.'

The barman looked at him quizzically. 'Funny-looking car? I'm not with you.'

'Yeah, a vintage job. Looked like something out of the forties; long black thing – a bloke in a uniform drives it.'

A gleam of comprehension registered in the barman's eyes.

'You mean Mrs Moffat's Daimler. She's a bit of a

character round here; bit of a recluse. That was her chauffeur you saw.'

Chris smiled thinly. 'So she lives round here, then?'

The man nodded. 'Yes, she's got an old place, really ramshackle, out on the coast road. Mind you, it used to be a lovely house; Victorian, I think.' The barman hesitated for a moment as he slid Chris's beer across the counter.

'When I was a kid we used to go there along the cliff path; you can walk right round to the next village, you know. Anyway, they had this green house in the garden with grapes in it . . .'

The man's voice faded into the background as the identity of the house dawned on Chris. He turned back to the man, who was still reminiscing about stolen grapes.

'Out on the headland,' he murmured. 'Looks deserted; got a huge garden?'

The barman nodded. 'That's the one.'

Before he could complete the sentence, Chris was on his feet. Pushing the money across the bar for his beer, he made his way unsteadily out into the night.

At the villa the guests had all decided to accept Alicia's suggestion of an early night. Outside, over the sea, the storm cracked and rumbled, bringing the promise of rain.

Francesca quietly closed the door of her suite. The curtains had been left open, flooding the room with the intense grey light of the coming storm. She went to the bathroom to change for bed.

*

Behind the two-way mirror, in the small room that adjoined Francesca's suite, Gerald had settled himself in a comfortable chair and was awaiting the show that promised to unfold. He pulled the chair a little closer to the glass and was not surprised that his hands betrayed a tremor of excitement as he did so.

In the room next door, Melissa was changing for her visit to Francesca's suite; she'd bought a new outfit for her friend's delectation. Beneath the smooth contours of her wrap, she had slipped into a tight little black silk basque; she opened the ties a little to admire herself in the mirror. The dark fabric was a sharp contrast to the creamy pallor of her skin. Her heavy breasts with their dark areolae pushed forward; already her nipples had hardened.

She leant a little closer to the mirror, her eyes stormy blue with anticipation and desire. From her make-up bag she retrieved her lipstick; with trembling hands she painted her plump moist lips before lifting the heavy curve of her breasts towards the mirror and rubbing the dark-red stick around her tingling nipples. She stood back to admire the effect; the disparity of the intense red against her pale skin was breathtaking. She ran an appreciative hand over their heavy curves and then, from a bag on the end of her bed, took something she had borrowed from Edgar's gallery collection during their afternoon tour. Closing her robe, she slipped from her room and crept silently along the landing.

*

Francesca, in her suite, had turned off the main light, leaving the soft glow of the lamps to illuminate the bedroom. She glanced at the mirror and then slipped into bed. She had let her hair loose so that it hung in soft curls around her shoulders. Her slim frame was draped in a sheer-white silk negligee. She sat up in bed and admired her reflection. The outline of her nipples was clearly visible through the almost transparent material; she smiled at her reflection and sat back, confident that her lover – whoever it might be – would not be long in coming.

After a few seconds she heard the gentle click of the door opening and then the soft pad of bare feet across the carpet. Framed in the doorway, Melissa stood for an instant, breathtaking in her beauty. Francesca gasped appreciatively and was rewarded by Melissa slipping her robe from her shoulders.

The blonde woman smiled, stepping into the pool of light from the lamps. 'So,' she purred, 'what do you think?'

Francesca grinned back at her. 'You look stunning.' She slipped from the bed to greet her.

In the soft lamplight they drank in the image of each other's bodies. Melissa was the first to put out a hand, her fingers lightly brushing the already hardened darkness of Francesca's nipples through the sheer fabric.

Francesca moaned and lifted her fingers to meet Melissa's delicate touch; catching her hand she led her lover towards the mirror.

'Why don't you come and admire yourself,' she said softly, turning Melissa around to confront the intense, scintillating image of the women framed in the cool glass. Francesca slipped behind her lover and lifted a hand to Melissa's breasts, gently taking their weight, her fingers seeking out the dark painted buds of her nipples. Melissa moaned and leant back into her caress as Francesca's other hand slipped lower, snaking around Melissa's waist to the blonde mound of her sex. Her finger slipped between the welcoming folds, seeking out the ridge of her clitoris. Beneath the press of her fingers she felt it tense and harden. She sighed; the evidence of the blonde woman's excitement made her feel heady, and between her own legs she could feel the soft moist stirrings of her own anticipation.

Melissa turned into her friend's arms and lifted her painted lips to find Francesca's; the first tentative brush of her lips sent an electric thrill along Francesca's spine. She opened her mouth and with delicate feathery strokes licked at the painted outline of Melissa's full lips. Melissa shuddered in her arms.

Behind the glass Gerald was holding his breath. Outlined in the mirror was the devastating curve of Melissa's full buttocks, framed by the dark contours of the basque. She parted her legs a little and he could make out the soft swelling folds of her lower lips, opening in response to her friend's kisses; already he could see the faintest trail of silvery moisture highlighting her blonde hair. He groaned and leant closer.

*

In the garden the promised rain suddenly flooded from the sky in a tumultuous roaring curtain on to the ruined garden below. A flash of electric-blue lightning illuminated the tortured shapes of the shrubs and, at the sea wall, the pale moonlit face of Chris as he fought to open the garden gate.

Francesca led Melissa back to the ottoman at the end of the bed, realising that, in spite of Gerald's attentions and the more exciting caresses of Catz, she had really missed the blonde woman and her intimate knowledge of her body. She knelt between Melissa's legs and, cupping her delicate rounded features in her hands, guided the woman's face towards her. Melissa's lips opened eagerly under Francesca's light enquiring kisses, her hips lifting spontaneously to meet Francesca's irresistible caresses. Francesca could feel the delicious touch of Melissa's hair brushing against her belly. She let her mouth slip down, kissing tenderly at the blonde woman's plump flesh until she reached the rise of her breast, her tongue seeking out Melissa's nipples. The sweetness of the lipstick against the lightest hint of salt made Francesca moan with desire. She sucked the hard dark bud into her mouth; Melissa sighed and slowly lay back, surrendering her body to Francesca completely.

With an almost compulsive need to taste Melissa's excitement Francesca moved her tongue down between Melissa's breasts, relishing the saltiness, kissing the tiny fasteners that held the basque in place. Her tongue snaked lower, pressing kisses against the soft bowl of her belly, drawing tiny circles along the smooth rise of her hips. Melissa moaned and opened her thighs to Francesca, her sex lifting towards Francesca's mouth. The smell of her excitement was electrifying, a delicate musky odour of desire and longing.

Francesca hesitated for a second, glancing up to admire the beautiful sensual lines of her companion, and then delicately she kissed the soft blonde hair of her swelling mound. Melissa whimpered and lifted her legs up on to the ottoman, her whole exquisite tracery exposed. Francesca slipped a tentative finger into the moist fragrant depths of Melissa's body; the blonde woman sighed, and around her finger Francesca felt the tantalising spasm of her friend's wetness contracting in anticipation.

Behind the mirror Gerald was totally enrapt; the scene unfolding in the room beyond was everything he hoped for. Somewhere in the distance he heard a muffled crash, but his concentration – his whole consciousness – was projected into the softly lit bedroom beyond the glass. He wondered when he should make his move, and a little trickle of anticipation shivered through his spine. Between his legs the hard outline of his erection pressed desperately against his evening trousers.

In the bedroom Francesca was beginning the slow circling kisses of Melissa's clitoris that would bring her friend to the height of ecstasy. The woman began to move softly under her touch, her head thrown back, her own hands lifting towards the painted outline of her nipples. Sleepily she lifted her head.

'I've brought us a little present . . .' she whispered throatily between hot little moans of excitement.

Francesca looked up and grinned. 'Now's a hell of a time to tell me you've brought chocolates.'

Melissa giggled, her normally languid blue eyes dark with passion. 'No, not chocolates; look under my robe. I borrowed something from the gallery that I thought might come in useful.'

Francesca uncurled from between Melissa's legs, smiling at Melissa's choice of words.

She lifted the robe; beneath it was the sleek outline of a creamy-coloured double-ended phallus lovingly carved from something cold and flexible.

She turned round and held it up. Melissa had pulled herself up on to her elbows, legs still open, eyes still glistening.

Francesca grinned and, running towards her, took a playful flying leap on to the crumpled bed, landing beside her.

'A screwdriver could be described as useful,' she said teasingly. 'Even a torch, maybe a tin-opener, but whatever else this is, the last thing it is is useful.'

Melissa moved towards her, kissing her lightly on the lips. 'Trust me,' she purred mischievously. 'It is very useful; let me show you.' She rolled over and took the dildo from her, kissing Francesca again; the light brush of her lips sent a thrill of expectation through Francesca's body. The blonde woman's hands lifted to stroke her nipples through the thin fabric of her negligée. They hardened into the cup of her palms. Melissa's hands lifted to slip Francesca's gown down over her shoulders; Francesca revelled in her attentions. Her painted mouth kissed along the curve of her collarbone, nipping, licking lightly. Francesca moaned and knelt up to face her. Face to face, they began to stroke each other.

Francesca glanced towards the mirror and was rewarded with the stunning image of herself and Melissa in profile, their breasts a hair's breath apart, the lift of their ribs sliding down to the rounded curve of their bellies and, below, the broad swell of their hips. Melissa turned too and for an instant they were caught together, their eyes suffused with passion and desire.

Melissa lifted her hand to Francesca's neck and anointed her lips with kisses. Francesca moaned languidly and drank in the woman's attentions as Melissa's hand snaked lower, and Francesca felt the light cool brush of the phallus on the tender skin between her thighs. She gasped and stiffened involuntarily.

Melissa stroked her neck and whispered, 'Hush, hush, it's all right,' her voice barely above a murmur. Her fingers brushed across the hard rise of Francesca's clitoris, softly, almost teasingly, tracing a light circle; Francesca felt every nerve ending flutter with excitement. Below, the cool head of the phallus crept closer. Francesca leant back, kneeling, taking her weight on her hands so that her legs opened a little wider. Melissa stroked her other hand down over her belly, her fingers sliding lower to gently part her swollen lower lips. Francesca, exposed now, let out a tiny whimper as Melissa let the heavy bulk of the phallus play against the sensitive folds.

'Relax,' murmured Melissa. 'Gently, gently.' As she spoke, she began to slide the phallus into Francesca's body. The coldness of it startled her, her body closed around it, she gasped again as Melissa whispered soft endearments and slid the dildo home. Francesca glanced down; between the dark hair of her outer lips the soft curve of the other end of the phallus protruded provocatively. Melissa caught her glance and looked down, too. She grinned teasingly. 'It suits you,' she said softly. 'Here, let me feel it.'

With great care Melissa leant back and slipped the other end into her own body. She opened her legs wide and encircled Francesca. The effect was breathtaking; they began to move, slowly at first, gently exploring the sensations.

Melissa's hand returned its attention to the bud of Francesca's sex and she in turn slipped her hands between the soft heavy folds of Melissa's body. The sensation electrified her. The blonde woman began to thrust her hips forward, setting a sharp intense rhythm. Francesca threw back her head and joined her, relishing the cool bulk of the phallus buried deep inside her and the expert stroking of her lover's knowing fingers.

In the room beyond the mirror Gerald could barely contain the heady waves of pleasure that the women's activities had created in him. His intentions to join them were retreating with every passing second. He was almost afraid to move, so close was he to the point of no return. In front of him the women were fast moving towards their own climax, their hips and fingers grinding out a tantalising rhythm. Gerald swallowed hard, trying to control the intensity of his own feelings. To one side of him there was a strange noise – a muffled crash – and then to his horror the room was flooded with light. He gasped, and swung round to be confronted by the furious red face of a tall, greying man, obviously the worse for drink.

Gerald clambered uneasily to his feet, still aware of the hard press of his erection against his belly.

'Who the hell are you?' he stammered.

The other man practically fell into the room, his face contorted in a mixture of fury and confusion. 'Francesca,' he snorted. 'Where is Francesca?'

As he spoke his eyes caught the light of the room beyond the mirror. He froze, a high-pitched whimper spilling from between his wet flaccid lips.

'Christ,' he whispered.

Gerald retreated into the dark corner of the room, his excitement suddenly draining away as the man moved closer to the mirror as if unable to believe his eyes.

Beyond the glass Melissa and Francesca were quickly working their way to the place of no return. Melissa had her head thrown back, her fingers busily engaged in the dark depths of Francesca's sex. Francesca was leaning forward, sucking at the blonde woman's swollen nipples, her own hand buried in the delicate blonde creases of Melissa's body. As they moved against each other, their hips beating out an intense driving rhythm, the shaft that joined the double-ended phallus was momentarily exposed.

The greying man's breath was coming in short ragged gasps. He turned to Gerald, his eyes aggressive narrow slits. 'What in God's name is going on here?' he spluttered. Gerald felt a cold chill of fear as the man moved towards him, fists tightening now.

Gerald's pulse beat in his ears. He wasn't an aggressive man and even in the face of the other man's intended attack his first instinct was to try to retreat further into the shadows. Instead he felt the chilling hardness of the wall against his spine as the other man lurched towards him.

'Get out,' Gerald whimpered, cursing himself for the shaky sound of his voice. 'You're trespassing on private property.'

The other man laughed in derision. 'You bloody pervert, it's you who's trespassing on what's mine. Do you know who that is in there?' His head jerked towards the mirror.

Gerald couldn't find any words. Instead he shook his head, afraid that his voice would betray his growing terror.

'She's my girlfriend.' Chris hesitated. 'I was going to marry her, you know. Do you understand, she's mine.' Gerald still said nothing. His silence seemed to infuriate the intruder and, stepping a little closer, the man took a wild swing and hit Gerald – who remained totally motionless – squarely in the mouth.

Gerald felt a sharp explosion of pain and his mouth filled with the coppery taste of blood. He gasped and then let out a strangled sob before sliding gracelessly to the ground. The man towered over him for a second as if to continue his assault, but he was interrupted by the frenzy of activity in the room beyond the mirror.

He swung around, seemingly mesmerised by the events in the bedroom. The women were now thrusting almost automatically; moving, touching, weaving their way towards their climax.

Gerald watched him; standing squarely before the glass, it was obvious that despite his fury the tall man was also captivated and excited by the images. He moved closer, his hands lifting towards the surface of the mirror. It seemed to dawn on him then that the events were occurring in the room beyond the barrier of the glass. He swore softly under his breath and ran out of the room.

As Chris left, Gerald struggled to his feet, the sweat pouring down his face. He lifted his fingers to his lips and winced. Moving close to the glass he pressed his aching head against the cool mirror and took a deep breath.

Next door in Francesca's bedroom the two women were gasping for breath as the waves of excitement began to flood through them. Francesca could feel the hot tight contractions of her climax closing around the smooth shape of the phallus. Against her face she could hear the frenzied beat of Melissa's heart. Melissa began to buck against her. Francesca moaned and then froze.

Across the room Chris stood framed in the doorway, his face set in a dark furious mask. Melissa looked up sleepily and turned to follow Francesca's gaze. She screamed in shock as Chris strode towards the bed and instinctively she tried to wriggle away from Francesca. Francesca rolled to one side, allowing the phallus to slip from her body. Her muscles complained bitterly, her other hand slipped lower and pulled it gently away from Melissa's body, breaking their erotic attachment.

Melissa, her eyes bright with anxiety, scuttled across the bed in terror. Francesca pulled her robe up over her shoulders and leapt on to the floor.

Chris stood over her, menacingly. 'What the hell is going on here?' he growled. His eyes moved across the wrecked bed to the stark outline of the phallus, still glistening with the women's juices.

Francesa stood her ground, feeling the glitter of white-hot rage growing in her belly, drowning out the intense waves of desire that had been there only seconds earlier. 'Get out,' she whispered furiously. There's nothing for you here.'

As they spoke, Melissa slipped from the bed and raced from the room. Both Francesca and Chris heard her yelling Catz's name; neither of them moved.

'So this is what you came here for,' he said icily. 'Why, wasn't this good enough for you?' His hand dropped to his crotch where his cock unexpectedly bulged hard and full of desire from seeing the two women.

Francesca sighed, suddenly feeling frustrated and sad rather than angry; her voice was softer now. 'Chris, it's over. You have to understand that. It was over the night you came to the cottage. What I do with my life is my choice. Now please, get out now before there's any trouble. What we had is over, gone – in the past. Please leave.'

Chris stepped towards her, his eyes dropping to absorb the erotic image of her body through the sheer fabric of her wrap. He moaned and tried to embrace her. 'Please,' he murmured. 'Stay with me. What we had was so good. Just come back with me. I can forgive you for all this.'

Francesca snorted furiously and moved away from his outstretched arms. 'Forgive me? Forgive me for what? There's nothing to forgive, Chris. I'm a grown woman. I can do what I want with my body, I'm free to make my own choices. What puts yon in such a superior position that you have the right to forgive me?'

As she spoke, she saw a flurry of movement at the door and Catz stepped into the room. He was wrapped in a thick white towelling robe which did nothing to hide the intimidating contours of his muscular body. His face was impassive, emotionless, as he spoke. 'I suggest you leave now, sir,' he said evenly. 'We don't want any trouble, do we?'

Chris growled aggressively, 'You bastard,' then snapped and launched himself full tilt at Catz.

Catz sidestepped him, allowing the man to make his drunken lunge. Grabbing one arm as Chris passed, he twisted it up behind Chris's back, effectively restraining him without inflicting any injury.

Chris screamed out in frustration and pain. Catz looked across at Francesca, ignoring the sodden man's writhing discomfort.

'Are you all right?' he asked gently.

Francesca nodded. 'Please just get rid of him, Catz,' she said. She caught Chris's eye and said evenly, 'I never want to see him again.'

Catz nodded and guided Chris, still swearing and protesting, from the room.

A few seconds later Melissa returned, her eyes bright with tears. Francesca stepped to comfort her at the same time as Gerald – still with a trickle of blood running from his mouth – stepped into the room behind her.

The three of them looked at each other, still all slightly stunned and shaken. Francesca was the first to recover herself. 'We'd better go and find Alicia.'

'That won't be necessary,' announced a familiar voice from the shadow of the doorway. She stepped into the light, wrapped in a large dressing-gown. She glanced at each of them, her eyes lingering for a second on Gerald's ashen blood-smeared face. 'I think we'd better make ourselves a little more presentable and then have a stiff drink. Catz will take our unwanted visitor home. I'll go and pour us all a brandy in the sitting room. Gerald, you'd better let me take a look at your lip, it looks quite nasty.'

*

A few minutes later everyone gathered in the sitting room. Melissa had now pulled on a thick dressing-gown to cover her basque and Francesca found the towelling robe from the bathroom. Only Gerald was still dressed, rather incongruously, in his dinner-jacket and evening trousers. Everyone still looked pale and shocked. Alicia joined them a second or two later and asked Gerald to pour the drinks.

Francesca, cradling a brandy balloon, began, 'I'm so sorry. I had no idea Chris would try something like this.'

Alicia shook her head. 'It's hardly your fault; let's hope Catz can talk some sense into him. I'll get him to check where your friend broke in once he gets back.' She paused.

On the sofa Melissa broke into a thin high-pitched sob and Gerald moved across to comfort her. Francesca realised that her hand was shaking. Alicia smiled supportively. 'It's all right,' she murmured and slipped her arm around the younger woman's shoulders. Francesca allowed herself to be encircled, and leant against Alicia gently.

A little while later Catz reappeared. Without a word Alicia poured him a drink.

Catz glanced around the room and then said quietly, 'I dropped him off at his house; he seems to be all right now.'

'He'd been drinking,' Francesca said flatly, settling herself in an armchair. 'I don't think he would have tried to come up here unless he'd been drunk.'

Alicia nodded. 'I believe now might be as good a time as any to consider leaving for London. Gerald, if you can arrange for Edgar's collection to be transported first thing tomorrow morning, I would be most grateful. There's no telling when our rather belligerent friend might return and it would cause all sorts of problems if he inadvertently stumbled into the gallery.'

Gerald nodded. 'No problem, Alicia. The carriers can be here by mid-afternoon. We'll complete the cataloguing in London.'

'Fine,' said Alicia. 'Well, when we've finished our drinks I suggest we all go back to bed. There's a lot to be done tomorrow; best if we make an early start.'

Gerald drained his glass and got to his feet. As he did so a bell rang. Alicia glanced at Catz, who had placed his glass down and was already moving towards the door.

A few seconds later he reappeared. 'It's the police,' he said softly.

Alicia Moffat glanced heavenwards and put her brandy balloon down on a side table. 'Show them in, Catz. It looks as if our friend has been rather busy since you dropped him off.'

Two uniformed police officers were shown into the sitting room. The more senior one smiled. 'I'm extremely sorry to disturb you at this time of night, Mrs Moffat, but we've had a report on the radio. A rather distressed gentleman rang in to say his girlfriend –' He paused and glanced at his notebook, '– a Mrs Francesca

Leeman, was in some kind of trouble up here. I wonder whether I might be able to speak to her?'

Francesca got to her feet. 'I'm Mrs Leeman. I'm afraid there has been a mistake, officer.'

Alicia interrupted, 'The gentleman in question broke in here this evening and made the most appalling scene. My chauffeur took him home.'

The policeman nodded. 'I see. Have you any idea why the gentleman might phone us?'

Francesca continued, trying to keep the emotion in her voice under control, 'I'm afraid he'd been drinking. He was drunk when he burst into my bedroom. We've recently split up and I think he's finding it very hard to come to terms with it.'

The officer scribbled something in his notebook, 'And so you are all right, Mrs Leeman; you're not being held here under any duress?'

Francesca shook her head. 'I'm fine, though I think we're all a bit shaken by Chris – Mr Pearce – turning up.'

The officer nodded again. 'Understandable, really, Mrs Leeman.' He turned to Alicia. 'So are you saying Mr Pearce broke in, Mrs Moffat?'

Alicia nodded. 'We haven't checked yet where exactly he got in. He burst into Francesca's bedroom and frightened everybody in the house. If it hadn't been for Catz, my chauffeur, goodness knows what might have happened.' She paused. 'He assaulted my other house guest, Mr Foxley.'

The policeman glanced at Gerald. 'And will you be

considering bringing charges against the gentleman?'

Alicia shook her head emphatically. 'No, no I don't think so. As Francesca said, I think Mr Pearce had had a little too much to drink, that's all.' She smiled. 'Would you like a drink, perhaps some tea or coffee whilst you're here, gentlemen?'

The officer shook his head. 'Nice of you to offer, Mrs Moffat, but we can't really stop.' He hesitated, glancing back at Francesca who was still sitting in one of the armchairs.

'If you're sure everything is all right here?'

Francesca nodded. 'Absolutely fine, officer. I'm sorry to have wasted your time.'

The policeman assured her she hadn't wasted their time and as they turned to leave, the first officer looked back over his shoulder.

'And if you do reconsider bringing charges against Mr Pearce, please let us know.'

Alicia waved her hands in resignation. 'A broken heart and a hot head – mixed with a few too many drinks – is a very dangerous combination.'

The man nodded and Catz showed them out.

After they had left Alicia sighed and looked at Francesca. Your friend Mr Pearce is rather emotional. I think the sooner we go down to London the better.'

Francesca drained her glass and stood up. 'I think you're right.'

# Chapter Ten

After the police had left, Francesca lay alone in her room thinking about Chris. Though the storm had passed the night was dark and starless. Sleep eluded her and in her mind she saw Chris's furious drunken face again and again; she pulled the covers up around her shoulders, trying to relax. In the silence she suddenly heard the click of the door of her bedroom opening; all thought of sleep vanished as she felt the hairs on the back of her neck prickle with fear.

'Who's that?' she whispered, frantically trying to find the bedside lamp.

'It's only me,' Melissa hissed. Relieved, Francesca snapped on the light; in the doorway the other woman grinned sheepishly at her.

'I couldn't sleep. I kept wondering if you were okay,' she said quietly, her voice trembling slightly.

Francesca smiled and turned back the covers. 'Come on,' she said, 'why don't you get in here. You frightened the life out of me.'

Melissa scurried across the floor and quickly slipped beneath the sheets. Turning off the light Francesca sank gratefully into the comforting warmth of the blonde woman's welcoming body.

'Are you all right?' whispered Melissa, slipping her arms around Francesca's waist.

'Yes, I'm fine now you're here,' she said, drawing the other woman closer and breathing in the reassuring scent of her soft body. Fleetingly their lips brushed as they snuggled together, warm and relaxed in the security of each other's arms. Sleep soon claimed them both.

The following day was a flurry of activity. Once they'd had breakfast work began with a vengeance to get the exhibits ready for Gerald's men to collect. No one mentioned the events of the night before, concentrating instead on packing, wrapping and labelling the artefacts from the gallery. The day seemed to be swallowed whole by the preparations. By late afternoon everything was arranged. Catz and Alicia stayed behind at the villa to lock up whilst the others followed the lorries back to London.

It was after dark when Gerald, driving Francesca and Melissa, pulled up in front of the Kensington house.

'Why don't you both come in for a nightcap?' Francesca suggested as she got out of the car.

Melissa followed close behind, pulling on her jacket. 'Sounds like a wonderful idea, though I'd rather have a coffee.'

Francesca looked back at Gerald sitting in the car. 'And how about you?'

He lifted his hands in mock surrender. 'All right, all right, but we can't stay long. I'm exhausted. We've got to make an early start tomorrow; the carriers should be here first thing in the morning.'

Francesca groaned. 'Gerald, you're a total spoilsport.' She turned the key and they stepped into the large dimly lit hall. Francesca turned on the central light and picked up a message the concierge had left by the phone.

'Alicia and Catz will be joining us later this evening, the dust sheets have been taken off the furniture in the sitting room and there's a cold buffet for us in the kitchen if we want it. Well, how about joining me for something to eat, you two? I am ravenous.'

Melissa grinned and nodded. 'Me too.'

Francesca led the way, through the house and downstairs into the kitchen, with Gerald trailing reluctantly behind.

Francesca got the food from the fridge and set the table with Melissa's help whilst Gerald opened up some wine and found three glasses. Far away from the events of the previous night, the party relaxed under the influence of food and a copious supply of wine.

By the time Alicia and Catz arrived, Melissa and Gerald had left and Francesca was curled up in the sitting room, with a magazine in an armchair, waiting for them. Hearing the door she hurried into the hall to be greeted by the familiar face of Catz – as cool and intimidating as ever – and Alicia wrapped in a fine wool coat. She waved Francesca back into the sitting room.

'Catz, we'd like a drink,' she snapped and followed Francesca. As she stepped into the room she sighed. 'It's so long since I've been here. Edgar and I used to use this as our main home at one time.'

Francesca smiled. 'I can understand why; it's a lovely place.'

Alicia sat down by the hearth. 'It seems very empty now. At one time the house was always full with friends, guests . . .' She hesitated, memories of their faces and long-forgotten voices suddenly flooding back. 'I think I prefer the villa now; it's much cosier. I've made it my home. We lived here when we were first married; it's too full of memories.' She stroked the deep leather of the chair and smiled.

'I was so nervous when I first arrived here. Edgar was sophisticated, so worldly-wise and I was afraid that I would disappoint him, though of course I soon realised it was my innocence and youth that attracted him so desperately. We travelled back here after our wedding reception, intending to travel to Paris for our honeymoon the next day.

'I remember the house was deserted and in this room there was a glowing coal fire and everywhere was lit with tiny candles set in crystal globes. It looked magical, like some strange version of Christmas. I was suddenly very, very nervous; all I could do was shiver. Edgar poured me a glass of champagne and brought me close to the fire. I'd already had several at the reception and it made me feel quite heady.

'As I stood here I realised I barely knew the man I'd married; since our engagement I had never been alone with him. My father was widowed; he was a friend of Edgar's and always insisted that either my aunt or one of my older sisters stayed with us when Edgar visited.

'It seems strange now but I had hardly spoken a word to the man I had just sworn to live with for ever. I had no idea what to expect from a man, particularly from a husband. My mother died when I was quite young. Anyway, I crept closer to the fire and he told me how beautiful I looked. I blushed furiously during his undisguised examination of his new toy. He refilled my glass and asked me if I thought I could grow to love him.'

Alicia smiled gently. 'I decided that perhaps I could, and he told me that he would never hurt me and would teach me things that would set me free from every constraint. I would be his fellow adventurer, and suddenly – I think it must have been the effect of the champagne – I felt very grown up, a grown-up married woman loved by this intimidating sophisticated man who could have chosen anyone to be his wife.

'He came closer and brushed his lips against mine, softly, the lightest and most delicate of kisses. I can remember it made him shiver; such a gentle persuasive beginning to our life together. He lifted his hand to the fastening of my dress and undid it. My fear returned, but all the time he whispered words of reassurance; his voice was very low and hypnotic. I didn't resist his fingers as they undid the buttons and my delightful little wedding dress slipped to the floor on the rug. I blushed at the exposure.

'I remember beneath my chemise I was wearing a cream silk camisole top and camiknickers, with white stockings rolled up to just above my knees. He stepped back and let his dark eyes move down over my body, drinking me in. His eyes sparkled in the candlelight – now I know it was desire – then I thought it was magical, as if his love for me had transformed his eyes into jewels.

'He asked me to untie my hair; it was still tied up in my headdress. I slipped off my veil and shook it down over my shoulders. He moved closer, letting his lips press against it, breathing me in, running his fingers through it. He murmured my name again and again and then he tipped my head back and began to kiss me. His lips were gentle, brushing, as they sought mine. I'd never been kissed by a man before and somewhere deep inside I could feel this strange alien little tremor of excitement. It felt like a tiny brilliant light in the pit of my stomach.

'I gasped and would have pulled back, afraid of the intensity of its glow, except that he held me closer, gently encircling me in his arms. His tongue slid between the tiniest of openings between my lips as his hands glided to the shoulders of my chemise. His touch was so slow, so smooth; as if nothing Edgar did could ever go wrong, nothing could ever be confusing or frightening whilst I was with him. I leant against his tall strong body relishing in the new sensations, though still with the flicker of fear in my belly, and now being drawn ever closer to totally surrendering to his persuasive gentle touch.

'He slowly sank to his knees and lifted the hem on my chemise. In my mind it was rather like watching myself from a distance; the champagne had relaxed me but it was his hypnotic touch that persuaded me. He slipped the silken fabric upwards, brushing the slim outline of my legs, kissing my knees until he pushed the fabric over my hips, lingering for an instant as his face passed my sex. He moved forwards and pressed his lips against it through the thick fabric of my drawers. I gasped but by then he was standing up and carefully lifting the chemise over my head. I knew I was blushing but his soft kisses along my shoulders and neck persuaded me that I was only complying with his wishes, doing what every good wife should do – permitting her husband a free rein over her body. He turned me round to face this mirror; in the reflection I could see him standing behind me, his eyes bright and dark. I could barely recognise my own reflection, my eyes glowed with the same intense fire as his, whilst beneath the thin fabric of my camisole I could see the soft curves of my tiny breasts tipped with little hard pink buds.

'As he kissed my neck he whispered that I was perfect – beautiful – that he would love me for ever and at that moment I believed him totally. His hands lifted to the straps of my camisole, slipping it down my shoulders. I gaped at my nakedness and the electrifying sensation as his hands lifted to scoop up the little swelling peaks of my breasts. He moved around me, his kisses more eager now – wetter, hotter, more intense – and he sucked my nipples into his waiting mouth.

'The sensation made me whimper and I stood unresisting as, above his bobbing dark head, I watched the mesmerising reflection unfolding before me. His hands moved lower as his tongue trailed back and forth between the little conical lifts of my teats. I couldn't resist him; part of me was afraid to deny him but another part wanted that magical gift he was offering me.

'Outside my drawers Edgar cupped my virginal sex, one finger very gently parting the lips through the fabric. I threw back my head at the indignity and the electric thrill of his touch.

'I had no words then to describe what it was he was making me feel. The intense sensations stood alone, described only by the feelings they invoked in me.

'My breath came out in a sharp desperate hiss. Now he knelt again, this time his hands lifting to the waistband of my drawers. Slowly he began to slide them down over my narrow hips and I was powerless to resist him. He whispered soft words of endearment, mouthing my name as he lowered them to the floor.

'In the instant that they whispered on to the carpet below I had this most desperate sense of panic. I was so exposed, so vulnerable, and suddenly terrified. Edgar looked up at me as if sensing my fear. I began to shiver and the heady effects of the champagne seemed to vanish instantly.

'He stood up and said softly, "Trust me, Alicia; trust

me and I will give you everything you ever dreamt of. I will show you paradise."

'I could feel myself blushing, the pulse beating in my ears. He lifted a finger to my throat, tracing the throbbing pulse, and then he turned to look in the mirror. I remember I looked like some wild little forest thing, with this great tangle of waving hair still scattered with orange blossom, my eyes dark with fear and excitement and a tiny smooth girl-like body.

'I could see Edgar's eyes moving over me and despite my inexperience could see the excitement and pleasure that seeing my naked body was giving him. He smiled as if I had caught him out and then he led me to a great armchair that was standing in front of the hearth and was reflected in the tilted mirror above us.

'His voice was even and calm when he spoke.

'He said, "Trust me to tell you what to do. I will never betray you."

'I nodded, afraid to speak.

'"Sit down on the chair." I complied wordlessly. In the mirror my eyes seemed darker, glints of golden candlelight shimmering through them.

'"Lift your legs," he whispered.

'I began to lift them together and Edgar shook his head, his face tight with emotion.

'"No, open them. Here, let me help you," he murmured. His fingers slipped under the crease of my knees and he parted my legs and lay one over each arm of the chair. I was absolutely horrified and felt myself flush crimson at the exposure. Awkwardly I began to wriggle forwards to try and get down, of course in I doing so exposing myself more. Edgar's eyes quietened me.

'"You are exquisite," he whispered. "Don't be afraid. I only want to admire my beautiful, beautiful wife."

'I could feel myself colouring even more; a thin sweat had broken out on my face under his undisguised examination of my naked, exposed body. His eyes moved down across my face, slowly taking in my tiny breasts, and then finally lower until his gaze lingered on the untouched virginal mound of my sex, its lips now gently parted as my stockinged legs straddled the chair.

'He whimpered and knelt before me, eyes alive; dark jewelled pools of desire and longing. Now without hesitation he kissed my mouth more firmly and in spite of my exposure and fear I found myself starting, reluctantly at first, to kiss him back. My mouth opened under the fierce exploration of his tongue and instinctively my hips thrust forward.

'I was so shocked at my body's instinctive reaction I almost pulled away from his kisses. His hands lifted to cup my breasts, brushing their tiny pink buds between his knowing fingers. I heard myself moan and then gasped as I felt his fingers moving lower. They brushed against the fine hair of my outer lips – a tentative touch – the lightest of caresses and I knew then I would give him anything he desired from me.

'The heat had begun to build in my belly. His tongue slipped lower, brushing my nipples, sucking them in and, below, my pelvis tilted up towards his caresses. He moved lower, blowing tiny tight kisses across my smooth stomach, and then the tip of his tongue found the secret place I never knew existed until that moment.

'His first fleeting kiss of my clitoris nearly took me to the edge of paradise he had promised me. I locked my hands in his sparse hair and lifted myself up to him, all nervousness, all coyness suddenly abandoned in my need to experience the sensations he was offering me. His tongue circled again and again and now one finger slipped lower, sliding very gently, very tentatively, between the swollen lower lips of my sex.

'The sensations of fear and desire seemed to grow alongside each other. He seemed to be opening me up; I knew I was wet, the mixture of his saliva and my burgeoning excitement was almost too much. I heard Edgar groan with pleasure as his finger slid inside. The feelings made me gasp and then I saw his hand drop to his flies. Now the fear returned; the intense spiralling heights of desire that had pressed so close and so compelling fled in their wake as he undid the buttons of his trousers. My eyes were locked on the growing opening beneath his fingers and I can remember clearly gasping with horror as he produced this huge curved object from the darkness of his crotch. I shuddered, eyes wide.

'Then he looked up at me; the same gentle loving expression was there, suffused by desire but still gentle, still benign. I'm sure my fear excited him but he disguised it well. I tried to back away from him as he knelt closer, the engorged head of his shaft moving slowly towards me. He smiled and one hand lifted to brush at my clitoris. I was lost; his other hand delicately parted the lips of my sex and he gently moved inside me. There was a sensation of hot resistance to his assault and from deep inside I felt a desperate hot pain and cried out, closing my eyes against the conflict of pain and pleasure that his body was bringing me.

'As the pain abated, and with the resistance gone, I felt him move deeper into the tight untouched sanctuary of my body. When I opened my eyes he was smiling down at me as if breaking through my hymen and the scream of pain had given him the greatest pleasure. Now he began to move against me, slowly at first, his fingers circling my dark hardened bud more intensely. I lifted instinctively to meet his stroke, moving rhythmically against his touch while desperately trying to accommodate his great phallus into the tight arch of my sex.

'He moaned and grabbed at my hips, pulling me down in the chair under the weight of his body. I slid compliantly under him, lifting my hips again and again in search of the sensation his body and his touch promised me.

'The first spasm hit me like a lightning strike; I bucked, so terrified of what I was feeling I almost tried to fight against it.

'Edgar whispered, "It's all right, all right," and in my growing excitement pressed himself home into me. The tightness of my body around him made me gasp, and I was lost as the spasms of paradise tore through me. I bucked on to Edgar's cock, impaling my sore tight little body on him again and again, desperate to catch hold of that instant, that heat for which there is no substitute. At the top of the arc I opened my eyes and saw him staring at me, his face tight with desire, and then he closed his eyes and joined me in the great surging wave of our mutual pleasure.'

Alicia looked up suddenly, almost as if she were waking from a dream. She glanced at Francesca and smiled sleepily. 'I'm so sorry,' she murmured softly, 'I do hope I didn't bore you with my reminiscences.'

Francesca, her face flushed, looked round the room and shook her head. 'No, no. It was beautiful,' she stammered. She paused, trying to compose herself, and then glanced back at Alicia who was looking into the empty hearth, as if her mind had already returned to the years long passed.

The next morning the first of the exhibits from the villa arrived early and within a few hours the whole of the ground floor of the house was transformed into a marshalling yard. Packages and crates were unloaded through most of the morning and the whole place was full of strange voices and strange men carrying things upstairs, into the gallery. After a little while Alicia excused herself and she and Catz left in the Daimler.

Melissa had packed all Edgar's records for the villa collection and so the job of cataloguing and sorting the pieces was relatively simple.

Melissa and Gerald stayed for dinner but it was a

quiet informal affair; the next day work would begin in earnest to transform the upstairs gallery into a viewing room.

One long tiring day stretched into another. Alicia let Gerald build bays upstairs in the gallery so that the collection could be divided into small groups for viewing. Upstairs the room was rapidly being transformed. Melissa and Francesca worked side by side to complete the listings and photography; under the prying eyes of the workmen there was little opportunity for the two women to enjoy the exploration of the artefacts or each other's bodies.

Finally the gallery was completed; illuminated booths lined one wall, each one containing grouped exhibits with a linked theme. The effect was eye-catching, and gave potential buyers a chance to examine the lots in privacy. When the gallery was complete, Melissa and Gerald left to make contact with the foreign buyers who were flying in for the viewing and the sale.

Alicia walked along the hall with Francesca to admire the finished effect. The mirror that lined the other long wall reflected the wealth of exhibits; the sum of one man's lifetime of collecting.

Alicia glanced at the mirror and smiled mischievously. 'Edgar would have loved all these little booths. They would have encouraged people to experiment; he would have relished that. Come, let me show you something.'

She took Francesca into the small office off the main gallery. It was untidy now, littered with cartons and stacks of packaging. Behind the tangle of debris Francesca spotted a familiar mesh grid.

'A door?' she whispered.

Alicia smiled. 'Of course. Edgar couldn't have coped with the idea of people visiting his gallery without an opportunity to watch them.'

She lifted the hidden catch. Inside was a comfortable room lined with padded benches and a few armchairs. Without the two-way mirror on the far wall it could easily have been mistaken for the sitting room of a gentlemen's club.

This will be an ideal spot for you and I to oversee the viewers,' she said. 'There's another door in the far end that leads back down into the main house. Perhaps I can convert you to the pleasures of voyeurism.'

Francesca shook her head. 'I don't think so.'

Alicia shrugged. 'I suggest, my dear, that you experience it before you dismiss it so easily. It's a heady addiction, one that sustained first Edgar and now myself. Believe me, it is not without its pleasures. The nature of freedom is to understand your needs and your limitations.'

They ate lunch together in the grand dining room on the ground floor. For the first time Francesca was aware that beneath the elegant exterior of Alicia Moffat there was something more vulnerable, something older and more fragile than the image she chose to project. In repose her beautiful face showed traces of the maturity she was so careful to conceal. Feeling herself under surveillance, Alicia swung round sharply and narrowed her eyes.

'Didn't your mother ever tell you that staring was rude?'

Francesca felt herself blush self-consciously. 'I'm sorry,' she stammered, 'I didn't mean to—'

Alicia held up a hand to quieten her and then laughed. 'It's all right. I'm sure in your position I would do the same.' She continued with a sly smile, 'Though I think I would be more circumspect in the way I did it. Selling this collection is a landmark occasion for me, one that I have contemplated for many years; it truly is the end of an era.' She sighed and picked up her fork. On her plate the meal Catz had prepared lay almost untouched.

'I know!' she said suddenly, her eyes alight with a mischief and youthful sparkle. 'We'll have a party, something to mark the end of this phase of my life, one final wonderful exhilarating burst of life, a firework burst – a crescendo.'

Francesca smiled. 'That sounds like a wonderful idea.'

Alicia got up and rang for Catz.

Francesca had never seen a party arranged on the scale that Alicia planned for what she referred to as her 'farewell performance'. The party was set for the night before the auction.

Despite a steady trickle of viewers and visitors to the gallery above, they arranged and oversaw the transformation of the first floors of the London mansion into a glittering elegant backdrop for Alicia's party. Every room had been dressed with tumbling concoctions of flowers, ribbons, balloons and candles. Mirrors glittered, crystals in the chandeliers and mantel ornaments split the light from the candles into rainbows, giving the whole house a magical jewel-like quality. On the lawn Alicia had arranged for a marquee with a live dance band for the more energetic party goers, and one of the back rooms had been converted into a casino, complete with croupiers, gaming tables and roulette wheel.

As Francesca walked through the house before the guests arrived, she realised this was just a small taste of the exciting, heady life Alicia had always been privy to. She went upstairs to change into the new evening gown she'd bought for the occasion.

She felt like a child before Christmas; the dress was a delicate confection of silver and blue fabric as thin as tissue-paper and cut like a dream. She had folded her hair back into a smooth pleat and, to complement her outfit, Alicia had loaned her a pair of diamond earrings and matching necklace. Francesca turned slowly in front of the mirror and smiled delightedly at her reflection. She looked and felt wonderful.

She met Alicia on the stairs. The older woman smiled at her appreciatively. You look simply gorgeous, my dear. I shall have to make sure you're not overwhelmed by offers of marriage.'

Francesca laughed and accompanied Alicia into the dining room for a pre-party glass of champagne. To her surprise Catz was standing by the window looking out over into the street beyond. He turned as they entered and Francesca couldn't contain a gasp of excitement at his presence. Alicia smiled and turned to take a glass of champagne from the waiter.

'I thought,' she said softly, 'as you hadn't got a partner for this evening you might join Catz. I hope you don't object too much. I'm afraid I will be rather caught up with playing the perfect hostess.' Francesca was speechless. Catz looked beautiful in his perfectly fitting dinner-jacket. He extended his arm and gracefully Francesca took it. He retrieved a glass of champagne from the tray for her, his eyes moving across her body. She felt herself flush.

'You look beautiful,' he said under his breath as they glided out into the hall.

Melissa and Gerald were amongst the first guests to arrive, each bringing with them one of the foreign buyers. From the dining room liveried footmen were serving champagne, whilst on the first-floor landing beneath the glitter of the chandelier a string quartet filled the house with music. Alicia glided like a stately goddess between groups of guests whilst, almost overwhelmed, Francesca moved around the house on Catz's arm to be introduced to famous and not so famous faces. Many of the guests were from Alicia and Edgar's past; some were potential buyers and all knew full well the nature of the collection in the long gallery above them.

Catz was a perfect and attentive partner, but he couldn't quite disguise the passion in his eyes as he moved around the groups of guests with her. As he squired her towards the bar his hand lingered a little

too long on the small of her back. The heat of his touch
made her quiver with expectation.

By late evening the house was alive with laughter, music
and the press of beautiful, elegant people having fun.
The crowd had thinned a little, leaving only the inner
circle of connoisseurs and their guests. Gerald was
standing under the stairs, deep in conversation with
Janic, the buyer from Germany. Catz pointed them out
and Francesca gasped. Gerald seemed transformed by
his friend's presence; in the shadows he moved with
ease, laughing and smiling. She looked up at Catz who
smiled mysteriously.

'The true nature of a man in love,' he whispered
playfully and took her arm.

In the subdued light of the casino they came across
Melissa who was playing *chemin de fer* in the company
of a large American businesswoman.

Catz guided her away from the tables and out into the
starlight. Behind them, from the marquee, they could
hear the soft strains of the dance band. He touched her
under the chin, tipping her head up towards him; she
instantly responded to him as his lips brushed against
hers.

'Later,' he whispered as she pressed her body to him.

They walked across the lawn towards the sound
of the music. Catz went to fetch them a drink while
Francesca found them a seat at a table on the edge of the
dance floor. A few seconds later Alicia appeared from
amongst a group of guests and made her way towards

Francesca. She smiled conspiratorially, her eyes alight. 'Time, I think, to retire to the peace and quiet of the gallery, my dear.'

Francesca glanced across at Catz at the bar. He nodded and lifted his glass in salute.

'Later,' he mouthed silently and took a sip from his drink.

Alicia turned to Francesca. 'You make a lovely couple. Now, are you going to come with me upstairs and partake in my own preferred diversion?'

Dumbly Francesca nodded, though her eyes were still following Catz as he moved between the party goers.

The back of the house seemed still and cool in comparison to the revels going on in the public rooms. Alicia led Francesca through the kitchen and up the back stairs to the gallery beyond. At the door Alicia hesitated and lifted her finger to her lips. 'Not too much noise when we're inside. I'm never sure how much noise carries from in here.'

Inside, the hidden room was suffused with a delicate mellow light cast from the gallery beyond the glass. Francesca was beginning to feel the effects of the champagne and tried desperately to control the heady sensations that bubbled up inside her.

In the booth furthest away from the door Gerald and his friend Janic were huddled over a display case. It didn't seem to occur to either of them that their liaison might be overlooked. They moved against each other tenderly, old friends, familiar with each other's needs and desires. There was something sensual and engaging in their easy familiarity.

The German lifted a thin, tooled leather whip from the wall; his gestures betrayed his excitement. Gerald moved closer and ran an appreciative finger over the thin end of the cruel instrument, his eyes moving back and forth along its length. Francesca recognised the glittering lights of arousal as he gave the whip a few gentle flicks as if getting the measure of it. Janic bent closer, whispering something into the auctioneer's ear. Francesca strained to make out the words but instead detected the slightest shiver of Gerald's shoulders as he turned and smiled at his guest.

Gerald's hands lifted to his bow-tie and Janic copied. Alicia touched her arm.

'Let's move along a little,' she purred. 'I would like to see what Gerald is capable of when he's in his element.'

But Francesca's eye had been caught by the shadow of two figures moving at the gallery door. Melissa was leading her new American friend into the first booth. The two blonde women froze for a moment when they realised the gallery was not empty. Francesca recognised the delicate flush of excitement over the shoulders and face of her lover, and knew that Melissa wouldn't be deterred by Gerald's presence. She turned now to the American woman and for an instant they faced each other.

Francesca gasped as the American woman leant forward, pulling Melissa to her, her lips aggressive and insistent. Melissa responded in kind, her mouth pressing hard in response. The American woman's hands slid to the neck of her own evening dress and undid the heavy draped neck; she pushed it down and the dress slithered to the floor, revealing a tight leather body suit beneath. Tailored to accentuate her heavy rounded body, it was studded and cut high on the thigh to show her shapely suntanned legs to their best advantage. The effect was both brutal and erotic.

Melissa shuddered and froze for an instant; the American woman said something, her painted lips curled into an aggressive sneer. Melissa stepped back, her face betraying a subtle mixture of fear and passion. Francesca knew this was the intoxicating heady mix she had experienced with Catz – a dark desire that fought against every fibre of your normal self and yet still compelled you to go on.

The American woman looked glorious, her diamonds and elegantly painted face a stunning contrast to the tight darkness of her body. She lifted a hand to Melissa's face, her long fingers stroking under Melissa's chin. Behind the glass Francesca held her breath as her friend stared into the dark pools of the American woman's eyes. There was a second when their eyes were locked and then Melissa let her tongue run along the woman's fingers and closed her eyes.

The American woman slid her hands down over Melissa's shoulders and firmly pushed her to her knees. Melissa sank slowly as the American woman's hands moved to the fastening of her own leather suit. Her hand slid provocatively between her legs and removed the panel that cradled her sex. Francesca felt herself flush; beneath the flap the woman's sex was shaved and two large gold rings pierced her outer labia. Mesmerised she watched as her friend leant forward, running her tongue over the smooth mound, unable to control a little shudder as her tongue discovered the American's slick nakedness and the heavy curve of the rings.

She turned back to Alicia but the older woman was watching the scene unfolding in the far booth. Francesca moved closer to her and gasped. Gerald was naked – hanging in the centre of the booth – both hands secured above his head in wrist-cuffs. Behind him Janic was gently moving the whip to and fro in preparation for his first blow. Francesca swallowed hard as she remembered her own introduction to the delightful kiss of the whip under Catz's tuition. The head of the whip lifted and tore a great arc through the air. Gerald bucked and even the thick glass couldn't muffle the ear-splitting shriek as the whip bit home. Gerald swung on the restraints, his face contorted, breathing hard as the whip cracked again. Janic moved closer, his hands travelling over Gerald's naked, exposed body. Francesca could see the livid red weals lifting on Gerald's buttocks as the German dropped his hand and cracked the whip again. Gerald spun wildly against his restraints, not able to disguise the arcing mass of his erection as the whip bit home again and again. Janic circled him now, his eyes narrow, face reddening with excitement and effort. Below, in the sparse greying hair at his crotch, a meaty phallus jutted forward, exposing his own desire.

Gerald opened his eyes, his face tense but his eyes alight with need. His companion smiled at him and moved closer, his thick cock brushing the back of Gerald's legs. The auctioneer's lips opened and behind the glass Francesca knew he was moaning with expectation. His tormentor gently cupped Gerald's genitals, his fingers moving tenderly along the tight throbbing shaft of his captive. His finger moved lower to trace the delicate swell of his balls and the sensitive skin behind. Gerald wriggled back against him. His guest smiled, resting his face against the narrow muscles of Gerald's back. He let the whip slip to the floor and slid his fingers between Gerald's buttocks. The auctioneer thrust back into his touch, opening himself. His guest did not deny him; instead he inserted the thick bulk of his phallus between the slim curves of Gerald's buttocks and gently pushed himself home. Gerald's expression was ecstatic. Janic's fingers circled his bound lover and grasped Gerald's cock firmly. In harmony now, the two men began to move against one another, their cries of pleasure muffled by the thick glass. Francesca was captivated; she couldn't tear her eyes away from the swaying, thrusting movements of the men as they struggled closer and closer to their climax.

Gerald's head was thrown back, his eyes tightly closed as he chased harder and harder towards the point of release. Behind him his companion was slick with sweat. Francesca realised that she was moving with them, her hips mirroring theirs. The realisation made her blush;

their pleasure, their desire, was overwhelming. Between her legs she could feel the intensity of their thrustings, her excitement growing – the fact startled her. It seemed as if she was there with them, could feel the heat of their bodies, the tight dark sensation as the buyer pushed home into the dark forbidden closure of Gerald's body. She swallowed, trying to regain her composure and, glancing away for an instant, caught sight of the bright violet lights in Alicia's eyes.

From the corner of her eye she could see the American woman in her leather suit thrusting back and forth against Melissa's stroking, searching tongue. She shuddered.

As a silent unseen observer she could watch it all, drink in every sweet sensation by proxy. The intensity of the others' mounting excitement crashed through her. The contrast of the women's bodies – their warmth and soft curves – to the harder sleek lines of the men was electric. She gasped and turned away, straight into the arms of Catz. He looked down at her, his eyes jewel-like and compelling.

'I didn't hear you come in,' she stammered, her colour rising.

He smiled at her and extended his hand. She took it and he led her back through the viewing room to the small door into the office.

In the gallery they walked by Gerald and his friend, who were oblivious to their passing. Catz stopped in the centre of the gallery and turned towards her. 'Stay here,' he whispered.

He moved across to one of the booths and switched on a light. In the centre was a large leather table. Catz glanced back at her. His features were as unreadable as ever, but above, his eyes were alight with mischief and desire. He lunged towards her – she laughed and squealed – he grabbed her shoulders and pulled her roughly towards him. Eagerly she stretched up to press her lips to his; they were hard, almost cold, and for a split second she wondered if this was part of the game. She wriggled away from him and he grabbed her wrists. She turned, bucking and pulling, to slip away from him and in return he held her closer, his hands moving to the outline of her breasts through the glittering tissue of her dress. She felt her nipples harden, felt the stirring between her legs, the beginnings of a trickle of moisture.

She spun away from him and his fingers grabbed at the fastening, slipping the catch. He dragged her to him and caught hold of the neckline. He slipped it down gently; the dress slid to the floor in a crumpled heap. Beneath she was wearing the briefest of soft bras and a tiny G-string. Catz let his eyes move across her body.

'I want you,' he murmured softly. She shuddered, his words electrifying every nerve ending. She stepped towards him and lifted her lips to his face. 'Not good enough,' she whispered throatily. 'Say it louder.'

Catz's fingers lifted to the tight dark buds of her nipples; they traced the outline, barely grazing the sensitive area. She gasped.

'I want you,' he said, and his emotions seemed

suddenly to close off to her, as if he had slipped behind a mask. For an instant it was almost as if he were a stranger. She shuddered and let him take her hand.

He led her to the table and lay her back on to the cool leather covering. He leant closer; his eyes had hardened to icy pinpricks of light. Walking around the couch he took her wrists and strapped them above her head, his lips lingering on the exposed and sensitive curve of her armpit, his tongue tracing the bowl with tantalising delicacy. She felt the familiar flutter of panic in her belly and welcomed its wash through her, accepting the trembling heady anticipation that came with it.

He surveyed her body, then his hands lifted to her breasts again and ripped away the soft curve of her bra. In spite of her compliance and desire she shrieked as the fabric bit into her flesh. He smiled thinly and moved lower to secure her legs. She fought against him, her body instinctively demanding that she be free. She felt the sweat break out on her face. He ignored her writhing and coldly grabbed her ankles, snapping them into the cold metal rings. The distinctive noise brought back intense memories of the first afternoon in the gallery.

Suddenly she felt vulnerable, her legs locked apart, her sex thrusting up towards him. He stood back to admire his handiwork, his eyes holding hers in a hypnotic predatory stare. She whimpered as he bent forward. His hands lifted to something below the table's padded surface and she gasped as the tabletop moved. Her legs slowly dropped down either side of the flat surface, leaving her hips and buttocks barely supported and her mound totally exposed.

His fingers moved across to the brief triangle of fabric that covered the dark hair of her outer lips; between her legs a single narrow strap held it in place. He let his fingers tease beneath it, lightly brushing her hair; in spite of the restraint, her hips lifted to meet his touch. He gathered up the fabric and pulled it tight so it slid up between the delicate lips of her sex and opened the damp fragrant inner folds; the material bit home. He leant closer; she could feel his breath on her body as his lips moved down, sucking in her breasts, trickling saliva down over her belly. She gasped and began to struggle under his touch.

His moist enticing lips pressed against the fabric of her G-string, breathing her in, heating her; she closed her eyes and drank in every sensation. Something lightly brushed the side of her face. Her eyes instantly snapped open and she looked straight into the deep pools of Melissa's dark, blue eyes. The blonde woman smiled sleepily and let her hands move to Francesca's breasts, still damp from Catz's kisses.

'Let me help you,' she murmured and climbed smoothly on to the table.

Francesca groaned as Melissa pushed herself up on to all fours, lowering her sex slowly towards her mouth. Above her, Francesca could smell the heady exotic perfume of Melissa's excitement and the brush of her breasts on her thighs as Melissa sought out a comfortable position. As Melissa lowered her sex within reach, Catz renewed his attentions to Francesca's sex, his tongue wetting the thin fabric, his fingers pushing aside the strap so he could slip inside her.

From within the viewing room Alicia moved closer to the glass. The new exhibit was stunning. Melissa was propped above Francesca, whose tongue was beginning a tentative exploration of the blonde woman's sex. Between her legs Catz was pulling aside the tiny silvery triangle that hid Francesca's mound, his tongue pressing against the gathered fabric, his fingers sliding deeper inside. Catz stepped back for a second and Melissa eagerly took over his ministrations to Francesca's eager straining body. Catz slipped off his evening clothes. His nakedness was delicious, the soft glow from the gallery lamps highlighting the firm musculature of his physique. Alicia was captivated.

Catz stepped towards the table; his fingers slipped past Melissa's tongue and grabbed the thin fabric of Francesca's knickers. Using his fingers, the fabric split easily to reveal the dark wet hair beneath. Melissa licked more frantically and beneath her intense kisses he slipped the smooth curve of his phallus between Francesca's outer lips. The dark woman lifted her hips, opening eagerly for him. He slid gently into her and with one fluid stroke was buried entirely. As he began to move slowly in and out Melissa renewed her attentions, her tongue moving smoothly between the hard dark bud of Francesca's clitoris and the smooth shaft of Catz's throbbing cock.

Around them in the soft light, several of the party

goers had gravitated to the gallery. From amongst the crowd the leather-clad American woman moved closer to the table. Her eyes were alight; she ran a proprietorial hand over Melissa's smooth buttocks. Melissa instinctively lowered her hips, her soft pink inner lips exposed and damp. The American woman slid one long painted finger into the damp inviting orifice.

Beneath Melissa and Catz, Francesca felt as if she would drown under the intensity of their attentions. Between her legs Catz's cock was buried to the hilt; her muscles grabbed at him, pulling him further and further into her. Above the hard probing bulk of his phallus she could feel the tight intense circles of Melissa's tongue, probing, nibbling, kissing against her clitoris, whilst over her belly she felt the electric brush of Melissa's heavy breasts. Above her was the trembling sweating outline of Melissa's thighs; her tongue had begun its spiral assault on Melissa's clitoris and the blonde woman's intense flavour flooded through her mouth.

As she moved back to caress the swollen inner lips, she met the hard, stiff chill of the American woman's fingers. She gasped and then lapped at them as they slid in and out, before moving back to the hard ridge of Melissa's clitoris.

It felt as if every nerve was alive and light; her senses reeled as Catz began to brush the rise of his belly against her. Melissa's tongue was like a red-hot torch bringing her ever closer to the moment when all would be lost. She felt the throb of her excitement growing beneath Melissa's tongue; a soft intense wave of white fire, it rippled and rose, suddenly spirally out from the tiny bud. Instinctively she bucked to meet their touch; Catz seemed to slip further into her. Struggling against her restraints she tried to rise again, forcing her hips upwards to meet their attentions. The white waves crashed through her, she let out a desperate strangled moan as Melissa dropped her body lower, signalling the first ripples of her own orgasm swamping her.

Melissa's tongue slipped away but Catz pressed again, his body lifting to take over from the blonde woman's tongue. Francesca could now feel the borders of pain as her orgasm reached its first peak. She thrust again, determined to ride on and out into the magical place beyond that Catz had shown her.

He bucked against her, his cock filling every aching fold. She heard herself scream against the delicate tight folds of Melissa's body and the press of the American woman's fingers. And then it was there; the golden throbbing intense sensations, tearing through her, ripping into the dark recesses of her mind, a great searing white light that seemed to go on and on and on, driving her to the fringes of unconsciousness. Her body screamed out in complaint as the tight straps bit into her wrists and ankles but the pain seemed abstract, distant, a faraway chill against the startling aurora of ecstasy.

She felt Melissa slip from the table and shuddered at the sudden coldness. In the seconds when she truly believed that there could be no more she suddenly felt the electric contractions of Catz's orgasm deep inside her; she moaned, writhing back and forth against the restraints as he pressed further into her.

Her body seized him, dragging him in, sucking him dry of every last magical drop of his essence. As he collapsed forward on to her sweating and exhausted body she heard a spontaneous burst of applause and, opening her eyes, she was astounded to find the table was surrounded by a crowd of the party goers. She felt a great flush of embarrassment flooding through her, which momentarily suppressed any last flutters of her ecstasy. From the corner of her eye she saw Alicia approaching the table, clapping furiously, and she closed her eyes as the older woman began to undo the leather straps at her wrists.

She lay for a few seconds when her bonds were released, relishing the weight and the heat of Catz's naked body against hers. Slowly he peeled himself away from her, his eyes two exhausted blue flames. He smiled and offered her his hand. Shakily she took it and, rising to her feet, joined him in a bow before Alicia wrapped her in the warm folds of a dressing-gown.

# Chapter Eleven

Alicia watched silently from her bedroom window as the first of the buyers arrived; taxis and chauffeured cars pulled up outside the house in a steady stream. Calmly she sipped her tea, ignoring the low hum of voices from the hall below. She had arranged with Gerald for ushers and caterers to cover the practicalities of the auction. Amongst the bidders she had spotted many familiar faces; friends, acquaintances and fellow adventurers from the days when she and Edgar had travelled the world. She stood the cup down on the sideboard; around her in the room were several large trunks in which Catz had packed Edgar's diaries for storage. There was nothing left for her to do. She touched the bell by the fireplace and then walked back to the window; outside the sun was shining brightly.

Catz crossed the landing and knocked on Francesca's door. She opened it and smiled. On the bed were her clothes, folded and ready for packing.

'Come in,' she said softly, pulling her dressing-gown more tightly around her. 'I heard everyone arriving. It looks as if there's going to be a good turnout; Gerald will be delighted.' She glanced at the clock by the bed.

'Not long now before they start. I was just going to get changed.'

'Alicia has asked me to invite you on a picnic.'

'A picnic? But I thought she'd want to be here to see the sale.'

Catz moved closer to the bed and picked up a thin blue scarf; his fingers lingered over the delicate fabric.

'No, she says it's too painful. She'd prefer to go to the park whilst the auction is going on,' he said, glancing across at her.

She could feel his interest stirring. She smiled; his brooding looks held no fear for her now, only the tantalising promise of things to come. Despite their knowledge of each other's bodies she still couldn't control the little flutter of anticipation in her belly. She took the scarf from him, brushing her body provocatively against his fingertips.

'I understand,' she said slowly, her eyes on his. 'Tell her I'd love to. Can you give me a few minutes to get ready?'

Catz nodded. 'We'll be leaving in fifteen minutes.'

She leant closer and lifted her face to his; momentarily their lips touched and she shivered at the sensations his nearness gave her. His hand lifted to her cheek, fingers cool and entrancing. She moaned and leant against him, drinking in the warmth of his body and the heady smell of cologne. His lips lingered for an instant, his tongue stroking along the line of her lips; then he pulled away, eyes alight with an intense longing.

'I have to go and help Alicia,' he purred.

She nodded and stepped away from him, the blue scarf fluttering to the ground between them.

Kensington Gardens was alive with walkers, joggers and families drinking in the heat of the summer sun. Alicia walked slowly along the meandering paths, arm in arm with Francesca, whilst behind them Catz walked to one side carrying the picnic basket and a rug. The sun was hot, the sound of the city only a distant hum.

Alicia stopped by a little stand of trees, Catz spread out the rug and the three of them sat down in the shade.

Alicia's expression had been closed since they'd arrived at the park; she seemed to be almost in a different world, her thoughts caught up in the past and the events in the London gallery. Finally she turned to Francesca and smiled; the effect was dazzling. 'I'm sorry,' she said softly, stretching as if waking from sleep. 'I'm afraid I'm not very good company today. I couldn't stay in the house to see the collection go under the hammer. I do want it sold but . . .' She hesitated. 'But I'd rather let its passing go unobserved.'

Francesca nodded. 'It's all right,' she said gently. 'I do understand. And when the collection is gone . . .' She paused and looked back at Alicia. 'I think it would be better if I went too.'

'Are you sure that's what you want?'

Francesca shook her head. 'No, I'm not sure at all,

but for the first time in my life I'm looking forward to the adventure of it. I'm free . . .'

Alicia smiled and then glanced at Catz who also seemed to be wrapped up in his own thoughts. She waved her hand at him. 'Catz, will you stop daydreaming. Let's open that damned hamper and have a drink. Did you bring the Bollinger?'

Catz nodded.

Alicia smiled conspiratorially. 'Wonderful. Champagne is the ideal cure for maudlin thoughts; let's crack a bottle and indulge ourselves whilst Gerald and Melissa earn an honest crust. Did you know that Melissa is hoping to accompany her new friend back to America? Apparently the woman has offered her an excellent salary.'

Francesca felt a strange disconcerting sense of loss and disappointment. She hadn't made any assumptions about their relationship – seeing it as a taste of magical and very special passion – but she now realised she'd hoped it would continue. She would truly miss Melissa. 'I'll be sorry to see her leave,' she said evenly, thinking of the rites of passage she had shared with Melissa in the sunlit gallery.

Alicia smiled and touched her arm. Her eyes more eloquent than any words. 'Don't upset yourselves with goodbyes. There are never enough words to say the things that really matter,' she said softly.

Beside them Catz had already got the picnic basket open and was removing two glasses. Alicia gave him a withering look.

'Catz, I do hope you've brought another one. I refuse to drink unless you join us.'

Catz smiled and produced a third from amongst the napkins with a theatrical flourish. Alicia clapped her hands with delight. 'Wonderful. Now hurry up and get the cork out. I think we're all in need of a glass of something joyously bubbly.'

The cork popped with a reassuring sound and Catz poured everyone a glass. Alicia glanced around the park; across the pathway, amongst the dappled shadows and below the trees, a young couple had begun a gentle dance of courtship. Alicia glanced at Catz and then at Francesca; her eyes sparkled mischievously.

'An ideal diversion, don't you think?' she said teasingly, sipping her champagne. She turned back to Francesca and Catz, her eyes narrowing a little. 'Instead of sitting here, why don't you two make the most of the weather. I'll be fine here; I've got champagne, food and entertainment.' She flapped her hands at them. 'Go, go. I need to be on my own.'

Catz drained his glass and extended a hand towards Francesca. 'Would you care to join me, lady?' he purred, his ice-blue eyes glittering. She smiled and finished her own glass before taking his hand.

'I'd be delighted,' she said and let him help her to her feet.

Catz took her arm and they began to walk along the shadowy paths; around them the soft dappled sunlight created a gentle and peaceful backdrop. Close by, Francesca could hear the soft tumble of running water and the summer blush of birdsong.

Catz slipped his arm around her. Francesca did not

resist, relishing the barely concealed strength of his touch.

'What will you do now?' she asked softly, letting him guide her.

Catz took a deep breath. 'That really depends on what Alicia wants.'

'Will you go back to the coast?' she said, glancing across at him. His expression was thoughtful; he shook his head.

'No, I don't think so; the summer is almost over. We'll probably go to France. We have a house in the south there.'

Francesca laughed. 'We?'

Catz smiled thinly. That's right, Alicia and I are married. Alicia Moffat is my wife.'

Francesca felt her colour drain. She spun round to face him. 'You're married to Alicia?' she whispered, unable to disguise her shock.

Catz nodded. 'We were married in the Bahamas the year after Edgar died.'

Francesca's mind flooded with questions. 'But . . .' she began. 'You are—'

Catz cut her short. 'I'm Alicia's housekeeper, chauffeur, chef and lover and I always have been. It was her suggestion we should get married.' He paused. 'I don't know if you will be able to understand but I have loved her since the very first day I met her. She is magical – special. She is the centre of my world.'

Francesca pulled away from him. 'I can understand why you love her, but,' she stammered, 'you work for her and you . . .' She thought of the way his body moved against hers, the passion they had shared. Everything she had thought about the nature of Catz's relationship to Alicia was suddenly thrown into confusion.

Catz shrugged. 'Someone has to take care of her; she needs me. When we met I was working in a bar, she was so alive, so humorous – so very, very beautiful. She offered me a job and took me to bed the first day I called at her house to find out what my duties would be.' He grinned. 'She was entrancing, and then after a few weeks she suggested that it would be better for both of us if she and I were married.'

'And nothing changed?' asked Francesca incredulously.

Catz laughed and stretched. 'No, nothing changed. I still loved her, I was still mesmerised, and that has never faltered. I love her now as much as the first day I saw her.' He looked at Francesca steadily. 'She set me free, free from poverty. She taught me English, she taught me to cook, to dress, to be a gentleman and when I was ready she taught me to love, to understand her body totally. She taught me about being free; she has made me alive.'

'And in return?'

In return I have given myself to her, willingly, gratefully, happily. A sweet act of sacrifice, with no compulsion, no force. A magical precious and mutual gift.'

Francesca shuddered. 'It seems so strange . . .'

Catz smiled and caught hold of her, his hands slipping around her waist, encircling her and pulling her to him. 'What part of Alicia have you ever seen that was ordinary or run-of-the-mill? No part of her life is untouched by the life she shared with Edgar. She revels in her strangeness, she is truly unique.'

He leant closer, his broad shoulders and head blocking out the summer sun. His brooding shadow engulfed her; she shuddered. His hands lifted to her neck.

'Come with me,' he whispered, 'I want you.'

Francesca gasped. 'But we can't, Catz. Not here; there are too many people.'

But he had already taken her hands and she didn't resist as he pulled her into a dense clump of bushes alongside the path.

'Catz . . .' she began to protest, but his lips crushed the words from her lips. His tongue was hot, invasive, as he pushed her back against the curved trunk of a tree. She shivered, excited by his undisguised eagerness and desire. Her hands lifted to his broad back, sliding up under his uniform jacket. She could feel the animal heat of his body under her fingertips and his muscles flexing under her caress. Desperately she pulled him closer to her.

He smelt divine, an intoxicating mixture of summer heat and subtle cologne. She moaned and returned his eager electric kiss, revelling in the sensation of his tongue seeking out the subtle contours of her lips and mouth. His touch made her quiver; nothing in her life surpassed the passion he invoked in her. She curled into his arms, feeling the intense press of his body against hers, his kisses making her head swim.

His hand slid up over her thighs, pushing up the material of her dress. His tongue moved down over her chin to lap along the tight arch of her neck, kissing at the tight glowing pulse in the pit of her throat. She thrust her hips towards him, her desire for him almost overwhelming. His hands slipped under the sides of her knickers and her own fingers hurried to help him, pulling the lacy fabric down and letting them slide unnoticed to the ground.

One of his hands brushed against the outside of her dress, sliding across her breasts, taking their weight, stroking the sensitive buds of her erect nipples through the fabric. She leant forwards and pressed her lips into the curve of his neck, breathing in his scent, trailing her tongue across the light covering of hair, relishing the. hot salty taste of his body on her lips. He moaned at her touch and, delighted at his response, she nipped and nibbled at his throat, glorying in his barely contained excitement.

His fingers slipped between her thighs, tracing up to the soft delicate pit of her sex. She opened her legs to him willingly and quivered as his fingers slid along the dark outer lips of her sex. His fingers moved back and forth teasingly; she whimpered and grabbed his hand to slide it home deep inside her. He resisted – teasing and provocative – then grinned down at her, She ran her tongue along the curve of his lips and grabbing his wrist guided him into her, pushing hard against him so that his fingers were buried to the hilt. He looked down at her and smiled.

'You're so wet,' he whispered.

She laughed softly. 'It's the effect you have on me. What am I going to do when you've gone?'

He shook his head, his fingers moving slowly in and out of the tight wet sanctuary below. 'You'll find someone else. Trust me.'

"I don't think there's anyone else like you, Catz. You're *another* strange one.'

He laughed, letting his thumb part the lips of her sex where they joined, in the thick bush of her pubic hair. He brushed down gently over her clitoris and instinctively she pushed against him.

'Maybe you're right,' he whispered, as he brushed the sensitive pleat again.

She was still holding his wrist and above she could feel the tight insistent push of his cock against her skin. She let go of his hand and moved to his flies, desperate to feel his excitement; her body ached for him. The hard bulk of his sex pressed against her touch as she fought to release him. The buttons gave under her insistent fingers and then he was free, the curving bulk of his shaft sliding between her fingers. She grasped him firmly and let her hands move along the reddened rigidity of his excitement. His flesh felt silky-smooth beneath her fingers, the engorged veins seeming to harden further under her caress. She moved her fingers back further to stroke the delicate flesh of his testicles; he moaned softly as she encircled them, cradling their weight.

Her hands moved higher so that she could push down the waistband of his trousers and slide them down over his slim hips. Her hands traced across the cool muscular curves of his buttocks, whilst beneath her touch he shivered and moved his hands to her hips.

She smiled sleepily. His body felt electric, wonderful; she wanted to drink him in, share every pleasure. She slipped slowly to her knees in front of him amongst the tangle of plants and bushes, her hands never leaving the curve of his sex and the cool intimidating smoothness of his buttocks. He stopped her for a second, his eyes alight, his expression intense. His fingers slipped beneath her chin and tipped her face up to meet his gaze. Slowly he slipped a condom from his jacket pocket. She grinned and grabbed it out of his hand. He looked down at her, his eyes stormy blue. She grinned and then, moving forward, grabbed the root of his cock firmly and with slow deliberation slid the condom smoothly down over him, engulfing his throbbing shaft. He shuddered at her light touch and arched back, gasping, as she took the very end of his swollen member into her mouth. She sucked softly, running her tongue slowly around the swollen delicate skin beneath the crown. He sighed with pleasure and pushed harder into her intimate caresses.

Expertly she began to move his skin back and forth, her grip firm and compulsive. She varied the rhythm, teasing; fast, slow, delicate, firm. Above her she could feel his excitement mounting, echoed by little animal noises of pleasure. Her fingers moved down to the delicate gathered contours of his scrotum and she took him deeper into her mouth, her lips tightening and relaxing rhythmically around the length of him while above her he closed his eyes and groaned. She felt his hands move to her hair; tangling his fingers in the dark waves he locked her close to him. She moved one hand to his buttocks to pull him further into her wet mouth and could feel him writhing beneath her touch, together with the tight electric hum just beneath the skin as he moved against her.

Slowly now, she let him go, her lips moving back along the length of his tight excited muscles, the hard outline of his cock damp with her caresses. He pulled her up to him, crushing her wet mouth with his eager, excited kisses, and then very gently caught hold of her under the arms, lifting her up on to him. She hissed softly and let herself slide slowly down towards the arc of his shaft, her hands locking behind his muscular neck.

Excitedly she lifted her legs to circle his waist and then held her breath whilst he delicately inserted the end of his cock between the soft folds of her sex. He lowered her slowly, teasingly, and she gasped at the intoxicating sensations as she felt the very tip of him enter the tight band of muscles around the opening to her body. He lowered her so slowly, letting her feel every tiny tight sensation of his penetration, and then he was inside, his great curving cock filling her to the brim.

His slow controlled entry sent her to the very edge of ecstasy. The way her body opened effortlessly under his caress made her shudder with pleasure; it was as if her body were made to accommodate him. Her body tightened around him and he began to flex his buttocks, the thrusts of his cock gentle and persuasive. They lay back a little so that her shoulders rested against the smooth cold bark of the tree, and then he began to pump harder. She let one of her fingers slip down to the hot moist union of their bodies. He glanced down approvingly as she began to stroke herself in rhythm with his thrusts. Her fingers trailed her juices over his shaft and then back up to the hard ridge of her clitoris. The first touch of her fingers against the glowing bud sent her hips thrusting forward. His eyes flashed and he renewed his thrust – harder now, more aggressively – and she echoed him, pressing her body home against him.

Her fingers began to move more quickly, circling, rubbing, and stopping briefly to dip lower to carry fragrant threads of her excitement up to lubricate the dark crimson hood of her clitoris.

He moaned as they began to make the journey out towards oblivion. She could feel her sensitive ridge growing harder and harder under her eager touch, and between her swollen excited lips she relished the potent thrust of his body into hers. She pressed harder towards him, her breasts straining, jutting forward against the bodice of her dress. She arched towards him, her fingers circling frantically as she felt their mutual excitement building.

She looked up at him, longing to see the expression on his familiar brutal features. His eyes were closed, his face wet with a glistening veil of sweat from their efforts. His expression was ecstatic; his obvious fight to maintain control added to her own excitement as she moved again and again, desperate to bring him to his climax. Below, against her fingers, was the growing certainty that she was close to tumbling over the brittle shining edge of her own orgasm. Catz moaned and she leant forward to press her lips to his; his lips opened under her tongue and she forced it home, seeking out his wet tongue.

As their lips met, the first white-hot lights flashed in her mind. She strained and arched, sucking him in, taking him further, dragging his passion to its magical conclusion. Below, her fingers brought her ever closer, the silky hot moisture of her sex bubbling up in the frantic throbbing space where their bodies joined. She dipped her fingers to feel it and let them slip to circle the root of his cock where it pressed against her.

Her touch seemed to electrify him. He bucked forward; his instinctive desperate thrusts were compelling, his excitement driving her on as she rhythmically tightened her fingers around the base of his shaft. Suddenly his climax was there. Beneath her fingers she felt the first great shuddering contraction of his orgasm crash up under her touch. The pumping rhythmic motion of his body was enough to bring her to the point of no return.

She shuddered, shocked at the intensity of the sensations as they glittered low down in her belly. They throbbed, rippling up through her, catching the breath in her throat as she pushed against his body and her fingers. The contraction of her own body around the bulk of his cock made him buck again, driving her higher, further. She gasped, and rode the delicious spiralling intensity of their passion, eagerly lapping at his tongue as it fought to push between the hot moist contours of her lips.

They both quivered, gasping and moaning in the intoxicating seconds of their mutual climax, and then suddenly they were still. Francesca could feel the pounding thump of Catz's heart against her chest as he lay back against her on the tree. She let her legs slip to the ground to steady them. They trembled as she took her weight.

Close by, from beyond the cover of the trees, Francesca could make out the soft voices of couples talking. She looked into the stormy depths of Catz's piercing blue eyes; he smiled gently down at her, stealing away any words she had in her mind. The air between them was totally still, honey-sweet; no words could convey the look that hung in the air, words unsaid and unnecessary as gently he slipped from her body. She left her arms locked around his neck, almost afraid to let go of him.

As he pulled his trousers back up over the hard curve of his buttocks, he leant forward to kiss her. Their lips met tenderly in air alive with unspoken emotion. His kiss was soft, delicate. He took her hand and slowly she followed him back on to the path.

Under the shadow of a huge chestnut tree Alicia sat peacefully on the rug in a pool of dappled sunlight. She'd tipped her head back to drink in the soft summer heat. At the sound of their approach she opened her eyes and smiled mischievously, lifting her champagne glass in silent salute. Francesca felt a tiny flutter in her stomach and then smiled. She folded herself on to the rug and did not resist when Catz lifted the bottle to refill her glass.

Alicia held out hers for a refill and then said softly, 'I have decided that I'm going to sell both the villa and the London house; they're too full of ghosts. It's time to move on . . .' She paused. 'I'm ready for a change.'

Francesca said nothing; there was nothing to say. They finished their drinks in silence and then Catz helped Alicia to her feet. Francesca fell into step behind them, watching the people in the park, whilst ahead of her in the shadowy light of the path she could see Catz was talking to Alicia. She had no doubt what he was telling her. She smiled and tipped her head back to drink in the heat of the day.

By the time they arrived back at the house the auction was nearly over. Alicia went to her room almost wordlessly and Francesca found herself alone in the sitting room. She closed the door, not wanting to run into Melissa or Gerald.

The air in the elegant room was almost still; only tiny filaments of dust floated around, trapped in the shafts of summer sunlight. Francesca let her eyes travel around the walls, taking in every detail of the elegant room. It was impossible not to speculate on the dark secrets it had witnessed that would now be lost for ever.

She stood for a few seconds in front of the mirror above the mantel, drinking in the glittering reflection; she thought about Alicia's wedding night and Edgar's dark tantalising obsession that had fuelled his collection

– all gone, now that the lots had gone under the hammer.

Behind her the door opened quietly. She turned; Catz stood silently in the doorway, his face expressionless. 'I've brought you these,' he said softly and extended his hand.

Francesca stepped closer. He opened his fingers; inside was a bunch of keys.

She looked up. 'I don't understand.'

'They are the keys to the villa. You'll need them to collect your things,' he said slowly.

Francesca swallowed hard, feeling tears push up behind her eyes. She shook her head sadly. 'I'm not really sure that I want this to end,' she said softly, gazing up into his dark closed face.

'Your things are still there,' he said again. 'Your manuscript . . .'

A single tear trickled down on to her cheek. 'I'd almost forgotten about it,' she said sadly, thinking about the pages of notes and her laptop left in the dressing room.

'And your clothes,' Catz continued. Francesca nodded and took the keys from him, closing her eyes tightly to hold back the tears.

'Thank you,' she said shakily and turned away, afraid that she would be swept away in a torrent of pain and grief.

'Would you like me to take you to the station?' asked Catz slowly.

Francesca shook her head, fighting to regain control. 'No, no it's all right, I'll hire a car and drive down tomorrow. I'll need to pack everything up once I get there.'

'What will you do?'

Francesca shrugged. 'I don't know; I must finish the book. I think there's still time to get it to my agent before the deadline.'

'Will you go back to the cottage?' he continued. His voice was tight and brittle.

'No. No, that part of my life is over. I'll find a flat; another cottage to rent maybe. I've got friends I can stay with until I decide what I'm going to do.'

'And Chris?'

Francesca detected the slightest tremor in Catz's voice. She turned back to him and smiled, trying to hide the sense of loss that was trickling through her.

'No, I'm not going back to him, Catz. I'm not prepared to give him what he wants from me. What he's offering isn't love but ownership. I've come too far to belong to a man like Chris.' She hesitated. 'Are you sure that Alicia doesn't want the same thing from you?'

Catz shook his head emphatically. 'No, she doesn't own me, Francesca. I have never been more free; my whole life with her is choice.'

Francesca closed her fingers around the keys. 'I'm glad,' she said softly. 'I hope you are free for ever.'

Catz leant a little closer and brushed his lips across her cheek. 'And you too,' he said gently.

The next morning Francesca left early to pick up her hire car. She drove back to the London house to say goodbye to Alicia and Catz but was shocked to find that it was already locked up and looked totally deserted.

Shaken, she rang the bell; she could hear it ringing through the house. After a few seconds the concierge appeared. She opened the door just a fraction on the safety chain and then smiled. 'Mrs Leeman? Hello.' She opened the door. 'Mrs Moffat said you would be back. I've left your things in your room.'

Francesca stepped into the shadowy hall, annoyed and at the same time desperately sad; unable to believe that Alicia would have left without giving her the chance to say goodbye.

Her footsteps rang across the deserted hall; everywhere had a look of desolation. She turned slowly back to the concierge. Through the open door of the sitting room she could see the hard ghostly outlines of the dust-sheets already hanging over the furniture.

'When did they go?' she asked, as she got to the bottom of the stairs. Her voice sounded unnaturally loud in the empty house.

The older woman picked up a pile of bed linen from the hall-stand. 'A few minutes after you left this morning, Mrs Leeman.'

Francesca closed her eyes for a second to hold back the hot press of tears and then ran up to her bedroom. Inside, her suitcase and holdall stood beside the bed and on top lay a tissue-covered parcel. She had wrapped it after they'd all returned from the park. It was a gift for Alicia; something that she had asked Gerald to exclude from the sale. She slipped the delicate pink ribbons off it and pushed lack the tissue. Beneath was the tiny framed watercolour of Alicia as a young woman.

Francesca sighed and rewrapped it. Alicia had been right; there were no words she could have uttered that could possibly convey everything she felt for Alicia and Catz. She slipped the painting into her holdall. She would see that Gerald got it back; he'd know what to do with it. She glanced around the room, her eyes not focusing. Instead, all she could feel was the sadness at their parting. She had desperately wanted to see Alicia and Catz just one last time.

The concierge had followed her upstairs and stood in the doorway. Now she stepped forward and touched Francesca on the shoulder. 'Don't be upset, Mrs Leeman. Mrs Moffat was never very good at saying goodbye,' she said gently.

Francesca nodded and thanked the woman. She collected her things together and hurried down the stairs. At the door she hesitated for an instant to whisper her goodbyes to the ghostly shadows and then stepped back out into the bright sunshine.

Outside in the street she looked back at the house. The windows glittered brightly, but it looked closed off now, silent and alone. She lay her luggage in the back of the car together with the wrapped watercolour, then climbed into the driver's seat, turned the key in the ignition and slipped out into the morning traffic.

# Chapter Twelve

Francesca drove out towards the coast, glad to put the roar and urgency of London behind her but feeling confused by the maelstrom of feelings that Catz and Alicia's rapid departure had created in her. On the dashboard sat the keys to the villa; they caught her eye over and over again as she negotiated her way along the narrow country roads. As the country became more and more familiar she wondered what she was going to do next. Although the fisherman's cottage was hers for another few months she'd been honest when she'd told Catz that that part of her life was over. She had friends in the country, people she could stay with who would be only too pleased to see her, and relatives she hadn't seen for years.

But she hesitated; the Francesca they knew had changed almost beyond recognition. She'd moved on and realised as the miles passed, she was now truly free; free of the past, free of Chris and unhappily, though inevitably, free of Alicia and Catz who had given her the key to her escape.

Finally, as she got closer to the villa she decided she'd find a hotel or guest house and then look for another cottage to rent; somewhere where she could begin again. She needed time to think where her life would take her next. The book had to be completed, and then she would begin another book, a book about the true nature of freedom. The memory of Edgar's diaries with their small rounded handwritten entries bubbled up in her mind. Perhaps Gerald might know where they had ended up.

A few miles from the coast she found a small motel and booked in for the night. She planned to spend the whole of the next day at the villa; one last chance before it was lost for ever to her.

As she drove into the gravelled forecourt of the motel the weather broke, flooding the road with crashing fragrant waves of late summer rain. It echoed her mood and she was relieved when she'd been shown to a small anonymous motel room. She slipped off her clothes, showered and curled up on the bed, her mind alive with new thoughts and possibilities.

The next day was clear but cool. Francesca got up early, slipped on casual trousers and a sweater and headed out towards the villa. The woman at the motel had found her some cardboard boxes. Ironic, she thought, pulling out of the drive in the hire car, that her newfound freedom had reduced her entire life to the contents of a few boxes.

*

The driveway of the villa looked the same. The rain had given the shrubs which lined the driveway a dark green sparkle, and fresh weeds had pushed up through the gravel. She parked under one of its tall hedges; beyond it the villa seemed abandoned and forlorn. She couldn't quite control the little tremble of emotion that shivered up her spine.

The grind of the key turning in the lock sounded uncanny, as if she were unlocking a gateway to another time. Inside, the hall was deserted and she noticed that someone had already thrown dust-sheets over the magnificent furniture. Her footfalls sounded loud, echoing around the walls, as she made her way across to the staircase.

Upstairs her room was exactly as she had left it. Her books, clothes, notepads – all the things that she had once valued – all left untouched; things from her life before Alicia and Catz. In the window the plinth was empty – the figures had been sold in the auction – and across the room the roses had faded, their petals lying in a dark brown drift across the table.

Packing her possessions she felt a strange sense of restlessness, the sensation intensifying as she carried each box and bag silently down to the hall. After the first trip downstairs Francesca stopped on the landing and looked into the empty hall below. There was something eerie about the house; not threatening, just disturbing. She had a strange uneasy and prickly feeling that she couldn't shift despite the reassurance of bright sunshine glittering in through the landing windows behind her.

It felt as if she were being watched, as if at any second she would stumble across Alicia or Catz. The sound of their names in her mind made her shiver. Hurrying nervously back up to her room she began to pack away her manuscript and laptop. Somewhere close by she was certain she heard a door open. The hair on the back of her neck stood up and for a split second she laughed out loud at her own uneasiness. The sound was uncanny in the deserted house and she had to reassure herself that the villa was empty – Catz and Alicia had gone.

It was almost midday before she made her final trip to the hall with the last of the boxes. Already through the windows she could see the garden, kissed by the first red blush of autumn. At the front door she hesitated, knowing that all she had to do now was put the boxes in the car and leave, but something else compelled her to stay a little longer. She turned and looked along the dark glittering corridors and then down at the house keys. One last look – one final farewell glimpse of the magic she had found there – was all she wanted. Laying the box down, she picked up her handbag and turned back into the house.

The little anteroom at the foot of the gallery staircase was in darkness, as it had been the first day Alicia had brought her there. Above, in sharp contrast to the shadows, was the same square of sunlight that opened on the gallery landing. Francesca took one step and then another, climbing slowly, imagining that if she turned, Catz would appear at her shoulder.

She felt a little *frisson* of anticipation as she emerged back into the sunlight. The gallery at first glance seemed empty, then she saw something under a dust-sheet, standing alone in the centre of the room; from beneath she could see a single black foot peeping out. Pulling the dust-sheet aside she discovered the familiar outlines of the dark woman and her secret lovers; the first object she had seen in the gallery. Taped to the top of the vase was an envelope with her name on it. The carved woman smiled slyly back up at her. Francesca lifted her hand to caress the dark contours of the woman's face, stroking the delicate high cheekbones of her beautiful frozen features.

The compulsion to walk around the back was too great to resist. She moved slowly around it, relishing the statue's dark secret. The woman's master still crouched excited and mesmerised, his tongue lifted in worship to the wide inviting crevices of the woman's sex; below, his handmaiden still serviced the hard meaty bulk of his phallus whilst her own fingers dipped into the hot pool of her own body, bringing her moment of ecstasy closer and closer.

The stimulating effects of its intense erotic imagery had not diminished. Francesca could feel the colour flooding through her face and the heat building in her belly. The statue was a celebration of erotic passion; every feeling, every desire of the dark trio was captured by the magical: talent of the sculptor. She leant forward and trailed one finger over the standing woman's heavy rounded buttocks, almost expecting that the woman would quiver under her caress.

'Francesca.' A familiar voice spoke her name in a soft low tone.

She spun around, her body trembling at the possibility.

'Catz,' she whispered.

He stood by the stairwell of the landing, dressed as she had first seen him in the hallway of the fisherman's cottage. His eyes were piercing and intimidating. Everything about him was threatening and mesmerising, just as she remembered him. She felt her pulse quicken and the plume of anticipation fluttered up in her belly. 'The statue is a gift from Alicia,' he said, slowly walking towards her. He moved like a predatory animal, smoothly, effortlessly. 'All you have to do is ring Gerald and tell him where you'd like it delivered.'

She nodded, unable to find any words. Her eyes never left him as he moved closer and closer. In one hand he cradled the thin whip he had used on her when they had first begun their journey of exploration in the gallery. Her eyes widened, she felt her pulse quicken and stepped back towards the door that led into the dressing room of her suite. She could see the glittering mischief in his eyes, sense the animal tension in his body and suddenly he sprang towards her.

This time she was ready for him. Anticipating his lunge she leapt sideways, twisting away from his extended fingers. His eyes were alight; she yelled triumphantly and snatched the door of the dressing room open, slamming it shut behind her. She heard his fingers on the handle and turned to run through the dressing room, pushing the door closed behind her. From inside she could hear Catz's efforts to wrench the gallery door open.

Exhilarated she ran through the bedroom, out through the door of the suite and into the hall beyond. She knew he would be close behind and sprinted across the landing, her shoes clattering against the polished boards. She felt the pulse rising in her ears, a subtle exhilarating mixture of excitement and fear. He was closer now; she knew it, sensing his trembling desire like static in the air. She grabbed the newel post at the top of the stairs and swung around, launching herself down the stairs as fast as she could. She slipped, regained her footing and was rewarded with the briefest, fleeting glimpse of the dark-green uniform back along the corridor as he closed on her.

She ran harder down into the hall. She glanced at the front door and snatched the key from the lock before running into the dark shadowy corridors beneath the stairs. Slipping into a shadowed alcove, breath bursting from her chest, she tried to be quiet, holding her ragged breaths under control so they did not betray her.

Francesca wanted Catz – she desired him almost more than anything else – but first he would have to catch her. She saw a shadow moving along the far wall and crept from her hiding place. He passed the end of the corridor; he was creeping, his shoulders hunched over in an effort to disguise his footfalls. She slipped off her shoes and moved to follow him on silent feet. As she turned the end of the corridor she caught sight of him again and something, perhaps her movement or the change of light, gave her away. He swung round, his eyes bright pinpricks in the shadows. He called out and lunged towards her triumphantly. She screamed and slipped away from him, diving back down the corridor. Now he was just a fraction of a second behind her. She surged forward, throwing open the doors of the breakfast room. Behind her he was so close she could almost feel his breath on her body. She spun around, frantically looking for a way out, wrenching at the French windows; they resisted.

Catz stepped into the room behind her, certain of victory. Now his face was expressionless, his breath controlled. He moved closer, slower now, savouring every second of her capture. She felt the key in the lock and turned it desperately. To her surprise the door gave way at once; she jerked it open and ran out on to the tumbled chaos of the terrace.

Her escape had taken him by surprise and gained her a yard or two. Leaping down the crumbling steps amongst the dark rolling creepers, she glanced back over her shoulder to see him emerge from between the French windows. His face was flushed, his blue eyes flashing and in his hand he still carried the light whip. She could feel the adrenalin pumping through her, forcing her onwards. Her breath burnt in her chest as she set off through the tortured ruins of the crumbling garden. Behind her she could hear Catz crashing through the undergrowth and calling out her name. An excited cry caught in her throat and she pressed further on through the ramshackle beds and great gnarled tussocks of grass.

She knew, despite her efforts, that she was flagging. He was gaining; her stomach ached from the efforts of trying to keep ahead of him. She could hear him closing on her and at last she turned round to face him. He was within inches, his hands flew out and, grabbing her, roughly rolled them both down amongst the intoxicating fragrant grass. He pinned her down, gasping, hot from the chase. She mewed and tried to wriggle away as he lunged forward and kissed her savagely, hard eager lips crushing hers. She closed her teeth on his tongue as it fought its way between her lips and strained against him, revelling in their desperate combat. His fingers dragged at her sweater, pushing it up to reveal her breasts. Beneath the fabric they were flushed with Francesca's exertions and her deep engulfing excitement. He tore his lips away from hers, leaving her feeling exhilarated and sore, and dived on to the soft flesh of her breasts, sucking them deep, answering her bite by closing his teeth around their sensitive buds. She screamed, trying to resist him as his hands ripped at the waistband of her trousers. She writhed under him, pummelling his back with her fists, fighting against the delicious conflict that threatened to engulf her. The buttons of her trousers gave under his desperate tugging, the zip bursting as his fingers tried to drag it lower. He lifted her up to him so that he could jerk the material down, dragging it over her hips and knees. Now his fingers locked in the tiny triangle of fabric that protected her sex, ripping it to shreds. She struggled against him instinctively, laughing and screaming almost in the same breath. Now she was exposed, her sex naked; he leant back to look at her, eyes bright with animal-like passion. Dropping the whip amongst the grass Catz pulled himself on to his knees, his hands moving towards his flies. With one desperate lurching thrust Francesca pushed him off and struggled back to her feet. She crouched for a second, her eyes alight, unable to suppress the excited triumphant whoop in her throat. She lifted her hands to the neckline of her sweater and pulled it over her head so she was completely naked and then, laughing, turned and ran away between the tangle of bushes. Catz pulled himself to his feet and gave chase again.

Her whole body pulsed with the exertion and yet she forced herself on, pushing aside the thick waving swards of grass, feeling the hot sting of the stalks as they hit against her naked glowing flesh. Behind, Catz had recovered from the surprise of her escape, was back on his feet and hurrying after her.

She glanced back at him and was delighted to see he was shedding his jacket. She grinned and turned away from him, trying to get to the sea wall and the gate that would lead them down on to the beach. As she turned she caught her bare foot amongst a clump of weeds and plunged headlong into a great bank of dried grass. The fall winded her; she moaned and rolled over on to her back, struggling to get up as Catz caught up with her, his dark bulk towering above her.

With his back to the light his features were unreadable but she could hear his breath coming in excited ragged gasps. She pushed herself back from him, trying to scramble across the uneven ground as his hands rose to his trousers and undid them. He threw his jacket down beside her and then slipped his trousers and boots off. She froze, mesmerised by his hard glistening body. His cock was already hard, jutting towards her like a wild insatiable animal. He knelt down and she could see the mischievous glint in his eyes.

'Gotcha,' he murmured breathlessly and rolled into the dried grass beside her.

She smiled and lifted a finger, stroking a line across his face. Taking her wrists, he pressed her fingers to his lips, his breaths still laboured as he worked his tongue between them. She sighed and pulled away, sliding down instead over the broad expanse of his chest, stroking amongst the tight hot curls.

Beneath her fingers she could feel the insistent beat of his heart, throbbing, excited. Wriggling closer she drank in the warm smell of his body and trailed her hot damp hair across him. Under her touch he quivered, as she dipped lower to take one of his tiny dark nipples into her mouth. She glanced up at him; his face with tight with desire, eyes burning. Locking his fingers in her hair he pulled her to him so their tingling skin met- and joined, her breasts pressed hard against him. She lapped again at his tiny closed bud and was rewarded by a soft moan; encouraged she moved across and licked at the other. As her mouth closed around the little hard peak she lifted her leg to straddle his hips. Behind, against her buttocks, she felt the excited tautness of his erection. His expression didn't change but his hips lifted to press it against her cool flesh.

'Well,' she said teasingly, rubbing back against his engorged shaft. 'Who's going to tell who that they want this? Or are we equal now?'

Catz grinned, the expression strange in his rugged features. 'I think we're equal. Here . . .' He pulled his jacket closer and Francesca slipped her hand into the pocket. Inside she could make out the familiar shape of a condom packet. She grinned back at him.

'Always prepared?'

He nodded. 'Always,' he murmured. She took out a packet and tore open the seal. He wriggled under her and she laughed.

'No,' she said softly. 'Lie still, let me.'

Moving back she lifted herself so that the smooth arc of his cock brushed against her sex and inner thigh. Catz shuddered. Gently she slid back on to his thighs so his shaft now arched up in front of her. She traced her fingers down from its tip to the heavy roundness of his testicles. The great reddened beast lifted its head eagerly under her exploration.

She smiled and gripped his shaft in her palm, working it back and forth. At the end a crystal droplet of moisture formed. She slid the foreskin back further and let her fingers trail around the rounded contours of its head, working the moisture down over it. He quivered deliciously beneath her touch. Slowly she unpeeled the condom and slipped it over the angry head, with a smooth delicate movement engulfing his manhood in its soft contours. Now she dipped lower to take him into her mouth, letting her lips nip and suck at him. He strained and moved against her weight while she relished the feel of his body moving under her.

His fingers moved to her breasts; gently, softly, stroking, caressing. She could feel the heat building under his touch and moaned, wriggling appreciatively, making her mouth tighten rhythmically around him whilst her fingers spun delicate little feathering circles across his balls. Between her legs she could feel the wetness from her sex pressing fragrant erotic kisses along her thighs.

He groaned and pressed her upwards, trying to bring her body closer. She slid off his legs, moving herself so that she was within his reach. Fingers brushed across the sensitive hairs of her mound; he moved slowly, smoothly, totally in tune with her aching desperate desire. Parting her lips he brushed a finger either side of her clitoris, sliding her outer lips between his fingers before slipping home into her sex. Her wetness engulfed him. Raising her lips from his cock, she grinned sleepily and slid away from his touch. He groaned in frustration.

She slid back on to his thighs. Her hands rested on his shoulders as she brought her wet opening tantalisingly close, the merest whisper away from taking him into her. She sensed his control was gone; the dominance and strength he threatened her with was lost as his desire for her body swamped him. She held herself above his cock and tipped it back so that she could guide it inside. He whimpered and moved his hands to help press his shaft home. Grinning, she pushed his hands away.

'No, Catz,' she whispered. 'Let me.'

She caught hold of the base of his cock and lifted it gently into her waiting body. The first tentative feel of him made her shudder. She let the very tip nestle between her inner lips, letting him feel her heat. He gasped but lay still to let her take him. She lowered herself further, her body slowly drawing his shaft inside until he was buried to the hilt. She hunched over him, trailing her moist hair across his face and chest, letting her nipples brush through the fine hair on his chest, dipping to take the dark curve of his nipples into her mouth. He arched his neck back and grimaced, trying to regain control.

She began to move against him, rolling her hips in hypnotic circles, slowly, slowly. She heard him gasp at the sensations and smiled triumphantly as she began to lift herself against him, brushing her engorged clitoris against the soft hair of his lower belly. Every stroke was a symphony of arousal, a brilliant rhythmic lilt, a delicate kiss of their bodies as her sex moved against the rise of his pubis and the delicate spirals of his curling hair. He closed his eyes and let her ride him. She looked down at his straining brutal face, peppered now with sweat and tiny leaves from their chase; he was truly beautiful.

Kneeling forward she brushed his lips with her breasts and was rewarded by him sucking one deep into his mouth. His teeth, teasing at the bud, made her gasp at the tiny silvery pain. As she lifted up, relishing his attentions to her breasts, his cock suddenly began to pump harder, his pelvis echoing the movement she had set in motion but much faster now. She shuddered and let him set the pace, drinking in the exhilarating brush of his body against hers.

She pulled back to kiss his eyelids, letting her tongue curve back and forth across the salty line of lashes. He moaned and renewed his upward arc. Suddenly his fingers moved to the moist throbbing junction of their bodies, his touch feather-light against her sensitive creases. Instinctively she jerked against his fingers and he buried his cock deeper still.

Part of her was content to let him ride her out beyond the crashing waves of their mutual passion, but another part – the part he had awoken – longed to take him higher, to drive him on. Instead of letting him set the pace she fought against his touch now, resuming her steady dip and rise. To her surprise he eased his thrusts, lying back to drink in her body's persuasive movements, letting her lead him.

She flexed her tight pelvic muscles inside so that her sex nibbled along his throbbing shaft, and moved again, slower, steadily with a slow, slow rhythm guaranteed to bring them both to the edge of the precipice. Sensing her growing excitement he began to move with her, echoing her arc, grinding his hips on the upstroke so that every last fraction of their bodies brushed together at the corded knot of their sexes. She whimpered and felt a delicate glistening heat trickling across her body. A thin trail of sweat broke out across her shoulders and face.

She dipped again, sensually, slowly – slowly. Under her she could see his face contorting with the effort to maintain his control. The muscles of his neck stiffened and she smiled before suddenly increasing the pace, a thrilling erotic acceleration that made him gasp. She felt his power growing inside her, felt him shudder. Suddenly she knew he was completely hers; his mouth fell open and his hips lifted randomly in a counter beat to her own thrustings.

His eyes snapped open and she reared up so she was sitting upright on his hardness; his eyes were unseeing, desperate, beads of sweat were rolling down his face. She grinned, relishing the sense of power and threw back her head, riding him out beyond the dark pulsating stars. As she felt the first exhilarating contractions of his orgasm pulsing deep inside, her body responded by renewing its tight grinding brush against his lower belly, and with his instinctive animal thrusting the bright lights of her orgasm crowded in around her.

A ripple spread up from the junction of their sexes; a shuddering intense wave that flooded up through her belly over her breasts and exploded deep inside her mind. Lost now, she forgot the slow dance of passion and bucked harder and harder, grinding the moist mat of her pubic hair into his. She heard a gasping screaming sob and in the next instant realised the voice was hers. Beneath her, Catz was pushing deeper, his heady contractions ricocheting through the swollen sanctuary of her sex, and at the point of no return he locked his eyes on hers and seemed to drag her mind into his.

She seemed to be able to feel his passion, sense his desire and the red crashing lights that drove him deeper still. Still he drove into her, still he pressed against her. The first euphoric waves of climax were surpassed by the fires of intensity that followed, taking her out beyond the barriers of pain once again, taking her out, out, until inside her dark frenzied mind she could see the coloured heat of their orgasm closing in again, hotter, wilder, more intense. She screamed out and knew this time the voice was hers. She screamed his name and embraced the red-hot crash of the returning sensation, riding across his body like a stormy wind.

His hands grabbed her hips, dragging her down on to his body. She bucked again and again, thinking that the sensations would drive away all reason. Her body tightened around him, leaving her dizzy and shaking. as finally the waves shuddered away. She gasped and let the last after-shocks ebb until at last they were both still. She rolled forward on to his chest, their sweating exhausted bodies glued together by heat and satisfied desire. It seemed as if nothing would part them. She rested her head in the curve of his neck and his arms lifted to encircle her. They lay still until Francesca gently disentangled herself from his embrace and slipped his cock from her satiated body.

He looked across at her, his eyes cold blue flames. Exhausted, she curled up beside him in the crook of his arm. He smiled sleepily and, pulling his jacket from amongst the grass, covered them both with it. Trembling, Francesca breathed in the heady aroma of his body and closed her eyes. Sleep claimed them both almost instantly.

When Francesca awoke, the light around them had subtly changed; she shivered, suddenly cold. Beside her, Catz began to stir, woken by her movements. He grinned across at her and, reaching up, encircled her neck, lifting his head to press his lips to hers. She ran her fingers through his short hair, letting her bruised lips linger on the moist contours of his mouth. Slowly she sat back on her heels and looked at him. He smiled under her examination, his hand sliding back to support his head. Beneath his armpit the curled soft hair was in sharp contrast to the hard outline of his biceps.

'One more story to tell Alicia?' she said softly, letting her fingers trail across the sleek muscles of his chest.

He shook his head. 'No, this one was for us. I waited for you. I knew it wouldn't be long before you came back here.'

She smiled. 'I'm flattered. Where is Alicia?'

'At a hotel. She'll be fine until I've finished here.'

'And then?'

Catz pulled himself up on to his elbows. 'We go south, chasing the summer.'

Francesca nodded. 'It sounds wonderful,' she said quietly, looking away to the growing shadows under the sea wall.

He watched her face. 'And have you decided what you'll do now?'

She nodded. 'I'm going to finish my book and then write another one, a better one. One day I'll be rich. I'm going to set myself free.'

He smiled. 'That's good.'

She pulled herself to her feet and started to pick her way back through the garden, stooping to retrieve her sweater. Catz clambered to his feet and followed quietly. She grinned back at him from over her shoulder.

'One thing. With you out of my life my clothes will last a lot longer!'

He laughed and threw her ruined trousers at her.

'Don't let it get too boring,' he said. 'Now you know what freedom is, make sure you never lose the gift.'

'I won't,' she said, wrapping her sweater over her shoulders.

At the villa they silently climbed the stairs to Francesca's suite. She turned on the shower and stepped inside. A second or two later Catz joined her and gently began to soap her sated aching body. She turned into his knowing comforting touch; her hands lifted to him and began to move across him, drinking in the strength of his muscles. Their movements were lazy, assured, confident. When they stepped from the tight hot blast of the water Catz wrapped her in a huge towel. He looked across at her as she dried herself.

'I have to leave,' he said flatly.

She nodded. 'I know, don't worry. I understand.' She paused. 'I wanted to say goodbye to Alicia, to say a million and one things, but she was right. There are no words to convey what I feel about her, or you.'

His eyes glittered and his voice was low. 'It's best if we say nothing,' he said softly.

She smiled. "Will you help me put my things in the car?' He nodded.

The last place they visited together was the gallery, to retrieve her handbag. Franceses walked across to the dark statue for one last look, then took the card from the top and slipped it into her bag. For an instant she and Catz stood side by side in the fading light. Catz turned.

'There truly are no words,' he whispered, stepping towards her.

She smiled looking up into his glittering eyes. 'I know,' she answered.

He stroked her cheek and then moved towards the staircase. Silently she turned to follow him back down to the hall.

Behind the wheel of the hire car she sat for a second or two looking thoughtfully out into the wrecked garden. In the shadow of the porch she could see Catz locking the door. She turned the keys in the ignition and pulled out of the drive. She had no need to look back.

Francesca drove back out along the coast road to the motel. The last of the afternoon light revealed that autumn was pressing closer. She pulled into the first restaurant she came to and walked in. Her mind was set now. She'd finish her book and be strong enough to live by her own rules.

As the light finally faded she finished her meal, deciding that one more night at the motel would be enough before she headed out on her new beginning.

She picked up her bill and, taking her purse from her handbag, went to pay the waitress. Inside, amongst the tangle of personal possessions, she saw the envelope that had been in the gallery with the sculpture.

She opened it and pulled out a thick vellum card. The inscription read 'BE FREE', written in Alicia's distinctive handwriting. Smiling, Francesca ran her finger over the dark inviting words and then opened the card. Inside was stapled a cheque – the amount made her gasp. She looked around, feeling the colour rising in her cheeks. Alicia's parting gift was enough to set her free for ever. She hesitated for a few seconds, the cheque resting lightly between her fingers. Her first instinct was to tear it up.

The old Francesca threatened to reassert herself, the sensible Francesca. Nothing she had done for Alicia warranted the gift. If anything, she felt it was she who owed the older woman something. Her fingers tightened, ready to tear the paper in half and then, from the corner of her eye, she saw someone move at a table across the room.

In the last light of the fading sun a tall man in a casual jacket was looking at her with undisguised interest, his dark eyes glittering with desire. She smiled at him. He coloured and looked away for an instant. Grinning she slipped from her seat. As she did, her bill fluttered to the floor; she saw him glance across, felt his eyes travelling over the sleek curve of her body. She turned a little and, crouching to retrieve the bill, let her skirt ride up, giving him an uninterrupted view of her barely concealed sex. She heard him gasp and choke on his drink. Francesca grinned, then glanced at the cheque thoughtfully before dropping it back into her bag. The new Francesca had no trouble accepting the gift in the spirit in which it was given. Alicia wanted her to be free.

Turning, she glanced out of the window into the countryside beyond. She picked up her bag and stepped towards the restaurant doors and then out into the evening. Behind her the man mopped half-heartedly at the front of his shirt.